THE LION-TAMER
AND OTHER STORIES

THE
LION-TAMER

and other stories

BY

BRYAN MacMAHON

SOUVENIR PRESS

First published 1948 by
Macmillan & Co. Ltd., London

This edition published 1995 by
Souvenir Press Ltd,
43 Great Russell Street, London WC1B 3PA
and simultaneously in Canada

ISBN 0 285 63229 9

Printed in Great Britain by
The Guernsey Press Co. Ltd., Guernsey, Channel Islands.

TO KITTY

CONTENTS

CONTENTS

THE LION-TAMER

As I entered the public-house I saw the man eyeing me through the meshes of froth on the side of his uptilted glass. He was seated by the fire. It is a characteristic of the older public-houses in the smaller villages that the bar itself is half bar, half kitchen. The fire was burning brightly in the old range and strata of underclothing were drying on the bars above it. The publican gave me the glare such persons reserve for strangers. I ordered a bottle of stout and threw him a casual remark about the weather. As he gave me the drink his face thawed into friendliness and he ordered me to pull over to the fire.

I did so and found myself opposite the man who had scrutinised me on my entrance; by this time he had placed his glass on the tiles at the side of the range and was balancing himself on the two hind legs of his chair. His prim eyes were on my every movement. I sat down opposite him and as his eyes dropped preparatory to taking up his drink, I appraised him as thoroughly as I could in the small span of time allowed me: he had a pale boyish face with the pimples of belated adolescence upon it; his nose was pointed to make his profile a shallow isosceles triangle with the vertex on the tip of his nose. A thing that struck me about him was his boyishness — his immaturity. I put his age at twenty-two or -three at the outside.

I am gregarious and convivial to a degree considered alarming by my friends. At that moment I was pining for company. The fact that my business in the village had been finished late in the afternoon necessitated my staying in the place overnight, and, according as one grows older, the prospect of spending a night out of one's home is by no means relished. I timed my imbibing so that the young man opposite me and myself should finish our drinks together. Then I was quick to offer to buy him a drink. His refusal came with the unexpectedness of a slap. " I prefer to buy my own drinks ! " he said. This type of brusque unequivocal refusal is rare in country parts. I accepted defeat, rankling not a little under the brutal and un-Irish nature of it. Just as I had begun to spin myself a cocoon of outraged reserve, his explanation was offered, and I was impressed by the rare directness of it : " A custom I learned in England," he said. " Treating is abominable — neither fair to the treater nor the treated. When two are drinking together it is impossible to have an odd number of drinks, and that is a limitation I can never accept. Nevertheless I am grateful to you for having asked me." All this came with the aplomb of one three times his senior in age. I called for my own drink ; he called for his. I paid for mine ; he paid for his. It struck me as unusual that the publican seemed to consider this arrangement entirely normal.

I was tempted to hang some cloth on the conversational peg of England. When I did so he spoke fluently and authoritatively of the Midland cities. I had spent six months in Birmingham, and each observation of his regarding that city struck me as objective, terse and accurate. As he continued speaking I found myself compelled to renew my respect for him. Before long we were chatting brightly but restrainedly. Putting a man at his job is an old trick of conversation ; so I indicated vaguely the nature of my business in the village. He rose to the bait with alacrity. Taking a sip out of his glass he sucked in his lips and laid down his drink with a good deal of ceremony. Then he said : " What would you say my occupation was ? " Followed the usual chit-chat and

mock-surprise. First, " You a native of this place ? "
(" Yes.") " Hmmm ! Teacher ? " (" No.") " Insur-
ance Agent ? Machinist ? Student ? Home Assistance
Officer ? " (We both laughed.) " Sacristan ? Clerk of
Works ? Engineer ? " The answer was always no.

" I give up," I said.

He sipped his drink with quiet triumph. " As a
matter of fact I don't blame you in the least. I could
have given you a thousand guesses and you'd never have
got it."

" But that isn't telling me what you are ! "

" I'm a lion-tamer," he said, " the only Irish-born
lion-tamer there is."

I lifted my drink to my mouth and threw him a glance
which must have spelled incredulity with a capital I.

He was quick to resent the fact that, in my own mind,
I was calling him a liar. " If you doubt my word," he
snapped, " I shall ask our friend O'Donoghue." He
swivelled in his chair to ask the publican to bear witness
for him, but Mr. O'Donoghue had vanished into the back
premises from whence the clinking of bottles came to our
ears.

I hastened to reassure him that I fully believed him.
" You look so young," I said in extenuation of my fault.

" Young as I am, I've seen a good deal of life and have
travelled more than my share."

There came a slight hiatus in the flow of our speech.
I thought he seemed inclined to bear away from the
absorbing subject of lion-taming. I hurried after him
and, conversationally speaking, caught him by the coat-
tails.

" How on earth, I ask, did you manage to become a
lion-tamer ? "

In lieu of response he took a packet of cigarettes from
his pocket, extracted one and tamped it deftly on his

knee. He did not offer me a cigarette.

" The story does me little credit," he began. " For my part of it I had always wanted to be a doctor. But my black friend here on the hob " (here he indicated his drink) " and his wee yellow brother said no to my dreams of medicine." I noted his lapse into the vernacular.

A pause. A smile flickered on his lips — it was distressing to see one so young smile so bitterly. " I ran away with the circus one night after a row with the stepmother. Ever hear of Vaughan's ? Not a top-notcher, but a good, honest little show as shows go. Vaughan's wife would have made a good sub. for the Fat Lady, only the old man never featured freaks. I remember a guy trying to sell the Boss a calf with six legs, but the Boss told him take the thing away. ' You'll gain two on the quarters of veal if you kill it,' the old man said.

" I found the tober hard graft. Taking down the Big Top of a wet night with your soaked pants clinging to your thighs was no picnic. I remember driving a wagon in the procession through the town — dressed as a cowboy I was — and my belly was back to my back with the hunger. Aye, and I had to turn every second minute to take a bite out of a raw turnip. I used chew it as strongly as I could to make the crowd believe I was chewing tobacco. Yes, and driving all night and trying to sleep on a pile of junk with the wind cutting through the slats in the wagon and every rut in the road rattling a panful of marbles on the floor of your skull. Right hard graft it was. But, by hell, I stuck it !

" The Boss saw I was frailer and finer than the ordinary run, aye, and that I had one hell of a tooth for the milk of the black cow. So he put me in charge of the cat — cleaning out from her and so on. The cat had four kittens, and this was the act : the cage was divided into two compartments and at every performance the trainer — he was an Edinburgh man — went into the cage and put them through their paces. First he went into the empty box. Then the four kittens were poked or coaxed out a small hole and McIvor put them up on four little stools — one in each corner of the box. When they were sitting pretty her ladyship was let out through a bigger slide and the tamer's job was to get her sitting on a big stool in the middle as if the whole cat family were posing for their photograph. The old lady was a sour old strap. During the performance three or four of us had to stand guard outside the bars with crowbars and poles ready to prise herself and Andy apart if she should take it into her head to maul him.

" I spent a few months cleaning out from Minnie. At times she had all the tricks of a real cat. I used stop and laugh at the way she'd stretch herself out and scrape at the wood just like your own pussy scraping the table leg. Maybe she'd get humorous and play with the cubs with those quick flicks that we see so often in the household edition. A lioness is only a Tab seen through a telescope. But frost played Molly Bawn to her and when hard weather came she was like a red devil out of hell.

" Andy McIvor was a tyrant of tyrants. He had realised his indispensability. Lion-tamers aren't two a penny, you know. The trade isn't listed in ' Careers for Your Children '. Most of the tamers come from European zoos and a few from England and Scotland. Whenever Andy had a row with the Boss, the Boss would be the first to pipe down. If he didn't do this the Missus would send for Andy and palaver him. Andy was inclined to go on the booze — not with me though : he considered me his inferior. The first portent of Andy's intention of hitting the bottle was his donning of a gold signet ring. The sight of that ring on his finger early in the morning was enough to set the whole show on edge.

He commemorated obscure festivals and obscurer anniversaries. On a few occasions he went into the cage paralytic drunk and called the cat a cowardly old so-and-so. Except for one rip on his arm he always got away with it. The others believed that he was immune because he carried a certain kind of herb in his pocket, the smell of which the cat loved. But I doubt it. I've watched him hundreds of times and he had only the four legs of a chair and a whip between him and the Jordan-box. His prat was a kind of continual hissing, the rhythm of which I was never able to pick up, no matter how hard I tried.

"Things went from bad to worse with Andy. The man became insufferable. 'Three lion-tamers in this blasted country,' he'd say, ' one tied up with —— (here he named a rival circus), one crippled with arthritis in Derry City, and the third is mysel'. Three of us in this blasted country. Pss. . . . Which of you fellows is willin' to go in to the cat ? Eh ? '

"One night just before a show was due to commence Andy was brought back stone dead corpsed drunk. The Boss was fit to be tied. The wife began to cry. When the time came for Andy to go on, the Boss pulled a fast one on the audience. He pitched a big yarn about the lion-tamer's arm being mauled and turning septic and that he craved the indulgence of his patrons. The country boys didn't like it a bit. They had planked their good money on the offchance of seeing a man mangled. They boohed, hooted and blackguarded. Country boys are like greyhounds : they get all their courage when they are in the pack, especially if the pack happens to meet in darkness. But the Boss had all this mapped out. He made himself heard above the noise and offered £100 to any man who would go into the cage and stay there with the cat for two minutes. That corked their bottle.

No one stirred. We had one of our own lads placed in the crowd. He was there to size up the situation and was to get in first if any country fellow made a move. Suddenly there was a jostling match among the crowd around the door of the tent. Then we saw that a big fellow who seemed to be half drunk was being pushed forward into the ring. Our man waited for a split second to see if the country boy was in earnest about going in. Then he jumped in and beat the yokel to the draw. The country boy looked nowhere and was pushed back into the people.

"The Boss began his patter. First he asked our man if he was willing to go in, and receiving a good gulp in reply he disclaimed all responsibility on behalf of the management of the Circus. Then 'Are you married ? Address of your nearest relative ? ' and a word of advice, 'Young man, in the cage make every move deliberate, nothing hasty, you understand ? ' The Boss took out his wallet, smacked it with the palm of his hand and stated that it contained £100 in £5 notes. After which he extracted his watch and bade the challenger to move in. Our man took off his cap, wiped the sweat off his face with it, swallowed his Adam's apple a few times, looked around wildly and finally moved towards the cage. There was a deadly silence. But the Boss had his head well screwed on. He had it all squared up with the two Civic Guards at the flap that if any country boy was idiot enough to risk going into the cage he was to be prevented from doing so. So at the tensest moment of the fake drama, the local Sergeant stepped forward, clicked his fingers and raised a legal hand at the sham adventurer. Immediately the pantomime warmed up ; the Boss shrugged his shoulders in a gesture of impotence ; the crowd went wild, our man grew truculent and was inclined to assert his constitutional rights to commit suicide if he so wished. Then at the height of the hubbub the Boss held up his hand for silence, drew a fiver from his wallet and handed it to the challenger, shook hands with him and made a magnificent speech congratulating him on his indomitable courage. The crowd liked this better than ever and cheered the hero as he resumed his seat. It was a first-class stunt thought up on the spur of the moment without any rehearsal. It worked so well that the Boss was inclined to keep it up and work it now and again — once, say, in each county, but when it was broached to a sober Andy he spurned the suggestion and said, ' By hell he'd be made a monkey of by no mon ! '

" It was in Ennistymon in Clare that Andy McIvor walked out of the show for good and glory. When the Missus came out of the living-wagon after the evening performance she saw the Boss and Andy rolling over on the ground. Vaughan was no daw in a rough-and-tumble and he chawed a neat semicircle out of Andy's ear. It's surprising all the blood that can come out of a man's ear. Like a tap spouting red ink it was. The Missus started to holler like hell. Gathering her breath she'd shriek down to nothing. Then again she'd swell like an insulted hatching-hen — all with the dint of gathering her screech. The ponies grew restive in the long tent. We closed in to separate the pair of them. Andy was frothing at the mouth and his ear was a show to God and the world. The Boss had a big beard of blood after the bite. Andy bucked about with three of us clinging to his back ; the Boss stripped his red teeth like a butcher's dog ; the Missus went off in a dead weakness. The village lads watched us from a huge stupefied circle. As Andy calmed down he shrieked perdition and punishment on us all. He called us all Irish this and Irish that and Irish th' other thing. He said we were for the Boss. Indeed that was no lie for him ; it was the Boss who was paying us, not Andy.

" Finally Vaughan was dragged into his wagon, and his Missus, who was prone on the grass, was slapped back to consciousness. Soon the Boss and the Missus were at it hot and heavy. In the heel of the hunt Mrs. Vaughan broke down and began to cry. In the meantime Andy had packed his bag and put on his signet ring ; he cursed us all squarely as he departed. A bus was going the road — Andy hailed it and went away. The Circus was minus its lion-tamer.

" About six o'clock that evening I was in the harness-wagon when the Missus came up. ' Is he gone, Tim ? ' she asked. ' Aye, ma'am, gone by bus,' I answered. ' Good riddance ! ' she says. ' There's as good fish in the sea as was ever caught.' With that she eyed me shrewdly. Then, ' Come down, Tim, I wan't to talk to you.' I came down. Then, ' Take me down to the town, Tim. I want a drink.' With that she took my arm. The woman was huge and would persist in wearing a fur coat. Going out the gate I could feel the eyes of all the other chaps burning holes in my back. The vision of the Missus waltzing out arm-in-arm with a circus hand had no precedent in circus etiquette.

" When we got to a pub the Missus started to drink gin while I stuck to honest porter. But after a while she started to throw whiskey down me. ' You're out of the ordinary run, Tim,' she said, ' and I've been on to the Boss to give you your chance.'

" ' My chance, ma'am ? '

" ' Aye, your chance, Tim.'

" Fuddled as I was, I started to put two and two together. I narrowed my eyes on her pneumatic side-face. ' This fat ould heap,' says I to myself, ' is aimin' to get me chawed up by the cat.' But she kept feeding me whiskey till she blunted the edge of my bitterness. Then I considered, ' Maybe I'm wrongin' the decent woman: maybe she *does* want me to go ahead in the world.'

" ' Three of them in all Ireland,' she primed, ' one with th' other crowd, a good man — even though he's on the wrong side of the fence — one in the City of Derry an' he crippled with rheumatism . . .'

" ' Arthritis, ma'am,' says I.

" ' Arthritis,' says she. ' And the third you know. A beast! A sot! A toper! A swiller! He'll never hold a job as long as he lives. None of the three are Irishmen,' she added regretfully.

" I sang dumb.

" ' Ah,' says she with an authentic Genevan sigh, ' Ireland produced a great poet in Tommy Moore, a great greyhound in Master Magrath and a great boxer in John L. But Ireland never produced a lion-tamer. Ah, the pity of it ! '

" There wasn't a sinner in the bar but the two of us, yet she leaned across to me conspiratorially and gave me the biggest wink I have ever seen. ' Dave got a letter from Ringling,' she whispers. ' Ringling and Dave are just like that,' with this she put one fat finger on top of the other. ' " Dave," says he in the letter, " I could do with a first-class cat-man. Can you help me ? " ' After she had let this sink home in me, ' I like you, Tim. I like everything about you. I like the way you clean out the cat's cage. I'm going to see you get your chance ! '

" When we got back, the band — our moth-eaten band — was playing in the Big Top. I was drunk but I was well able to put my legs under me. Dimly I saw a knot of people around the ticket wagon. The slide hadn't gone up as yet. The Boss came against us with question-mark written all over his face. ' Dave,' says the Missus, ' did I ever in my life cross you ? '

" ' Never ! ' says he.

" ' Well,' says she, ' don't deny me my request. You've got to give Timmy Moran here his chance to see what he's able to do with the cats ! '

" ' I'm a man of quick decisions,' says the Boss. ' We'll bill you as Moranni. Wash your face in cold water. Get into that fellow's wagon. Pull up the duds on you and lie down until I call you.'

" Jacko and Drumshambo came from nowhere and took me in hand. They led me to the lion-tamer's wagon, dragged the togs on me, then heaved me into the bunk and left me.

" When I awoke I was perished with the cold. The two boys were pummelling hell out of me. I heard the band playing and listened to the machine-gun fire of hand-clapping breaking across the music. When the applause ceased the stentorian voice of the Boss boomed out in a build-up for the aerobats Vivo and Vivienne.

" Jacko and Drumshambo were working on me with a sponge and cold water. ' Snap out of it, Timothy,' they said, and slapped and splashed me as seconds pummel a fighter who is all but out on his feet. Then a voice spoke from the misty oblong of the caravan door : through gritted eyes I saw what looked like an up-ended sperm whale standing on the steps of the wagon. 'Twas the Missus, and whatever it was she was wearing it gave her the genuine sheen of something huge out of the ocean. She kept whispering ' Tim, Tim,' in a quavering voice. I fuddled out under the stars. The Boss bustled around from the back-flap. At first he was agitated, but on appreciating that I was actually erect, his agitation subsided. ' Come on,' says he, then, ' Don't let the cat see your face — and keep crouched. 'Tis a living cinch, I tell you ! And always remember that we're there with the crowbars. And as soon as ever you see the cat and the four kittens sitting pretty, give your bow and get out.

Above all, don't forget to make your bow ! '

"When, with my trembling retinue, I got inside the tent, Vivienne was down on the strip waiting for Vivo to come down out of the air. I saw her sequins glittering though my eyes were the eyes of a dullard. There she stood with her Little Jack Horner pose until eventually Vivo thudded to the mat beside her.

"I put my nose sideways and upwards and searched the air for the odour of lion. Receiving it, I felt my face grow haggard. Hitherto that smell had connoted but a repugnant chore; now for me it had become charged with a novel deadliness.

"'The Great Moranni . . . jaws of death . . . dangers of this amazing feat . . . accentuated (the Boss always pivoted on this word) . . . by the fact . . . female of the species . . . cubs . . . defensive instincts of the lioness . . . African home . . . movement not wholly in harmony . . . intrepid Moranni . . . limb from limb . . . Ladies . . . gentlemen . . . privilege and pride . . . the Great Moranni ! '

"All the small noises of the circus ceased. I felt myself being propelled forward to make my bow. God forgive me, I did my level best to bounce out gaily with my hands up at ' Ou-la-la-la ' and my crop flashing down to slap commandingly on my high boots. Uppermost in my mind was an access of retrospective appreciation of Andy McIvor. Roar after roar came from a circle that was studded with a thousand smoky blobs.

"The cage had been moved up to the verge of the outer ring. I turned to it. Jacko gave me a short, light iron bar and Drumshambo held out the chair. ' 'Tis as easy as pie,' said Jacko. Dirty Dan was there with a long iron pole. ' You poor so-and-so,' he said. Dirty Dan and I were old foes. I got up those steps, bent and went into the empty compartment. The Boss began to bark :

now and again he gave an agonized look across his shoulder at me. I found the apprehension in his voice contagious. I got a squint at the Missus who was quivering like a bladder of lard in a hot corner. When the Boss had finished, the drummer picked up the thread of the tension and began to send his eerie peas hopping on the skin of the kettle-drum. This was designed to get the customers down, but, God's truth, it affected no one more than it did the Great Moranni. Iron poles clanged on the cage-bars as the men poked out the cubs through the smaller opening. It seemed to me that the cubs' heads had come together on the rim of a wheel and that the wheel had begun to spin violently. I blinked my way out of that spasm. I was fairly familiar with this routine, and after a good deal of tugging and hauling I got the four of them on their stools. The band pleaded for applause, got it, nourished it, fattened it, then killed it abruptly.

" Two things had begun to bother me : Number one, which of the poles clattering on the bars belonged to Dirty Dan ? Number two, what was the jabber Andy carried on to Minnie when she came out ? All I could think of was ' Allez-oop ! ' and that would have been acro-jabber, only any acros. I knew said ' Huppie ! ' or ' Hup ! ' Still, in a pinch I reckoned ' Allez-oop ' better than nothing.

" As the big slide came across — in pardon to you — I began to retch off my stomach. But I had the presence of mind of half turning my back on the people who at this moment must have been closely watching the cat. The whiskey — subtly altered by my stomach-juices — began to dribble down my chin and neck. Some of it leaked out of my nose as out of a poteen-still. I felt so weak and banjaxed that I didn't give two hoots in hell whether it was on my leg or my hand that the lioness began to chew. Minnie came stalking out. Once again

my tongue filled my mouth and I was racked by the
second spasm of vomit. Through my tears I saw the four
cubs eyeing their Ma's dinner. I grew conscious of voices
nursing and cursing me alternately. I palmed away my
dribbles and feebly raised the chair to shield me from
the cat. She came padding towards me. I backed away
from her. She put her nose to the retched whiskey and
turned away without appearing to register any reaction
except an ominous boredom. She looked at the kittens ;
then yawped ill-temperedly in my direction. The iron
poles poked in through the bars. Which was Dirty Dan's ?
— that was the one that would let her in to me. I woke
up, gathered my courage, crept towards her and started
saying ' Hiss ! ' and ' Allez-oop ! ' in an endeavour to get
her up on the centre stool. First she backed away from
me ; then she stopped and walked towards me. All the
while I was hissing like a goose. I peeped from behind the
chair at her face and I knew by it that she was itching
to maul me. Just then one of the cubs put a trial paw
towards the floor of the cage. I put down my hand and
bundled her up again. The movement, simple as it was,
made me sweat like a bull. As I was straightening myself
my knees began to knock. Up to this I had thought that
one's knees knocking was a figure of speech, but if anyone
tells you that it's not a physical fact, you can call him a
liar and quote me as your authority. Then I got a brain-
wave. I began to scrape the seat of the perch with one
leg of my chair. The lioness put her nose to the point
of scraping, so I brought my scraping to the offside of
the seat from her and her inquisitive nose pursued it. I
lowered the chair and scraped on the floor on my side of
the seat. I'm blessed to God if she didn't jump up on the
stool to view the situation as a whole. Immediately I
pronged her with all four legs of the chair and put her
sitting down.

THE LION-TAMER

" The deed was done! The kettle-drums rattled up and up and on and on. In barged the trumpets and brought the crowd to the peak of the huzza. The place swirled around me — cubs and lionesses and stools in that infernal wheel. My nostrils were assaulted by the fumes of whiskey and the unconquerable odour of lion-dung. Somebody called on me to bow. I backed against the side of the cage; my knees buckled while I gave the crowd as much of my profile as I could afford without even once taking my eyes off her ladyship. Again the applause backed up like a suddenly dammed river. I heard the gate clang open behind me. Inch by precious inch I retreated until my buttocks found the aperture: then the lads dragged me to the ground. I can't remember whether I took a second bow or not. Then the clowns spun out in cartwheels of colour and the feed banged in with his bright patter.

" The Boss and the Missus were there to congratulate me. Pride was flowing down off the pair of them. ' Leave it there! ' said himself, extending his hand. ' At last Ireland can boast that she has a lion-tamer.'

" I stayed with Vaughan's for two seasons and, believe you me, before I was finished I could cuff that old cat across the ear. Like all women, she was contrairy now and again: once she gave me the hooks in a little place in North Tipp., nothing worth talking about, but still . . ." Here the young man made as if to tug his shirt over the back of his belt and show me scars and weals, but on my counterfeiting squeamishness he desisted.

" I left Vaughan's to start on my own — on a small scale, you know. I picked up a performing bear dirt-cheap from a chap in Dublin and ran a Pick-and-Win joint for three months, making as much money in that time at that racket as I had made in my whole circus career."

THE LION-TAMER

A clock struck. "Oho!" said my friend, glancing up. He finished his drink hurriedly and bade good-night to myself and the publican. I ordered a nightcap. The publican put his elbows on the counter and nodded towards the door through which the story-teller had gone. I saw pride lighting in his eyes.

"Isn't he good?" he asked.

"Damn good!" I agreed.

"What was it?"

"Eh?"

"It wasn't the Lizard in the Cardinal's Pocket?" The man's eyes pipped in anticipation of tiny triumph.

"Eh? No no."

"Nor the time he operated on his mother for appendicitis?"

"No no."

"Let me think. Don't tell me. Was it the Litter of Elk-Hounds he sold in Cruft's?"

"He said he was a lion-tamer," I faltered.

The publican grew solemn; then wan. Suddenly he brightened in parochial pride. "Blast me if I ever heard that one before." Then, ominously, "Isn't he able to put them together well?"

"Never heard better," I said.

The publican cupped his face in his palms. "What gave him the lead to that one?" He ruminated for a moment. Then his face splintered into the joy of discovery. "Blast me if it isn't Miss Evans's cats!"

"Miss Evans's cats?"

"Aye! he's feeding them while she's away. He must have a lead. Cats — lions, see? The Lizard story — he got the lead of that from a kid who brought a frog to school in his handkerchief. Once they took him as far as the Falls of Doonass on a Confraternity excursion and he came back with a grand story about Niagara. I'd say the Niagara story is his best. That's all we have in this place, him and the Caves ": here he dismissed the hamlet with a gesture. " The caves are about a mile up the hill — spikes comin' up out of the floor and more hanging down from the ceiling. There's a big name for them. Would you remember what it is ? "

" Stalagmites and stalactites," I said.

He repeated the words, savouring them. Then, " The Caves are damn good, too." I pondered on the shade of meaning latent in the addendum " too ".

I finished my drink, bade the publican good-night and walked up the village towards the tiny hotel. The night was still and frosty with a wealth of stars above. I heard the crunch-crunch of two Guards' boots on the gravelled path a hundred yards behind me. Lemon lamp-light glowed in a few houses, on the side of the street. On my right-hand side the bulk of the hill was clear against the northern sky. The place where the hotel stood was at the higher end of the street, and when I got to the top of the little eminence I looked back on the twenty or thirty mongrel houses in the village. Odd to consider, I pondered, that after all these years it is in this shabby insignificant hollow in Ireland the reincarnated spirit of Munchausen has found flesh fit to cover its shade.

THE CLARINET

I was squatting on an orange-box at the kerb. Branded on the end of the box was a circle enclosing the words, "Zebedeila Citrus Estates, Transvaal". It was the sleepiest of afternoons in the peak of August, and behind my back the final motors of the day were passing through the little square — sneaking as it were, as if they had done something felonious, though in reality they were simply going out to the seaside. Remembering the great heat of that evening I deliberately chose to rechristen the little square a piazza, which, though alien, is a fine sunny word, even if it is a little wall-bounded in its connotation. In the act of rechristening the place I could do little but offer the area the applause and the congratulation of my tilted face. I remember the wasps, too. A team of them, dressed in Kilkenny jerseys, were playing a hurling match around my boots.

Oh, but the heat in the piazza was wonderful, wonderful, wonderful. It had the force of a large animal's breath, but the smell of the sun was there to incense it and the strength of the sun was there to show up the many motes in it. The great belch of heat and light had stilled in the piazza, and there, willy-nilly, it had to remain, prisoned but cushioned by the air-palms of three thoroughfares. True, now and again, a rebel something in the air made a gallant effort to ripple, to move, to proceed. In short, to revolt. Again and again I tried to find that vital something, but I failed. Then I concluded that it was nothing but the muscular reaction of the dead day; nothing but the purely physical phenomenon illustrated by a just-dead body or a just-beheaded chicken. And

18

then another thought occurred to me when I raised the wet penthouses of my eyes and looked at the tall houses. Then the walls became the sides of a pitcher, for the houses had taken the heat and had held it as a vessel takes and holds a liquid.

The legs of the step-ladder were on the flags of the pavement. The passage between my knees and the ladder was narrow, but while I was squatting there no one passed by. Stevie Egan the painter was on the step-ladder, and on the lower narrow edging of Mrs. Devane's shop he was lettering: "NORA DEVANE LICENSED TO DEAL IN TOBACCO". Mercifully enough, the projecting top-heavy fascia board and the lucky swinging of the sun gave him the tithe of shadow necessary for his hands and the work under his hands. Even at that, the bright show-board made a desperate attempt to blind the man. Devane's was a corner house and against the inevitable electric-light pole at the corner, Jack the Yank was standing, the blade of his sole against the pole. Jack was flabby and small with a great stomach on him. I'd have to clasp my hands together and put them away out in front of me to illustrate the kind of stomach Jack the Yank had on him. Under the broad rim of his hat the corners of his mouth kept clicking. Turn and turn about, click, click, just like that. If only I could have mustered the energy to look up at him, I knew that with the first click I should see the gold-filled second bicuspid on the right of his mouth, and with the second click the ditto on the left side of his mouth. So there he went over my head, click, click, just like two mouse-traps snapping side by side, or like the ball-bearing hatch in a pub-snug opening twice.

Stevie Egan the painter pouted down at me. In the aperture under the axilla of his amber-and-ochre-stained jacket I could see that he had lettered the "LICEN" of

THE CLARINET

"LICENSED". Then I saw that Stevie's eyes were heat-jaded and that pin-points of sweat were jack-frosting his face. He flung me the question:

"A *c* or an *s*?"

"An *s*," I answered.

"Education is a grand thing," said Stevie, striking me across the face with the hand of his sarcasm. But then to prove his impartiality, he added: "Twenty-five years I'm writing this damn thing an' I can't ever think whether 'tis a *c* or an *s*. I should be shot, so I should."

So off he went, licking the waist of his little *s* with the tongue of his camel-hair brush. The kernel of interest hardened in my eyes when I saw how sweetly the shape of the *s* came to him. Wrist levering on wrist he worked and then, hanamandeeul! just when the letter was perfect, a last foolish and superfluous lick gave it an ugly belly-protuberance. Stevie's face instantly rejected that protuberance. I rejected it with him. Stevie spat the letter from him as he had spat the heat. I dropped my eyes for fear he should notice that I had witnessed his small ignominy.

An itinerant clarinet player shuffled off the pavement and walked out into the sun. He was perhaps fifty yards from us. Outside Dinny Dineen's door he stood still, licked the salt off his lips and started to play "Bonny Mary of Argyll". Jack the Yank jerked his head up and around the pole to see the musician. He never moved his body and his face grew strained and changed colour before he let it roll back. Stevie Egan turned his head too and glowered at the clarinet player for a long while. Then Jack and Stevie smiled contemptuously at one another.

"God be good to you, Shone Cronin." Jack's voice was warm yet bitter.

"Amen! Amen! Every time," sang out Stevie, at

the same time throwing the clarinet player an evil look.

" There was a bandsmaster for you ! "

" Put it to Ireland's ground, Jack. Put it to Ireland's ground."

Jack and Stevie had what they wanted — an audience. I was the audience. Jack the Yank went off, " Myself and yourself, Stevie, playin' the E-flat clarinets. God be with the days."

" Remember the day we went to Youghal ? "

" And the excursion to Killaloe. Shone Cronin out before us an' his head up for height. It often struck me since that the Killaloe people must ha' thought we were daft."

Stevie brought the brush smartly to his left hand. He inclined his palm at an angle that was barely ten degrees off the perpendicular. " The streets of Killaloe were like that," he said to me.

" And Joe Devlin's meetin' ! Will I ever forget it ? Same as if you'd spill it out of a bucket."

" Rain, rain, rain! Shone Cronin standing in front of us an' he like an Archangel superintendin' the deluge. Mrs. Callaghan comin' down to pull her Patsy away an' she sayin', ' Faith, 'tisn't that cracked oul' Shone Cronin 'll tend you if you get knocked out with pneumonia.' An' Shone lookin' us over an' he sayin', ' Here we shtay if the Heavens opened an' swalla'd us. Th' oul' Independent Band will never let it be said.' "

" Say, Stevie, I bin tryin' to figger out for a long time who else was in the B-flat clarinets besides Paudy Ryan and Rory Mulcahy ? "

" Wasn't it Jody Ryan-West and Nelius Ahern the harness-maker ! "

" Aye, 'twas indeed. An' poor Jody's dead too. Jody was a dandy clarinet player. He was jest dandy. But not comparin' the livin' to the dead, Stevie, he wasn't a patch on yourself. Best day he ever was, he couldn't hold candlelight to you."

"Aw, I wasn't all the bad. Jody was your sweet player, though. Pity he lost his teeth so soon."

"Tell me, Stevie, outa curiosity. Twen'y nine, Shone Cronin died. Say, did the band play him to the grave?"

"Of course they did. I wasn't there, though. I was gettin' fired for rheumatics above in St. Joseph's. An' I'm not jokin' you, Jack. The ward window was open over my head. I could hear the music quite plain. 'Twas lonesome for me to be there listenin' to it an' to be able to do nothin' about it."

"Aye, tha' was twen'y-nine, wasn't it? Wha' was I doin' then? Twen'y-nine? Peddlin' sars'parilla an' coca-cola in a little soda-parlour, corner of 38th Street and 3rd Avenue. . . . Americo Lauretino's. Tha' was it, Americo Lauretino's."

Jack the Yank allowed himself a short interval of silence in which he indulged in American reminiscence. Then he broke the silence.

"Say, Stevie?" he said with a large shining face. ("Well!" from Stevie.) "About that funeral. What were they playin'? 'Return from Fingal,' eh?"

"Guess again."

"Don't tell me, Stevie. Don't tell me. Lemme figger it out for myself. 'O'Sullivan Leavin' the Mountains'? No? 'Green Woods o' Slew'?"

"I'll give you wan more try."

"Aw! sure o' course I got it. 'Will Ye No''!"

"Tha' was it. 'Will Ye No' Come Back Again!'"

As I looked up I noticed that another inner warmth had been added to the sun's warmth in the painter's face.

The clarinet player in the street was coming to the end of the first verse of "Bonny Mary". Now you know the part near the tail of the song where the music goes sailing up on the " of " that comes before " Argyll ". Here the " O-o-o-o " notes are up-scooped or grace-noted or semi-quavered in proportion to the player's incompetence or personal vagary. In spite of their talk, Stevie and Jack the Yank had their ears cocked waiting for the boyo to come to this part. Come to it he did. And sure enough he bogged in it, tore at it, gartered it. Finally he got out of it with a rip, a stick and a tear and with a penultimate noise not unlike a man sucking his shoes out of swampy ground. Then the poor creature floated into the placid waters of " Argyll ". Jack winced. Stevie winced. Indignation went out and met with indignation.

Jack the Yank criss-crossed his forehead in thought. " Say, Stevie," he began, and then he lapsed into the calculation, " '25, '26, '27 ". He spoke up again. " Say, Stevie, remember my old clarinet ? You know ' O'Reilly, Dublin ' branded on the mouthpiece ? Remember I handed it in at your place the morning I left for the States. Outa curiosity, Stevie, outa curiosity, say what became of it ? "

Stevie twisted his torso, then screwed up his face to squeeze the sun out of it. From beneath the peak of his cap he focused two eyes as heavy as binoculars on the clarinet player. By turns he grew leery, artful, secretive. He tongued out a carbuncle on his cheek with the dint of his garotting of good humour ; gazed up at the tall walls to adjust his fiddle-face of innocence ; then looked Jack the Yank straight in the face.

" Ask me tha' question ag'in, Jack. Maybe I didn't hear you rightly. My ears do stunts sometimes."

Jack the Yank grew more bland and more acquiescent. " Outa curiosity, Stevie. I'm only askin' you outa curiosity."

THE CLARINET

"Outa HELL!" Stevie detonated joyfully. Then with all the ominousness with which he could invest the little action, Stevie laid the brush across the upturned lid of the paint-tin. Then he wiped his fingers on his sleeves. Examined them to see if he could whistle on them. He grimaced at them as they were still too paint-soiled.

"Gi' tha' fellah a whistle!" Stevie was peremptorily addressing me. I scuttled out of my objectiveness.

"Who? The clarinet player?"

"Who the hell else is there to whistle at?"

I gave him the full four-finger blast. It did more than penetrate the man's playing. The whistle split the sunny sleepy street wide open — whyttt! like slit silk. The clarinet player cocked an eye at us, rotated on his axis with his mouth still full of music, irresolutely played a few bars, ceased, made a dumb show with an opening-and-closing hand, semaphored that he was on his way, and finally never drew bit or bridle until he had shuffled up to us with the spurious sprightliness and the still more spurious servility of the street musician.

"Bless ye all, gentlemen, bless ye all." Just the usual old man with the usual cold nose that a thousand of Africa's suns could not warm. There he stood, finger to mock-servile forehead. Jack the Yank and I disowned him deftly. How we did it was damn good. We impaled his eyes on the fine points of our gaze, swung them around in an arc that floated out into mid-road, and swung them to the top step of Stevie's ladder. "Here, Stevie," we seemed to say, "here are his two big eyes."

Jupiter descended one terrace from the mountains. He aimed a lethal forefinger at the clarinet player.

Jupiter Egan cannonaded. "Where did you get that clarinet?"

Again the spurious sprightliness. "Bigor, sir, I have it ever an' always, so I have. Myself an' herself have

24

been together this many a long day. An' if you'll excuse me sayin' so, 'tis many's the pint of porter . . ."

"Where did you get that clarinet?" Reverberation upon reverberation . . .

The old man's memory buckled. He pummelled his cold nose with a reminiscent knuckle. In so far as the sun allowed him to, he eyed the sky. "Well, now, as you ask me, sir, maybe 'twas Buttevant, or maybe 'twas Abbeyf'ale or Rickale. Shtop, maybe I'm a liar — 'twas Noocashtle or Charleville. All thim towns around here look all the wan to a man on the road, so they do, sir. I'm goin' back now the besht part o' ten or twelve years. An' so it was comin' on for Chris'mas an' I was playin' an oul' bit of a thing held together by spits an' wax coard an' glue. An' so I was that cold, didn't it fall outa me fingers an' busht to flithers on the road. Fair fit to cry I was, sir, an' me way o' livin' gone on me. So there was this man watchin' me from the other side o' the street an' he listhenin' to me playin'. An' it bein' Chris'mas time an' all, the fellah I'm tellin' ye about walks up to me, an' as sure as God is my judge, sir, an' I'm not tellin' ye a word of a lie, didn't he say to me, ' Throw away that pinny whisthler o' yours an' I'll gi' you a present of a nate clarinet. A sweet little clarinet with " O'Reilly o' Dublin " cut in the mouthpiece.' So he carr'ed me into a house an' gev it to me, sir. As sure as . . ."

Stevie Egan's face was beatific. Suddenly the light of a remote star of memory reached the old musician.

"Beggin' your pardon, sir," he wheedled, "but would you ever rise the peak o' your cap wan small tashte till I see would you have a sort of a strawberry mark high up in your forehead?"

As far as Jack the Yank and myself were concerned it wasn't necessary for Stevie to lift his cap. Jack the

Yank and myself were all tangled up in threads of laughter.

" Gi' me up that clarinet ! " said Stevie.

With the instrument in his hand Stevie mounted one step on the ladder. He put the cover, upside-down as it was, on the paint tin, and then hung the tin on the spear of a Gold Flake sign. He sat on his grug on the top step with his legs pulled up to him. He wetted his lips with a gentle relish as if he were enjoying the bouquet of a rare wine. He put the instrument to his lips and was appeased and pleased when he had brought the mouthpiece to his own mouth's heat. I could not help noticing that his love for the instrument had triumphed over his revulsion to the itinerant's spittle.

" What'll it be, Jack ? " he said, cocking a bright eye at Jack the Yank.

" What'll it be, Stevie, but ' Will Ye No' ' ? "

Stevie played. We listened. We prayed too. Our prayer was short and sweet. It was, " God be good to you, Shone Cronin." Now I'm not claiming that the clarinet is the king-fish of all the instruments. But the right man can handle it. And the right man was handling it in Stevie Egan. If I was asked out of cold blood if I had ever heard a finer player than him I'd have to admit I hadn't. And indeed and indeed, if the old street player wasn't a good warrant to play — well at least he knew a good player when he saw one. As the people say, if he hadn't been to school, he had met the scholars. There he was in a dead set like a red setter. I did my best to bring order to unruly emotions. As for Jack the Yank, his face had become soft and sagged. All the American harshness had drained out of it and an Irish softness had flowed home in it.

And then they all came out ! Aye, man, the whole damn place knew the touch, the turn and the twirl. First

to come was Jackie Geraghty the shoemaker with his
apron coiled up around his middle. There he stood,
light-blinded yet smiling, with the dark straight lines his
trade had ruled across his face. I remembered Jackie as
a trombone player in the old Independent Band. Then
Nelius Ahern the harness-maker stamped out on the
pavement. In his hand was clutched the shining rapier
of a collar-iron. Nelius, of course, was one of the B-flat
clarinet players. The ghostly figure of Dick Harrington
the baker came up out of an alleyway. I remembered
Dick as a sort of Laocoon perpetually struggling with the
serpent of a circular bass. Mr. Bovenizer the jeweller
sauntered respectably to his doorway as indeed a jeweller
should. I had a vague memory of his mincing with
an instrument that was delicate and genteel and wholly
in harmony with his social standing. Nora Ryan-West
waddled out of her apple-and-onion shop and stood
sponsor for her brother Jody the clarinet player who was
dead and gone. No one knew the tune and its implications better than she. Fat Nicholas Deenihan the
publican came out — I remembered to have seen his
bloodied head on the black-and-brassy charger of a big
drum. Lastly the Goose Allison came striding slowly and
grandiosely out of Friary Lane. As he approached us
he took off his cap and started jigging it in glory above
his head. He was roaring out the words of the song as
if he were drunk. " Sweet the lav' -rock's note -and lang,
lilt -ing wild -ly u-up the-eh glen. . . ." Then I remembered the Goose Allison as a funny little boysheen bawn
tipping the triangle in the Independent Band.

And then, as sure as God made small apples, the
queerest thing in the world happened. Perhaps after all
it was nothing but my fancy. Mind you, to me it was
not wholly unexpected, when our town, that compact,
intimate huddle scooped out of Kerry rawness, stirred in

its foundations, sprigged and jogged, bucked and lurched, heaved itself up to the sun, levitated freely and sweetly, stretched its neck like a flighting mallard, proceeded softly through warm ether and after an aeon or so, complete with its waterworks, its fishery courts, its solitary privy and its sawdusty pubs, snuggled down into a land that was alien and wondrously sunny. Perhaps it was the Campagna, perhaps it was Castile, perhaps it was Carinthia. Wherever it was, it was a place where music is as vital as mother's milk, as indigenous as grass. And there in that changeling air, high on a dais on a bright piazza, a great musician was playing a lament for a dead maestro.

BALLINTIERNA IN THE MORNING

ONE clear cold morning in November two young men boarded a south-bound train in Kingsbridge Station, Dublin. Both were bareheaded and wore shabby tweed overcoats. That they were fitters was a fact indicated by a black timber attaché case which one of the men was carrying; there were also tell-tale smudges of grease on their cuffs and on the edges of their overcoat pockets. Their names were Bernie Byrne and Arthur Lowe: they were being sent by their firm to repair the boiler of a country Creamery in County Kildare.

Byrne was an albino; his complexion was over-fresh and his eyes were the eyes of a tamed white rodent. His hair was cut short to avoid attracting undue attention, but the irrepressible pink of his body had bubbled up through his scalp. His expression had a disconcerting trick of trading idiocy for sagacity at the most unexpected moments. Arthur Lowe's face gave promise of being cadaverous before he was twenty-five. He had a facial tic. He was so sallow that one could not imagine his intestines to be other than grey rubber tubes. His humour, of which he was extremely niggardly, was slow, droll and deliberate. His dyspepsia, already chronic, had made him a person subject to sudden bouts of unreasoning irritation.

During the journey down — a bare hour's run — they remained standing in the corridor with their elbows resting on the horizontal guard-bar of a window. Since they were young, they resented the fact that they were wearing their working clothes while travelling — this was the reason that they did not enter a compartment. The corridor was ammoniac and stale and had little to offer them except the beginnings of train-queasiness. Despite this they found the ride slightly exhilarating, and it was with an unmistakable, if indeed somewhat subdued, sense of adventure that they looked out into the widening day. People passing to the lavatory crushed by them with barely articulated apologies. The young men gave room with excessive readiness as if to compensate with manners what they lacked in clothes. Looking downwards at an angle of forty-five degrees Byrne saw in the compartment behind him a sickish girl of four or five who was mouthing biscuits. The compartment was crowded; at a station he heard a stout woman praise the virtues of Aylesbury ducks. Some time afterwards he heard a voice from the other side of the compartment begin : " There's nothing on earth the matter with my husband, but . . ."

The men alighted at a small station in County Kildare. An impish boy of twelve with a red head and a freckled face met them. That he was a playboy was instantly obvious. His face cracked up with contagious glee as he asked : " Are ye the men to mend the Creamery ? "

" We are ! "

The albino was laughing. The boy's face set for a moment as he examined Byrne's face and eyes. The albino resented the examination.

" The manager says I'm to show ye the way. If ye like, I'll get the case sent up in a Creamery car and ye can take the short-cut across the bog."

" Across the bog? "

" Aye ! "

" That'll suit me fine," said Byrne.

The boy roared at the porter who, on closer inspection, proved also to have a red head and was obviously a brother of the guide : " Hey, Mick, send that up in the next car ! "

BALLINTIERNA IN THE MORNING

When they came out of the station they saw the trees. From an old oak depended the tattered remnants of summer finery now eked out in ragged brown bunting; a mendicant beech held out in emaciated hands the last of its unspent coppers; the furze was flecked with in-between-season gold. Beneath the trees they saw the bogland. As they approached it they lost interest in the trees and were taken with the as yet finite landscape. Following the boy they crossed the fence between the trees and were then on the floor of the bog.

Before them a turf bank reared itself in a great black rectangular box with planed-away corners. Drawing near they saw that, close to the surface, this rampart had crazied into fissures that had oozed irregularly shaped knobs of semi-dried peat. Clean rushes in tight clumps sprang from the chocolate-coloured ground. Bog-holes were filled with ink or quicksilver according to the light's quirk. A not repulsive odour of old sulphur came up out of the mould underfoot.

Their guide was agility itself. He sprang to a step in the black bog-wall, gained purchase and leaped up. The two young men followed. Then they saw the country-side in its entirety. It had all the variety of a display of tweeds in a shop window. Under their feet it was prune and orange and vermilion, with sometimes a lichen blazing up in a brilliant green. The leathery heather swished hungrily around their boots. The large white bones of fallen and stripped trees were flung here and there in the canyons of the cutaway. The sun had bleached them and the wind had antlered them. Two or three newly erected labourers' cottages were placed around the periphery of the bog: what with their red roofs, green doors, white walls and tarred plinths they had a wholly fictitious prettiness. A disconsolate black cow moved dully beside each of these dwellings. The sky

31

was a wash of grey clouds. On the near horizon they saw the scarlet and white hulk of the Creamery. Beyond it were the crisp orthodox hills of the Irish skyline.

The men strode along, singularly braced by the morning air. To breathe it was in itself an adventure. Since the ground underfoot was reasonably dry they had the sensation of walking on eiderdowns. On their left they saw a hollow square carpeted with fionnán as white as wood fibre. It was growing in great tufts which were heavily matted in one another. The hollow seemed as snug as the bottom of a delf-crate. Their guide dropped into this hollow, at the same time signalling to the men not to make unnecessary noise. Byrne and Lowe followed warily. The youngster had his hands extended with the palms turned backwards. He was tiptoeing forward, his pert head turning this way and that. Suddenly he stood stock still and the wings of his nostrils widened. His eyes were fixed on a tuft of grass before him. Seeing him standing thus the two men halted. Then the boy threw himself forward on the ground. Lying prone he scrambled into a ball, bringing his knees up to him and clawing at his belly. The men heard a squeal coming from beneath the boy. For all the world it sounded like the complaint of an injured infant.

" I have him! I have him! I so-hoed the hare! " The youngster's voice was blotched with an excitement which immediately communicated itself to the men who began to laugh and query eagerly. Lowe's tic began to beat furiously. Meanwhile the little actor was making the most of his moment on the stage. He rolled over to his knees, thence to his feet, all the while clutching something in the pit of his stomach. Then the men saw the elongated whitish body trimmed with red-brown fur. They saw the cut and carve of the great hind legs, the squashed ears and the huge protuberant eyes. Carefully the boy gathered the animal together, all the while keeping the hind legs under firm control.

All three grew strangely intimate after sharing this experience together. With a nod of his head the boy indicated the hare's form in the grass. The albino immediately crouched and bared the snug little arch. They all saw where the bones of the hare's buttocks had bared the clay. Byrne and Lowe in turn placed the backs of their hands on the floor of the form and remarked that it was still warm. As they stood up, each man shrank and shrank in imagination until he was a hare in the form peering out at the world through the tangled stems of the grasses.

Then Bernie Byrne asked: "Hey! what are you going to do with him?"

This was a question the boy had not asked himself previously. He took refuge in a laughing vagueness. But the actor in him suddenly provided the answer.

"I don't know . . . unless I kill him!"

"Will you give him to me?" asked the albino readily.

"Alive?"

"Yes, alive!"

"Sure I'll give him to you. I'll put him in a bag above at the Creamery and you can take him with you."

Arthur Lowe had recovered his moroseness. "What do you want him for?"

"I don't know. . . . I'll do something with him." Byrne smiled and grew remote. This withdrawal irked Lowe who said, "Come on or we'll never get this job done."

It was night when they returned to the city. A frosty river-wind caused them to shudder as they emerged from the station. Arthur Lowe was carrying the timber case:

BALLINTIERNA IN THE MORNING

Byrne had the hare in a bag. They took a bus to O'Connell Bridge.

Looking up the great thoroughfare, Byrne suddenly discovered that he had been granted the power to view his city with novel eyes. For one thing the balusters of the bridge were now wondrously white. The diffused light in the street was almost as impalpable as floating powder: it hung in a layer perhaps twenty feet in height and then it fined upwards into the windless city rigging. Over this was the unremembered night sky. Dan O'Connell himself and his satellites in bronze had all fused to form a drowsy octopus; Nelson was a cold hero on an eminence waiting to be quickened by a brilliant anecdote. The trams were lively enough, but they had gone to great pains to conceal their pattering feet. To the left and right Neon displayed its inability to form a right angle. Now and again a ragamuffin wind, shot with gaseous green slime, clambered up the ladders in the river walls and shrugged its facile way in and out of the arcades and the ice-cream parlours. The curves of the lamp-standards interpreted benevolence in terms of cement.

The people, too, had altered. In a remote nook in the street cerulean lanterns were busy transforming the passers-by into death's heads. The theatre queues were composed of sexless, friendless, kinless persons who had voluntarily assembled thus in batches to make it easy for them to be gathered to God. The managements of the eating-houses had scraped circles or triangles or squares or lunes in the frosted rear glass of their windows through which the prudent could observe the imprudent eating lime-green hens. Objects in breeches and skirts trod on the grey-green cellar lights and applauded themselves for their intrepidity. A girl with her partner passed by hurriedly; a shell-pink dance frock was show-

34

DATE:06/07/2008   TIME:19:11:43
TERMINAL   LK457050

WITHDRAWAL FROM CHECKING

CARD NUMBER   ************9965
BUSINESS DATE   06/08/2008
SEQUENCE #   5647
AUTH #   008933 16

AMOUNT REQUESTED $80.00
AMOUNT DISPENSED $80.00
TERMINAL FEE $2.95
TOTAL AMOUNT $82.95
BALANCE $0.00

736.16
276.51
782.00
_____
68

338.
_____
1.69

ing below her dark coat. Suddenly she leaned forward and, egging her face onwards to a gambler's vivacity, said sweetly, " But, Joseph . . ." Two workmen passed by ; one of them was saying vehemently and gutturally, " Play yer cards, I said, play yer cards."

The albino had halted by the O'Connell Monument. His eyes were luminous in the dark.

" Hey ! " called Lowe. " Whatta yeh doin' ? "

Byrne did not answer. He stepped softly in under the statue where it was semi-dark. He ripped the slip-knot on the sack's mouth, caught the sack by the bottom, and spilled the hare out on the ground. The animal was cramped : he gave three sorry hops, then crouched against the base of the statue. Above him Octopus O'Connell gave no indication of ambling.

(A hare is composed of three delightful ovals with swivels at the neck and loins. First there is the great oval of the body, balanced above and below by the smaller ovals of the head and hind quarters. The oval of the hind quarters is fragmentary but may be indicated satisfactorily enough by a simple illustration. The flexible ears are propellers, the tail a rudder. After that it is a question of power propelling a mechanism that is in perfect equipoise.

But wherever the power of the animal is generated, it finds expression in the spatulate hind legs which have the gift of spurning the world. Spurning the world — that's the secret out ! That is what makes the hare so surpassingly gallant and his beholders so chagrined and superstitious.)

Sallowface was very quiet as he watched the albino. The tic flicked in his morose features. His face cleared as he gradually acquitted his companion of blackguardism. Byrne had begun to smile curiously ; he crouched with legs set well apart. His two palms began to aim the hare towards the lighted street. The animal moved in the desired direction but, as yet, his gait consisted of despicable lopes. There was no indication that he could be so transcendently swift. Suddenly he stopped and began to cosy himself on a tram-track. Then he looked like an illustration of a hare in a child's picture-book. A breath of river-wind came upon him and eddied his fur : this wind also edged the albino's anger. He stripped his teeth and shouted, " Yeh-Yeh-Yeh ! " He raced his heavy boots and cried " Hulla-hulla-hulla ! " as he slipped his imaginary hounds. The somnolent hare became suddenly charged with violence. First he sprang erect until he was a vibrant red loop laced with white shadow. His ears were tubed to the street. Then he began to pelt up mid-road. All the while the maniacal teeth of the albino were volleying " Yeh-Yeh-Yeh! " behind him.

At first the hare's passing occasioned little comment. The people continued to stilt along or stand in lack-lustre lumps. Then someone began to cry out " The Hare ! The Hare ! "

(You have seen the breeze impishly test the flexibility of a barley field ; you have seen a child's hand ruffle the tassels of a countrywoman's shawl ; you have seen a window-wind bring to life the dead hair of a deskful of schoolgirls.)

" The Hare ! The Hare ! "

Passion sprang up in the people as if it were a Jack-in-the-Box. The alert among the six thousand persons began to gesticulate and run. " The Hare ! The Hare ! " they shouted. The street rocked in its own uproar. The rushing, roaring people miraculously had sons and sisters and friends.

" The Hare ! The Hare ! "

Meanwhile the animate talisman darted here and

there, setting his red torch to the golden thatch of the street. Now and again he stopped abruptly. When he did so, no part of the street was hidden from his exophthalmic-goitrous eyes. His ability to stop was fantastic. There was no doubt whatsoever that he was terrified, yet his body was incapable of demonstrating dread and thus his terror masqueraded as alertness. He seemed to be aware that the milling people were roaring for his blood. And the people ? They continued to demonstrate that mankind is a huge wind-rocked stone balanced on a cliff-face. Either that or (absurdity of absurdities) the greyhound is present in everyone, together with the bittern, the plaice, and the elephant.

Then the blazing galleon of a tram bore down upon the animal. He lost the sense of his exits. He raced towards the lighted street wall which miraculously opened before him in the form of an entrance to a subterranean barber's shop. He sped downwards, breaking the many parallel gleams of the metal stair-treads.

The barbers stood in reverent ranks attending to the customers. With long cool hops the hare passed through and went in the half-open doorway of an inner store-room which was roofed at its farthest end by opaque cellar-lights. The room had a repulsive smell compounded of superannuated combs and hair-oil in semi-rusty tins. Along one wall was a long bench. The hare lay down beneath it.

The crowd from the street surged down the stairway. They were a shade intimidated when they saw the hieratic gestures of the barbers. The head barber came forward — he also owned the premises — and began to shepherd the intruders with his scissors and comb. His name was Richard Collis and he had the urbanity that has come to be associated with commercial competence. The man had a skull the shape of an inflated pig-bladder ; his complexion, though a trifle over-scarlet, was undoubtedly first class. The points of his moustache were his twin-treasures and compensated in some measure for a child-less marriage. His thinning hair was as a large cross placed on his bare shoulders. With every step he took towards the intruders he filched the significance from their entrance and made it appear a vulgar brawl.

" It's a hare, mister."

" A hare's after coming into your shop."

They took refuge in defeated laughter and the in-evitable puns.

Richard Collis brought the full searchlight of his suavity to bear on the crowd on the stairway. Those nearest him were light-blinded by its rays. But his rear was unguarded : he felt the nick-snip of the many scissors die down behind him and whenever a snip did come it seemed as if one of the younger barbers were cocking a snook at his poll. He turned to his staff and rebuked them with a glance. The music of scissors and razor began again, but at a much slower tempo. Turning once more, he found the people at the head of the stairway quite merry and mutinous. It took all his charm and tact to expel them without appearing undignified.

Then a young barber pointed and said : " He's gone into the room, sir."

Richard Collis asked his customer to hold him excused. He entered the store-room, switched on the light and closed the door softly behind him. He saw the hare beneath the bench — a brown huddle which had achieved an unmistakable domesticity. The animal's panting was difficult to apprehend. Step by step the barber stole nearer. The hare swivelled his head but did not move away. Richard Collis got down on his knees. The hare watched him, first with friendliness, then with apathy. There came a sudden lull in the minor thunder of boots on the cellar lights. The barber stayed thus watching the hare for an appreciable while.

Then Richard Collis's countenance sagged, spruced, then sagged irretrievably. The skin of his face, as yet under some small control, proved to be covering a volatile squirming flesh. Unsuspected nerves jerked in patches like wind-flaws on still water. His tongue had ballooned and was filling his mouth. His lower lip essayed speech a few times before it succeeded.

" Wisha, God be with you, Ballintierna in the morning ! "

He continued to kneel thus in trance while high in his mind the years clinked by like silver beads. Gradually his face grew less ruined. At last the renewed thunder of the boots on the cellar-glass aroused him. Then he arose and returned to his shop, closing the door reverently behind him.

YUNG MARI LI

FATHER DAVID NEALE was parish priest of Aaron (pop. 8104), Montana. When he was returning to Aaron (pop. 8104), Montana, after a six months' holiday spent in his native Tarmoneerla, in County Limerick, he took with him a sod of turf. The task of selecting this sod of turf was, he found, by no means easy. He demanded of his selection that it be a typical sod; but what constitutes the typical has always been an oyster-bed of argument. Father Neale had visualised his typical sod as having an attractive texture and appearance; then it would have to burn well in case an unbeliever in Aaron, Montana, should doubt the authenticity of the souvenir; average size was also desirable; and, *nota bene*, it would have to smell well. To smell well, Father Neale repeated — almost aloud. To smell well!

He examined numerous sods from numerous bogs before he eventually selected one approximating to his definition. He learned a good deal about turf in the course of his search. Some sods, he found, are base-bred, gloomy-looking blackguards, and, with every aperture sealed to gaiety, they sit in peasant stolidity, resigning themselves to the advent of the day when they shall be re-purchased by fire. And then at the last, when they are in the midst of the conflagration, they have a habit of breaking out into the laughter of flames and revealing themselves as ill-judged honest folk. Other sods are nincompoops. They release a granular titter even at wee provocation, seem to clasp the fire eagerly, and then, if you please, have the insolence to peter out in a prolonged, slow-dying sniffle of smoke. Others are perfect in texture, but are huge awkward louts of fellows in appearance : others are so small that when you look at them you say : " These were cut by mean men with mean sleáns on mean mountains ! " However, Father David Neale eventually did find a sod to his entire satisfaction. It was a good human sod, satisfactory in gloss and weight, its ebon solidarity fining out to a small combustible tuft at one end. Father Neale was thoroughly satisfied with his selection and kept tapping his right nostril to give the world some indication of his approval.

Returning to one's native place after an absence of twenty-eight years occasions major adjustments to one's mental machinery. The day of departure is recalled. Heigh-ho, after the inevitable drive in the trap to the station with the two yew trees, you stand at the window of a carriage and clutch your bright-ribboned breviary. There over the heads of your lugubrious kinsfolk is a normal traditional Ireland, all wolfhounds and geometric sunbursts and round towers and shamrocks. The train pulls out and you carry this precious photograph in your heart for close on thirty years. And then, by golly ! you plump back into electric cookers and a bewildering iron alertness. It's not fair, your poor mind squeaks, when in dark prank the mahogany stool of traditional Ireland is pulled from under it. However, there had been compensations. When he did return, the trees were staunch around the new houses, the cool whistle of peace was through it all, he had nephews fit to answer his Mass, aye, and nieces big enough to turn the heel of his stocking.

From the deck of the liner he looked back at Ireland, patted his nose and said, " Good, good, good ! " Taking it all-in-all he rather approved of this Ireland that he had not seen for twenty-eight years, so much so that a prompting from nowhere tempted him to revise certain fixed principles of his regarding the use of physical force.

Then, with a sigh, he turned from the wisp of Irish shore and looked about for Irish ears into which he could empty his stock-in-trade joke of " Come back to Aaron, Montana, Montana. . . ."

Aaron is an open town within striking distance of Montana's glacier district. Bears walk out on the black highway a few miles from Aaron. Anglers catch prodigious numbers of trout in the mountain streams. The mountains north of the town have generous selvedges of snow, rich long laps of it under the blue tops. Laps and selvedges are greedy for the sunlight seeping through the first slats of day. Whatever about Ireland, *that* had not changed.

Back in harness, Father Neale was at first inclined to view the place with alien eyes. Gradually he eased into the old ways. He cut a few knots of procedure, rebuked three persons in so far as God had built him for rebuke, shied predictably at the deaths of two notable parishioners, and stolidly listened to his curate rendering a desultory parochial account over several meals. Then he made a few adjustments to a typewritten list which he kept in his desk. He struck out the names of twenty-four dead, inserted the names of thirty-three born, added the names of eight new arrivals, subtracted the names of fifteen of his flock departed and computed that the list of his flock now contained 1126 names. Finally (as a result of the curate's rendering of account) he wrote thoughtful notes, in the space for remarks, after the names of five of his parishioners. He folded the pages sadly and carefully and replaced them in his desk. As he did so his eyes lighted on the sod of turf. His drooping spirits rose. Suddenly he grabbed his hat and went out.

He went along Main Street to the office of *The Aaron Advertiser and Post* and made enquiries about having

a poster printed. He was satisfied with the plan the
printer sketched out for him. The printer himself irritated him : the man was too workaday, too nonchalant.
And besides, the priest fancied he saw a sniffle to the
nose under the steel-rimmed spectacles. Still, he found
in due course that the man had done his work well.
Father Neale liked the type-face used in A SOD OF TURF
and also the fact that that lead was dead in the optical
centre of the poster. The border was sturdy and solid ;
whatever qualms he had had, that solid border squashed
them. His own name was, as he had intended, in no way
obtrusive. He puckered a little at the word " Lecture ",
but after a little thought he allowed it to pass as a subterfuge. When he passed the proof he tapped the side of
his nose slowly and ponderously and said, " Good, good,
good ".

At first his parishioners were disposed to be amused,
but each one of them retreated two steps into solemnity on
finding no responding humour in the priest's face. Without vehemence he succeeded in conveying his absolute
earnestness ; he did it chiefly by the resolute stare in
his eyes and by the set tilt of the jaw. Thus he had
always tried to transfer his iron sincerity to his parishioners,
mostly Irish, Irish-born and second generation, with a
sprinkling of Italians and mid-Europeans. He knew that
without this humourless sincerity all his plans would be
defeated : all his little conspiracies to prevent the shred-
ding of his community, each new token of which he had
noted through the years with troubled eyes — the first
zoot-suit on a hobbledehoy named O'Connor, the marriage of Sally Donegan to an Anabaptist salesman, the
open rebellion of old Jim Deenihan's son.

He entrusted the task of posting the notices to his
curate, but only in the outlying portions of his parish —
in Red Springs and Kanahook. The posting in Aaron

he reserved for himself. One morning he strode out, the
posters fingered to a careful figure of eight lest the fresh
ink would kiss and blur. He called first on Charlie
Meehan. Charlie became a fanatic at once. Charlie
was a person of some consequence in Aaron : he owned
twelve chain-stores in the State, and everywhere you
went in Aaron you found a sly old lady on the bill-
boards pointing to her bulging reticule and screaming,
" Meehan's for Me ! " Charlie's main store was on the
principal crossing of Aaron, and while the priest was softly
explaining the matter to him, Charlie was away ahead
of him in fierceness. Charlie had the admirable dexterity
of the fat, and while the priest was speaking through
well-dressed lips and with round noble gestures, Charlie
was proving his markmanship with accurate movements
of his hands and perfectly timed interjections such as
" Sure ! Fine ! Fine ! Sure ! " When Charlie began to
speak he did so with such concentrated vehemence that
one looked everywhere for the person who was contra-
dicting him. He manipulated his coloured words as if
they were snooker balls. In his agony he bit off the end
of a cigar, looked at the cigar truculently, then stowed it
away quickly as if it had almost tempted him to national
apostasy. " Say, Father," he said, " how about lapping
the old sod in a white silk scarf and putting it on the
centre of my big window ? Get one of the School of Art
stoodents to do a pretty deckle-edged card, say ? Stick
ribbons and arrows and ticker-tape all around it, see ?
Make it kind of mysterious like ! Give it the whole
darned window, see ? On one condition, Father. One
condition, Father Neale. I gotta see the sod myself, see ?
And handle it myself, see ? You gotta grant me that,
eh? You gotta grant me that ! " Father Neale said,
well, he hadn't figured on showing it to anyone before
the night of the lecture — thought it a point of honour

like — but seeing that it was Charlie Meehan and that Charlie . . .

By noon the priest had but one poster left. Fingering it nervously he slowed down his pace outside a jeweller's shop in Lime Avenue. The shop was discretion itself. It was painted black, and over the doorway MARY YOUNG was written in gold leaf in a rather elaborate script. The name was flanked by two scrolls bearing the legends JEWELLERY: ANTIQUES. But the priest passed the house and then his steps lost momentum. He tapped the side of his nose but he omitted the concomitant " Good ". The tappings came slowly and thoughtfully at first, but then they worked up to a crescendo of inner battle and ended with a decisive tap that was tantamount to a blow. He turned and pushed open the glass door of the jeweller's shop. In the act of entering, one of his eyes blinked silver in the left-hand window while the other blinked brass in the right-hand window. The opening door rang a bell above his head. A German shepherd dog lying inside the door raised his jet head from the cream whorls of his chest and tilted his eyes to an angle of intelligence.

Mincing and prinking, the assistant wove among the showcases and, pouting her lips, sweetly said " Yes ? " She had all the awareness and unctuousness of a black pullet. Father Neale raised his hat. " Miss Young, if you please ? Yes ! Miss Young." The girl bowed and turned towards a brass-studded door behind the glass trays. The door had an oblong inset of hammered glass. The door swooshed out, but the return journey was baffled by its patent-closing and it whispered home with considerable dignity.

The priest was alone with the dog. It was like being alone with a Christian. Softly, very softly indeed, the priest rustled his fingers, but the dog had abandoned him as if saying, " I have no further interest in you; you conform to the standard of respectability this establishment demands." The priest ceased rustling his fingers. He leaned gently against a showcase and raised his head to the ceiling. There he read an old entry in the Baptismal Registry of his church in Aaron. " Mary Young (Yung Mari Li). . . . Father's name, Yung Seng Li. . . . Mother's maiden name, Bridget Collins . . . hmm . . . sponsors . . . yes, yes . . . gap of a year and a half between date of child's birth and child's baptism. Mary Young . . . Yung Mari Li." And then the priest thought of the very last name in that typewritten list in his desk : Mary Young ; and the blank after her name in the space for remarks.

Bridget Collins, the mother, he had never known. She had died previous to his appointment as parish priest of Aaron. But the father — wryness drew its needle across the priest's lips as he remembered Yung Seng Li and the two skirmishes he had had with him perhaps fifteen years before. Father Neale still carried two tags of Confucius as scars from those little frays. And then he remembered his single encounter with Mary Young after her father's death. The girl was then twenty-five. She had heard him out, not without blandness and gentility, but afterwards there was the poise and the shrugging : " Yes, of course . . . Baptism . . . one's time is so occupied, Father . . . one does never quite get the opportunity . . . you understand how it is. Duty . . . of course . . . duty, but one's conception of duty, even of belief, is so, shall we say personal ? . . . arbitrary ? Yes, yes . . . if you don't mind, the telephone. . . ."

The priest looked over the glass showcases and the silver and the brasses. The intestines of the watches are now in a workshop at the rear, he concluded. A good

deal of tone since the old man's time. The old man was
a brassworker but he had never quite mated his trade
with that of jeweller. His girl had succeeded. There
was discretion here, even opulence. He smiled at a pair
of brass snakes with tails coiled in an attractive standard
and mouths gaping to receive tall tapers. He looked at
the die-direct edges of the showcases; at the cut glass;
at four silver mannikins. He looked at the sleek dog.

Mary Young came out through the brass-studded
black doorway. She bore her Oriental face before her as
if it were a shield of brass embossed with a nose, a brow,
and a pair of eye-sockets. Her dress was the correct
black. There were pearls at her throat. When she joined
her defensive, her suspicious fingers, a diamond ring
flashed a low warning at the priest. In the centre-parting
of her black hair the skin of the scalp glowed lime-white.
The hair was gathered to a spinsterish bun at the nape
of the neck. Approaching him she tilted her Eastern head
to remote belligerence and her ten cyclamen nails formed
a purely negotiatory cradle. Without speaking she conveyed: " At the risk of tediousness I must repeat that my
attitude towards certain matters is entirely unaltered."
The priest made a quick calculation and reckoned that
her age was thirty-nine.

Smiling, Father Neale raised his hat. Then, replacing
it, he energetically took refuge in his solitary poster.
While his head was bent he resolved to play the part of
an old priest whose stock reaction was benevolence. Then
the imp of his temporary embarrassment began to urge
him to play his part more fully by doddering. But
behind this absurd play-acting he was tremblingly alert.
Yet when he raised his head, his face held the incipience
of a counterfeit pastoral palsy. " A whim of mine . . .
our schools, Miss Young . . . repairing. . . . In Ireland. . . . Turf . . . peat you know. . . . Display it . . .

according as we grow older . . . primary importance."
All the while the alive eyes were seeking a cranny in her
visage of beaten brass.

Mary Young grew amicable. Her eyes said, " Yes
. . . yes . . . is that all ? . . . Is that all ? " But when
she acceded, was she eager to accede? No, no, he must
not betray his eagerness to recognise her eagerness. He
thanked her with a facile sliding into complete senility
and fumbled his way out on to the sidewalk.

There he tossed aside the fiddle-face of his weakness.
He dismissed the sham saggings of his body by the natural
expedient of throwing himself upwards and outwards
towards the fullness of his great frame. Now again he
was a man with a task before him.

But had it all been a waste of time ? How much —
if any — of her mother went to her composition ? Was
there even a tithe of Bridget Collins in Yung Mari Li ?
Or was she wholly her courteous, inexpugnable Confucian
father ? He shrugged. He had much more to do, many
people to meet, numerous letters to write.

Late that night he brought the sod out to Charlie
Meehan's. Charlie had a spacious house on the fringe
of the town. The house was ablaze with lights to welcome
him. Charlie had allowed his kids up late to see the
sod of turf. There they were, whooping in the hallway.
Charlie's American wife was as astute as blazes ; she had
reserved her role until she had observed her husband's
face for a while. What she saw in his daft eyes decided
her against chaffing. All through the evening she thanked
her stars that she had not made the most grievous blunder
of her life by falling headlong over the cliff of facetious-
ness. Charlie handled the sod reverently and thrust it
under the nose of his eldest son with, " Get your nose to
that, you damn Yankee, and get the smell of home ! "
The man was roaring ; but his sorry bulwark of harshness

was as thin as tissue-paper. Yet the next morning the appearance of the wrapped sod with its panoply of streamers and arrows in Meehan's window engendered widespread hilarity. Hilarity and some fierceness. Father Neale was pleased when he heard the rumblings of this fierceness. He tapped the side of his nose and said, " Good, good, good ! " By way of superfluous explanation he added to himself, " Fierceness is cement ! "

On the night of the lecture the hall was full. Father Neale was at the door shaking hands with the Irish. His curate was busy inside. The Irish had come out of their houses — every man-jack had come. There they were, Jack Mulcahy, Teddy Lysaght, Peter Flynn, Anthony English, Dan and Michael O'Connor, Joe Feehan, Dinny McGinley, with their wives and children, some of them with their children's children. Old Mrs. Sloan (née Broderick) drove down from her mansion in the hills. A sprinkling of Italians came. Giuseppe Salvini was there — the richest man in town — and his gargantuan midnight glittering wife with him, waddling up the narrow pathway, circling from leg to leg as a heavy box is trundled by a railway porter. Father Neale pressed Giuseppe to appear on the platform, but the Italian said, " No, the Irish to-night," and after this he telescoped ten no's.

Charlie Meehan, Tim Foley, Anthony English and young Sloan the attorney were on the platform. The wrapped sod of turf was on the table with the carafe of water beside it. Charlie and his fellows were portentous as haystacks. Then, precisely on the stroke of eight, Father Neale appeared on the platform. The people cheered. The priest looked well. He possessed the unpurchasable and wholly natural gift of ceremony.

But though it was clear that he was pleased with the size and zeal of his audience, yet some fraction of him seemed wholly not at peace within himself. Some essential lustre was absent from his lips, and now and again scrawlings came out on his forehead. His tongue readied his dry lips ; he walked forward and looked at the Poles, the Austrians, the Italians — and the Irish. Just then, in the pause before he began to speak, Mary Young entered the hall. Sprucely and trimly her body moved forward through the people. The minor ripple of whispering that s-s-s-ed forward and broke upon the priest's boots indicated that the woman's presence at a Catholic meeting was considered abnormal. Father Neale eyed her keenly and nodded to a youngster who immediately vacated his place in the front row. Mary Young graciously thanked the boy and then yielded her face up to the speaking priest.

Now, I cannot tell you with any degree of accuracy what the priest said to his people. My mouth and the priest's mouth are two different mouths. Come, now, be honest with yourself! What would *you* say about a sod of turf in Aaron, Montana ? Or in any five other places, pin-pricked at random on a kid's atlas ? Emotion is emotion anywhere, even in Aaron, Montana. His end and his beginning was home, and the things of home. Home. Home. Home. Beyond the beloved bits of ceremony he was a baker and his people were dough. He was a potter and his people were clay. He was a sculptor and his people were stone.

When he came to the unwrapping of the sod the Irish, for the most part, were blatantly on the point of tears. Home. Home. Home. God dear ! God dear ! Home. Over the hills and the steeples and the towers and the salt water. Like the passing of a great wind every single one of them was having daybreak in his chest and a hundred cocks crowing in his heart. These poor drugged Irish were galloping like thunder at the heels of their priest.

The women were crying and they didn't give two hoots in hell who saw them either. They snuggled against husbands who had grown wondrously fierce, each man's face the hue of a cock's comb. The husbands resented such advances lest they be considered effeminate, and unangrily clucked their womenfolk away. A miner who had come all the way up from Butte took his short pipe out of his mouth and said loudly, " Wisha, Glory on you, Priesht up there ! "

And then, when their emotion was at its peak, the priest, by an unpredictable flippancy, smashed the wondrous glass of their mood. This was no error on his part. It was carefully calculated.

He protested his own inadequacy to deal with his subject. If 'twere his brother Dick now or Jim Joe, they could talk on turf till Tibb's Eve. But he ! Here he held up his milky-white hands and the people gave back the guffaw he had expected. He reckoned that this breaking would now set them the communal task of gathering the fragments and setting them together again. Ultimate individual fracture, he knew, would have in any case inevitably followed.

He urged them to talk now : Charlie Meehan started off and his naturalness proved infectious. Narrowed down to the intimacy of a family group the men were soon speaking without shyness. They spoke hesitantly thus :

" Would you believe me, Father, when I say I seen turf cut under the red strand of the seashore ? In Bally-heigue it was, and 'twas cut out at the low-water mark ! Cut in a great hurry, too, and then 'twas saved on the brink of the sandhills. . . ."

" I seen a son a flamin' sleánsman and the father before him as awkward as Euclid. . . ."

" In our place we'd pelt the brúscar on to the top

51

of the rick so that it'd soak the weather. Doin' it of a windy day 'twould blind the two eyes inside your head and . . ."

" Say! Good turf rings even when it's leaving the sleán. It squeaks under the prongs of the pike. The wax in it is sort o' slow to leave go its hoult on anything."

" Good turf darkens on the bank within the hour. Then it glistens, man, like a pony's back. Like a pony's back and her feed thickened with linseed oil."

" Footin' turf is a job you should second to no man. Rogues footin' your turf for you mightn't stir the dead man in the heart of the grogue and then . . ."

" On the mountain in our part we'd pull the single scraw from it. Up 't'd walk with the little cubes of solid dark turf dangling off the grass threads. Beggin' your pardon, Father, but 'tis like nothin' on earth more than skulldraggin' a woman down a shtairs. . . ."

" Do you know what it is, but the breenshin' man has a proper animal's job, so he has. . . ."

The priest was happy now. The place was crackling about him with vivid yapping. Women were eager that their husbands should be heard. No woman spoke. Instead she pulled at her husband's sleeve to make him the vehicle of her contradiction or her addition.

" An odd time the sleán'd strike a gusher. A gusher, man, and then all the water in the wide world'd boil out under your boots. . . ."

" Well, God be with the mornin' I so-hoed a hare in a snug truppal at the butt of our reek of turf. I remember it well. 'Twas a mornin' in June and the mountain was fair drowned in clear blueness. . . ."

" I got a trálach in my wrist pikin' turf of a day and I declare to the Man Above if . . ."

" I dare say there's none among ye but found the lovely red bog-sally ten sods deep in the clay. You'd find yourself nursin' it in your hand for the full round of a day. . . ."

The priest handed down the sod to be passed from hand to hand through the hall; he thought it good that each person smelled at it deeply as if to capture even one camera-click of the lost world at home.

And then, when the harvest of words was almost reaped, it happened. Yung Mari Li was on her feet. The Irish was out on her yellow face. Out on her face like a torch. Silence weaved through the groups. The woman's face swung from priest to people, from people to priest. And then she spoke:

" My mother was Bridget Collins from Tobbernagoneen, near Knocknagoshel in the County of Kerry, Ireland. Tobbernagoneen is Gaelic and it means ' The Well of the Rabbits '. Miles on the land-side of Tobbernagoneen is Tournafulla which is a name as strong as a blow of a fist in the mouth, for it means ' The Bleachfield of the Blood '. When my mother was a child growing up she spent all her time out on the bog. She wore a red flannel petticoat you could see two miles away. Tobbernagoneen is a townland with nothing in it but bog. My grandfather Joseph Collins had the grass of three hungry cows on the cutaway but he had up to sixty acres of bog. He used to let it to the farmers around at five shillings a bank for the year. I remember, too, my mother saying that a sleán of turf is what three men would cut in the run of a day, one man cutting, one man breenching, one man spreading. A sleán of turf worked out about thirteen rails. My grandmother Maria Collins used to make pillows out of the canavawn that grows on the bog. I recall my mother saying that a noted fiddler named Kevin Regan was drowned in a boghole on my father's turbary. My mother said that he used be heard playing ' The Job of Journeywork ' there afterwards and that she and her sisters were mortally afraid to stir out after dark for fear of Kevin Regan's ghost. . . ."

Invisibly the arms of the women were out, groping about to embrace the Chinawoman. Their arms stopped short of her, repelled by the foreignness in her face. Then again the poor bewildered women sent up their arms to clutch at the garments of their priest, to pluck at him, to hook him, to ask him, "What? Why? Who? Why? Why?" And the priest was tensed and relaxed and meticulously sensitive to their pitiable queries, and hinging his face over them he chided them silently (even dangerously, lest even their clumsy breaths should knock over his lovely house of cards) and they interpreted his eyes and mouth as saying: "This is utterly normal; utterly normal, remember! I tell you that a good deal depends on it that you should believe that this is utterly normal." Then, after the small negation, the wave of their perplexity ebbed and they were at peace. The priest approved of their acceptance and lidded up his eyes till he looked like an old hen. He began to stroke his face in thanksgiving; he put the pads of thumb and forefinger on the lids of his eyes, stroked briskly out over the cheekbones, ran them up the lip corners and vouchsafed the finger-tips a minor osculation in the middle of the lips.

Afterwards the people went home through the dark.

The priest allowed five agonizing days to elapse before he called on Mary Young. As he expected, he found that she was eager to receive him. Even then, he spent five minutes lipping the tittle-tattle of the town. He skilfully avoided the topic that was a mutual urgency in them both. And then the guard of her grandeur was down. . . .

"An exclamation of my mother's," she said: "Reen-anangel! What does it mean?"

" King of Angels," the priest said.

" King of Angels ? "

" Yes ! King of Angels ! "

Then they both said " King of Angels " together.

After that she was nothing but an unsure groping woman. She indicated the studded door with its rectangle of hammered glass. " If I'm not taking up too much of your time, Father ? " Then, " Miriam ! " she said, clicking the girl to her station. She put her carmine fingers on the studded door and the door shrank open. The dog saw the priest's grey head pass in, high and mighty amid the splendour of the brasses.

BLACK NETS

As the tide brimmed slowly in, its mounting green fluid began to shorten the long-legged cliffs. Far out in the dazzling western world sky had mated with water until the horizon was imagined rather than seen. To the north and south small clouds, no larger than gun-puffs, decorated the heavens. Over the strand the gulls moved beautifully, the blades of their outstretched wings finding the grain of the timber sky.

The seaside resort nestled under the northern cliffs. Southwards the fawn strand flowed in a curve that was roughly three miles in length. The strand ended on the slobby estuary of a river, beside which lay the fishing village — an excrescence of tarred sheds and thatched cabins. Beyond this huddle, on the other side of the river, loomed a large hill dotted with lime-washed cottages. Seaward from the estuary the southern horizon was formed mostly by the bell-tents of three mountain peaks. To-day these peaks were gauzed in sun-heat.

The sandhills between the seaside resort and the fishing village were divided equally into two zones of influence. Southward for a mile and a half went the golf links — the undulating emerald axminster links. Standing on one of the many domesticated dunes it contained, one saw the admirable switchback sweep of the fairways, the flawless cosy greens (each decorated with a brilliant red pennant), the tortured and defeated bent-grass, the collapsed and untenanted rabbit-holes (untenanted, for the rabbits had been efficiently gassed). The whole course seemed to be whispering the word " Civilisation " over and over as if it were a prayer. For the greater part of its southward journey the links saw to it that they kept a stout dune between them and the uncivilised sea. But the thirteenth green, like a foolish virgin, peeped out over the sandy cliff and recoiled astounded at the barbarity of what it had seen. Instantly the links swung inwards and north-wards towards home, sauntering unadventurously through the smooth fields.

But southwards from the thirteenth hole the sandhills were untamed bristling upheavals of scabby, mangy ground that brightened with a thousand rabbit-scuts on a sudden handclap. Here and there the dunes were slashed into huge valleys of dazzling white sand — the sand studded by the further brightnesses of shells and stones and bones. This savagery of land raged and roared southwards till it whimpered out in blown sand beside the fishermen's cottages on the estuary.

A boat was hauling on the Long Strand a few hundred yards to the south of the thirteenth hole. As the boat moved out to sea it cut the flecked flanks of waves of average strength, which lifted, then lipped tentatively, finally spilling like tumbled churns of milk. The boat itself was of an unusual make, rather resembling a canoe in timber : like the canoe it had a high prow and stern. It was called a " ganelow ", which word, as likely as not, was a corruption of " gondola ". The three fishermen in the vessel were Pompey Connors and the two Cour-nanes. A youngster of sixteen or so named Danny Martin was standing on the strand " shoring ", that is, he was holding the head of the net-rope. The men were fishing for the rearguard of the spring salmon or the van-guard of the peal.

Pompey Connors was as black as the hob of hell ; he had a squat powerful body. His arms were the arms of an ape. Under the visor of his dirty cap the two jet pupils of his eyes were set in startling whites that might have belonged to a negro. The whites were terrifying in the sooty stubble of his face. His eyes, the old people said, had not been given him for his soul's salvation. His lips made a letter *s* lying on its side : they had been twisted either by a cerebral stroke or by an unusually sardonic outlook on life. When his great mouth opened it was seen to contain a ruined temple, with the broken amber pillars of his teeth fallen haphazardly on the red sand of his gums.

The two Cournanes were cousins, a fact proclaimed less by their red colouring than by the similar bone construction of their faces. One, who was perhaps fifteen years older than the other, had begun to acquire the grizzle of the forties ; the younger of the two was dressed in a suit of rags. Both cousins were barefooted. Pompey wore heavy old boots with uppers well slashed to let the sea water in and out.

After a morning of fruitless fishing Pompey and the younger Cournane left the boat and walked up the sand. Danny Martin turned southwards and went in the direction of the village. The older Cournane remained in the boat. He had shipped the unwieldy oars and was resting his weight across one of them. The younger Cournane mooched disconsolately about the sand ; he picked up a belt of madra-ruadh seaweed and began to pull it apart in his spatulate fingers. Tiring of this, he looked out to sea. He called Pompey's attention to a large flock of gulls attacking something in the sea about four miles from the shore. After hooding his eyes and looking out to sea for a space, Pompey said it was a school of mullet or else a dead sea-pig. That ended the conversation between them.

Between the sandhills and the sea was a great rampart of rounded stones which raised itself in three distinctly marked tiers. Pompey threw himself down on the lowest

tier, took out a shortened pipe and began to smoke.
After a while the younger Cournane also threw himself
on the stones, about thirty yards south of Pompey.
Lying down he looked like a bundle of old clothes or the
body of a drowned sailor cast up by the sea. As Pompey
smoked, his eyes instinctively sought the resort under the
dark northern cliffs. His gaze lingered thoughtfully on
the white hotels with annexes that looked like children's
arks or playboxes painted lime green. He slipped deeper
and deeper into rumination.

Half an hour passed thus. Pompey's pipe grew cold
in his palm. His eyes had grown as soft as a cocker's.
Then young Cournane came up. " I might as well get
the jar for you," he ventured deferentially.

" Aye, you might as well," said Pompey, not without
surliness. He spat as he looked out at the barren sea,
at the boat slumped at the tide's lip, at the irritating
figure of the older Cournane crouched over the oar.

As young Cournane took the earthenware jar from
under the stern seat or " deck ", his cousin lifted his face
and ran his tongue over the salted crevices of his lips.

Returning to Pompey the young man set the jar down
on the sand. Pompey's ruined yet powerful mouth was
opened in a grimace of twisted humour. Cournane
waited respectfully while Pompey built up an effect by
scrutinising some coins in his palm. Then the dark face
twisted towards Cournane.

" Did you ever hear what the mountainy man said
as he looked at his sow ? " asked Pompey.

" What was that ? "

" He said, ' God direct me whether I'll ate you or
drink you.' "

" Ha-ha-ha " went Cournane's raucous laughter.
Then " Ha-ha-ha " again. Pompey looked at the syco-
phant in open disgust. Cournane's glee puttered and

ceased. Pompey rose and spat on the sand. He gripped the jar by the ear and strode up the hill of rounded stones. Though he did not make noise by displacing even a single stone, the older Cournane lifted himself in the boat and watched him until he disappeared through a gap in the wall of the dunes.

A long time after he had gone a woman in a rose-red ruched bathing costume walked down the strand towards the boat. She was a young woman and her fair hair was sculped in the air behind her. Every movement of her body gave glory to God. Gradually the man in the boat raised himself to watch her. A head appeared on the bundle of rags on the stones. When the woman was perhaps a hundred yards from the boat, she turned abruptly and walked away.

As he was returning from the resort with the jar of porter, Pompey cut diagonally across the golf links. This was a route he had never before taken, but to-day he found the jar a load on his cramped fingers, and besides, the heat of the sun was beginning to suck the sap of strength out of his body. He began to tingle and smile as he felt the elastic pile of the grass beneath his heavy boots. He was experiencing the thrill of the unchallenged trespasser. Whenever he put down his boot he churlishly saw to it that he placed it on a shrivelled daisy or on a tiny winsome heartsease. Once or twice he laughed aloud. Suddenly he felt an urge to trumpet a challenge into the green corridors of the links. He walked on to a green, and then it seemed to him that he was a burglar in a bedroom of a mansion. He lifted the flag-pin out of the hole and speared it home. It fell with a clang into the metal cup.

At first he was taken aback on finding a four-ball approaching the thirteenth green. His tendency to halt was a natural reaction, but he overcame it and walked forward with hooded menacing eyes. The men were approaching the green; the nearest man to Pompey was a short stout man dressed in a fawn windbreaker and black trousers. Pompey walked out into the rough and drew level with this man just as he was taking an iron from the caddy. Pompey noted the sun-crimsoned fleshy face with its protuberant eyes, the greying head and the stumpy neck on the bottle-neck shoulders. Pompey was momentarily puzzled by the whiteness of the man's throat. Then the black pants the golfer was wearing led him to the conclusion that the man was a priest. The priest seemed to be labouring under a sense of grievance, for his lips were pouted and the preliminary swings of his club conveyed a sense of ill-temper. The caddy's face, too, was extra alert to anticipate displeasure: at the slightest glance by the priest in his direction he was quick to feign apprehension.

Pompey sauntered past the priest. His pace lagged down as he waited to watch the stroke. The priest gathered himself in a lump over the ball and began to address it. He broke his stance and looked at Pompey as if requesting him to cease walking. As the golfer resumed his position, Pompey halted; this seemed to disconcert the priest much more than the walking had done. Pompey rolled his tongue in his mouth and hissed softly through his nose. After the priest had played and failed to make the green he looked at Pompey as if blaming him for the mishap. Pompey's dark eyes coolly took the reprimanding glance, and as the priest moved up to the green he followed leisurely, all the while keeping at a discreet distance in the rough. The priest's next stroke brought him to within a yard of the pin. Pompey was now squatted on a small dune over the sea with the green directly beneath him; he had laid down the jar, and his eyes were firmly fixed on the golfers. Again the priest began his ungainly address, but he seemed to be irritated immoderately at finding himself thus gaped at by the fisherman. His brogues became uneasy and unsatisfactory; the movements of his head and body frankly expressed disgust. At long last came the ill-timed loose tap that muffed an easy putt. None of the others commented on this. As the priest bent and snatched up the ball, his eyes roamed to measure his companions' reactions. Then he looked up at Pompey on his perch. His face hardened, for he fancied that the fisherman was smiling at him.

As the golfers drove to the fourteenth, Pompey still retained his position and eagerly watched the balls rise gracefully in long parabolas and fall far down the fairway. All except the priest's, which swung determinedly in a powerful yet graceless curve into a bunker to the left. Again his eyes put the blame on Pompey.

There was a workmanlike rattle as the caddies slung the bags high on their shoulders. The sudden noise seemed to break the tension. Then Pompey's face hardened; he rose from his crouch, walked forward slowly but deliberately, and placed himself in the priest's road. At first the priest could scarcely credit the obvious fact that the fisherman was bent on obstructing him. Then, after the perceptible pause that followed on this incredulity, he steeled his face for a rebuke. But although Pompey was fully equipped to read the portents in the priest's face, he stubbornly stood his ground. His boots were rooted in the turf. He did not consider it his duty to raise his cap since the priest was not wearing his collar. When at last the fisherman spoke there was no trace of servility in the tone of his voice.

"You'd better do something for us, Father," he demanded.

The priest's brows came down abruptly. He was

having trouble with his refractory mouth. " Do something for ye ? " he asked.

" Aye ! do something for us ! " Pompey's voice was now coloured with a deep emotion.

The priest hesitated. Anger or tolerance ? Curiosity and his training for the priesthood urged him to be tolerant. He was aware that his companions had halted and had become acute witnesses of the little duel. At last he raised his eyebrows in the most tolerant of unspoken queries.

For answer Pompey curtly nodded downwards and indicated the boat riding at the tide-lip. " Black nets!" he said.

The priest looked down. He saw the idle boat with the man asleep across the oar. He saw the ragman slumped on the round stones. He saw the youngster returning from the fishing village. Turning again to Pompey he looked him up and down. His gaze stole towards his fellow golfers.

" Oh ! " he said, almost making the fatal error of laughing. Then, with remote amusement, " What do ye want *me* to do for ye ? " His face had bloomed up in the full flower of tolerance.

Pompey's reply came with the accuracy and speed of a cobbler's hammer. " That'd be more your business than mine, Father," he said.

Under his summer crimson the priest's colour momentarily changed. He opened his mouth to speak, but thinking better of it, drew in a quick breath and clamped his teeth tightly together. Air came from his nostrils as he walked round Pompey and drew away to join his companions.

Pompey was left alone on the higher ground. His jar of porter lay behind him on the turf. His face had darkened to malevolence. His eyes had become objects that could inspire terror. Despite the great heat of the day he had begun to tremble. His rose tongue (a peace-making woman) crept out to quiet the brawling masculinity of his lips. He stood there watching the players walk away into the grassy hollows. Far below him he saw the priest approach his ball, saw him select a niblick from his bag, saw him crouch, saw him strike, saw the ball lift over a small dune, saw it bound dead on the pin. As Pompey watched, his broken nails were digging into his palms.

The excellent stroke restored his buoyancy to the priest. It brought gaiety back to his carriage. It was as if the loose faggots of his nerves had been suddenly bound in a trim bundle. He was walking sprucely up to the green when, inexplicably, he halted dead in his stride. He turned and looked back at the dark figure on the dune. For a moment it seemed as if Pompey and the priest were alone in all creation. Their thoughts began tangling and twining across the intervening space like seaweed swaying on the sea-bed.

Then, on a sudden, the priest turned seaward, raised his hand, and scrawled curiously in the sky. The golfers watched him intently, even embarrassedly.

As for Pompey, he began to laugh like hell. Grabbing up his jar of porter he commenced to run awkwardly. Out through the fawn gap in the dune wall he ran, while the loose sand tried in vain to clog his passage. He plunged down the slope of stones, making a great racket as he moved. Seeing him, the boy returning from the village began to quicken his pace, the sleeper in the boat raised himself, and the bundle of rags on the stones began its resurrection.

Pompey placed the jar on the sand and then laughed richly out into the tide. He was shouting at the Cournanes: " We'll try one more haul ! " Then, as a surprising after-

64

thought, in a curious tone of voice ". . . in the name of the Father, Son and Holy Ghost." The Cournanes looked at him : their dullard lips were wide apart.

Pompey leaped into the boat and paid out the net as the two Cournanes rowed. Danny Martin held the net rope on the strand. " Pull, blast ye, pull ! " roared Pompey. When he stood erect in the boat he seemed to dominate the sea. The circle was quickly completed, and jumping out into the shallow water, Pompey and the elder Cournane began to close the haul while the younger Cournane joined Martin. Slowly the necklace of blackened corks moved inshore. Even the incurious Cournanes began to show signs of excitement. Their eyes lost their natural stupidity and their mouths widened in a strange sagacity. They took a pace or two nearer the net and were soon up to their collops in the tide.

It was then Pompey began to roar, and the noise his mouth made was like the sound of a hound baying. He was pointing here and there along the dwindling semi-circle of half-submerged corks. Then, as on a signal, the great school of trapped salmon began to drive smoke out of the net.

A cormorant flew low across the sea. Its flight was determined and urgent. Over the horizon hung a great dark cloud and from behind it the sunlight streamed down in seven strong shafts.

THE MAN WHO DETESTED MOVEMENT

THE man had but one abnormality and that was his unreasonable detestation of movement. An important characteristic of this hatred was that it remained wholly inoperative until he was preparing for bed or just in bed. Then his detestation became all-powerful and clamant within him. In the first onset of bedroom darkness his ears became as pointed as an elf's : only on the firm assurance that his house was the soul of stillness could he fall asleep. Lying there before slumber it was his un-varying custom to examine the conscience of his house, asking, " House, house, are you wholly still ? " Times the query became an admonishment : " House, you owe it to me as a duty to be still ! " Times it became a whine : " House, to-night I am utterly weary ; won't you please be still ? " Times the examination culminated in a snarl or even a roar : " House, house, for God's sake be still ! "

More often than not the house was obedient and pleasing. Nights there were, however, when the building would play the sneak, the liar, or the rascal. Then the man would be conscious of secret movement, although it was often a nerve-rending task for him to locate it. Each night he went to bed at 11.30 P.M. His wife had preceded him by half an hour ; the intervening half-hour he had spent reading by the fireside in the living-room with his stockinged feet high on the fire-canopy and his tongue searching out the vestiges of biscuit-mush that clung to his gums.

At 11.30 approximately he laid aside his periodical or paper, lighted a cigarette, and began the prelude to his little game. " Movement ? movement ? " he whis-

66

pered. Years before, it had been an interesting game: ears aiming at movement — taps dripping, curtains swaying, mice scampering, smoke eddying. But with the passage of time what had begun as an unimportant pastime became a dangerous game. Finally it assumed the proportions of a tyrannical obsession.

The man was realist enough to appraise the implications of the problem clearly. Quite early in the self-scrutiny he had estimated correctly that the potency of his phobia ebbed and flowed with the tides of his physical condition. When, for instance, he was on a seaside holiday, healthy, sun-roasted and sea-washed, he was more than master of this dread of nocturnal movement. If he could have had his will he would have wished it to be always summer, always sunny days. When he was bathing in the sea he considered that never did great green wave shatter itself on a more fearless chest. On emerging from the water his claret bathing-trunks contrasted flatteringly with his clear skin — both trunks and skin kept reassuring him of his masculinity: of his strength. But away from the sea, the first quavering of winter's dusk brought an answering quavering of terror to his heart; dead leaves scurrying on flagstones roused the echo of morbid flutterings in his soul. His spirit, which loved the sun and cliff-tops and open day, was powerless when November's fog allied itself to his own anaemia. Each night then the fear of movement while he slept was a rat gnawing at the angles of his cheekbones.

A superficial observer would have reckoned him happily married, would have gone so far as to state that, for a sensitive man, the fellow had found the ideal mate — the woman was large, global, unimaginative; even earthen. In the early days of their married life he had confided fully in his wife in the hope of securing a buttress for his crumbling mental masonry. But receiving in return a dull but studious desire to please and keep pleasing — which irked him by its very blundering animal nature — the man had ceased his confidences abruptly. The upshot of this amputation, this cauterisation, was that he had grown secretive, repressed. Within him the pet of his fear grew fat.

Two children, both boys, completed his family. One of the boys was nine, the other seven. In the daylight, and especially in the summer daylight, they occupied a large place in their father's affection.

One evening in spring the younger of the two boys brought home a tiny fish in a jam-jar of water. While showing the fish to his father the boy's face kept blazing with excitement. The father was sitting on a rustic seat in the garden when the child rushed out to show his treasure. The man smiled dutifully at the fish. "And Daddy! there's millions of them in the Green Stream!" the excited child bubbled. "Millions!" smiled the father; then out through lips pursed in fun — "and tell me, is this all you've caught out of all the millions?" Father and son chortled. The boy said, "Isn't he a beauty, Daddy?" The father hummed assent. Since the jar had now been level with his eyes for a few moments he had no alternative to examining the fish closely. He saw an ugly lime-green head over an orange throat. The little minnow was staring out through the convex glass at him; the mouth kept opening and closing as it chop-chopped the water. The indolent but graceful movement of the little fins was barely discernible. Then the jar was lowered as the child's arm tired. "I'll put him on the shelf of the scullery and feed him in the morning," the boy said. Then, as an afterthought, "I wonder what he eats?"

That night the man read at the fireside as usual. At

THE MAN WHO DETESTED MOVEMENT

11.30 P.M. he dropped his book and began to give the house its customary examination. Suddenly he became aware of the presence of the fish in the house; his first reaction was one of inverted pleasure at discovering this novel source of movement. But after the initial exhilaration he realised coldly that he was confronted with an entirely new problem. He rose abruptly, quenched the lights and went to bed.

To bed, but not to sleep. He read for a short while before attempting to sleep. Sleeping for him had always been a positive action; he never simply "fell" asleep. Latterly, getting to sleep was becoming a process akin to clambering on to a horse's back. Before the essay of sleeping he was addicted to reading stories of violence and vivid movement, tales of shipwrecks, battles, and explosions, with blood spilled by the pitcherful. On ceasing to read, he invariably experienced a delicious sensation of escape. Then, after the light-switch had clicked under his fingers, he grew conscious of his tremulous ability to terminate violence at will. He ceased to reflect that the violence was wholly imaginary; it pleased him to delude himself that in this instance at least he possessed an attribute normally associated with the Godhead; that in the matter of putting a period to violence he was master of his destiny. The danger of this flirting with violence attracted him, as the danger of leaping from the water must possess some attraction for a fish. Then, after a brilliant minute or two of reflection on his powers, the man's senses went arrowing into every part of the house in quest of movement, aiming at wind-shaken cords, at busy beetles in their crannies, at the electric disc in the meter, at the flies making approximate figures of eight around the focal point of the extinguished kitchen bulb. Later, his mind settled for a space on the old problem of the pendulum, which over the years had grown curiously dear to him, as an old corn or a short thorn in thick skin is dear to its possessor. Compromise had been reached on the problem of the pendulum, but to-night — there was the problem of the fish.

He began to argue by analogy. Fish and clock! He spoke to himself with candour : If once, even once, I stop the pendulum of the kitchen clock I am irretrievably lost. For if this happens, an imperious and exigent narcotic will have assumed powers that cannot thenceforth be denied it. The ten womanish fingers I have been fondling will have tautened on my throttle. The pendulum, I appreciate, is the acid test. The problem of the fish is annoying ; the fish is not permanent in the house. A few days and it will have died of stale water, or of excess of sunshine, or will have been exchanged for three sticky sweets, or will slide down the sink when the child is renewing the water. This fact must be appreciated with some degree of clarity if the problem of the fish is not to be continuous or even recurrent. Yes, yes, the problem before me to-night does not involve basic principles. But in so far as it leads to a violation of the truce between the pendulum and myself it is vitally important. The fish is unique ; it is domesticated and still untamed. Its domestication is of a curious type — it cannot be bracketed with a cat or a dog. It is not even one per cent sapient. Yet it moves, and its movement cannot be controlled by any subterfuge of mine, short of killing it. In the matter of the pendulum my solution was astute and diplomatic. It was the folk-lore that provided the answer (when the owl caught the bat, the bat protested that it was a bird ; when caught by a hawk the little creature protested that it was a mouse). So thuswise I addressed the clock saying : Clock, I have been examining you for a number of years, cursorily perhaps of a Monday, perfunctorily of a Tuesday, and so on with varying degrees of indifference through the week — but deeply and analytically on Sunday. And after keen consideration extending over a number of years I am resolved that you are gifted with animation—even with cerebration. You have clearly a face, hands, and a heart ticking covertly in your chest. Since, then, I have established that you are animate, I cannot deny you the right to wag your pendulum all through the night if it so pleases you. I am resolved to catalogue you among the uncontrollables — with, say, the rain and the wind and the iron hailstones. These, since I can in no satisfactory measure control their movements, I find but serve to act as sedatives for me. Perhaps, clock, you question my ability to bestow life and to end it. Ignoring the fact that the mere fact of your querying thus argues reason in you, I would remind you that in the matter of termination of violence in the form of battles, shipwrecks, and explosions, I have demonstrated conclusively that I do indeed possess certain powers normally associated with the Creator. Believe, clock. Have faith, clock. Trust, clock.

In this fashion the irritation of the clock had been allayed and a truce signed with the swaying pendulum. A moderately satisfactory solution indeed! Not so now with the fish. Before him in the darkness he saw its hideous lime-green head riding on its pale-orange body; he saw its protuberant eyes penetrating his head, its dying-man's mouth generally chop-chopping the water, the remotely descried fans of its fins never ceasing to move. Movement! Movement! Undeterred, unslackened by darkness or glacial convexity. Movement! Secret movement!

Twelve o'clock chimed. One o'clock . . . two o'clock. . . . Hellish infernal movement!

The man opened his eyes and let them tiredly ride the gloom of the room. Beside him his wife snored like a herald. He turned violently on to his right side, half-hoping in his viciousness that the abrupt movement would wake his wife and so ensure that she would share his anguish. The woman snored on determinedly, as if she were brilliantly mimicking a woman snoring. Presently the pillow began to blaze under the man's cheek and temple, and deducing from this that it would be equally futile to try for coolness on his left side, he turned on his back, where the chances of head-fire were minimised, since the point of contact of poll with pillow was bony, not fleshy. In this position the mind moved ever upwards towards an intensity of clarity.

Closing his eyes he tried as a last resort two mental tricks. He took the tyres and tubes off his bicycle, shod the rims with plum-coloured velvet and, briskly tautening a light cable across the chasm of a quarry, he began to cycle across on the velvet-shod rims. After he had cycled noiselessly for a short distance the cable became endless and undulated in great soft waves. This trick rarely failed to send him asleep. To-night it was of no avail. The fish came swimming against him as he rode the cable.

He tried his second trick. It consisted of firing a small but powerful cannon at a lime-washed wall which had the ability to return to immaculate unity after having been shattered. This, too, to poor purpose—the fish came floating out through the breaches in the wall.

The man put his arm outside the clothes and began to beat his forehead with his palm. Impervious to all this tumult, his wife snored on.

Finally came the cursed reiteration that the problem was novel ; that if it could be but checked and harnessed it was capable of offering rich and ingenious sources of amusement. But unwittingly the mind found itself more and more forced to the conclusion that this unique spring of delicious torment, unrepeatable and tantalising as it was, admitted of but one crude brutal solution. Tedious to argue its uniqueness, its utter lack of congruence with other problems considered and solved — a dripping tap could be tightened till the finger bones ached, a rattling casement could be clasped, re-clasped and if necessary plugged ; a cat (although the little bloody bellows of lungs would continue to be inflated and deflated beneath his erect chest-fur) could be thrown plup ! on to the damp concrete of the yard. Not so the fish ! The fish, argue pro and con as he would, admitted of but one solution.

Three o'clock chimed through the sleeping house.

Suddenly it seemed to the man that the fish in the jar had got hold of a bugle and had begun bugling through the silent building. The sound was unusually resonant, as though the house had been stripped of furniture, wall-paper, and carpets. The man was amazed that no one heard it but himself. He sat up in bed. At the movement his wife lunged away from him, moving a great hillock of clothes with her as she went.

He pivoted to the floor. His tired face prickled ; the bones of his face felt as if they had been scraped ; his stomach soured. His toes groped for his slippers while his hands felt along the coverlet at the bottom of the bed for his dressing-gown. As he opened the bedroom door the draught from the stairs made him shiver.

Switching on the scullery light, he saw the fish just as he had seen it in imagination. For a while he stood watching it intently. The fish wheeled in the jar and stood at the ready, watching him. The man tapped with his finger-nail on the glass beside the minnow's head and the fish swirled away, but shortly returned to its original position. The man went into the kitchen, turned on the light, and took down a darning-needle from the pin-cushion. Back to the scullery again, where fish and man recommenced their mutual malevolent surveillance. A breeze from under the back door caught the man's calves and urged him to hurry. He tightly grasped the darning-needle between thumb and index finger. As he did so the uselessness of the unnecessary weapon struck him. He stuck it into his dressing-gown.

Taking the jar, he held it over the sink and tilted it; the water slowly leaked through his fingers. The fish tailed downwards with the falling water, but when its tail touched the fingers it immediately darted upwards to the surface of its dwindling reservoir. The man became more careful in his draining. Presently there was little water left in the jar; the fish was kicking in the few precious drops caught in the groove of the vessel's neck. The man turned the jar, letting the fish fall to the bottom, where it began to spring and flicker and pant. Its sides began to heave and its mouth began to chop-chop the air. It did not die easily, however; the man let about as much as would fill an egg-cup flow into the jar from the faucet before he found that he had been premature in his supposition of death, for on receiving the water the fish began to show signs of life. He drained the jar again, replaced it on the shelf and began to pace the kitchen floor.

He took cigarettes and matches from the pocket of his dressing-gown and began to smoke as he paced. Now and again he stopped and looked out into the scullery. He kept pacing for a long time, lighting cigarette after cigarette. Finally he threw a half-smoked cigarette into the ashes of the kitchen range, and went out to the scullery. He placed the jar under the faucet and turned on the water. The sudden jet afforded the fish a spurious but momentary semblance of life. After the jar had become filled and the faucet turned off, the minnow wheeled downwards with diminishing speed, finally reaching the bottom of the jar, where it keeled over till its belly was turned upwards. It was slow to achieve stability and it seemed as if the slightest movement of the jar would cause it to become buoyant.

THE MAN WHO DETESTED MOVEMENT

The man thoughtfully padded upstairs. On the second landing he lighted a cigarette and looked out over the roofs of the sleeping town. A huge moon was riding high in the sky. Here and there the slates of outhouses gleamed golden in the moonlight. A single light was burning in the window of a house on the other side of the town. The man stood there, watching and smoking. Suddenly he found his ears pointing to impale all the insignificant noises of the house. Their sharpening was not fruitless. Deep down in the building the clock chimed the half-hour.

BY THE SEA

ONCE on the gravelled path of the village the Boy Scouts squinted up at the bus-top. But the summer sun was a sudden splash of limewash in their eyes and their screwed faces faltered and fell. Down the broken gapped village street drove a wind tinctured with the sea, and immediately the boys began to laugh and twitter and twinkle like a flock of sparrows bathing in a deep well of road-dust.

Canvas, poles, tinware utensils, rucksacks and boxes came perilously down from the bus-top. Little hands clawed chattels safely home. Finally, all the gear was piled on the pathway; the conductor offered them his absolutely final company smile; a woman in the rear seat of the bus fisted a clear circle in the glass; the exhaust jetted blue-purple and the bus churned away. It left a huddle of blue-clad boys tangled in a medley of mostly green gear.

They trudged up to the higher end of the village. When they saw the sea they cheered. Between them and the sea, the sandhills below the village held creamy flanks lipped with generous shocks of emerald bent-grass. Out on the ocean there were no waves. There was little sound except the half-imagined, half-audible whisper of the inshore ripples, repeating " Lipsss, lipsss ". To the right were the sun-drenched cliffs; to the left, the long, attenuating scimitar of red sand. From their place of vantage at the end of the village the boys halted to appreciate the sea, the squirming and crawling of it, the slithering and sidling of it, the terror and delight of it. Capricious highways of green ink wandered in its spurious blueness. Under a short cliff to the right floated a dirty blanket of unmoving foam which seemed independent of submarine movement. The sun, swinging ponderously above the cloudy mountain camps across the bay, threw its royal image along the sea even to the strand below. Seeing, hearing, smelling, tasting and touching became luxuries. Luxuries, indeed, since there was nothing worth seeing but the sea; nothing worth hearing but the soft inshore " lipsss, lipsss "; nothing worth smelling or tasting but that which came to nostrils and palate in wild salinity; nothing fit for the body's touch but the velvet stroking of the waves.

Christy Hickey roused them. They turned from the sea and dragged themselves up to the Castle gates : the gates were set in a high corner of the green above the ocean. Over the gapped demesne wall they saw the great hulk of the burned building — its battlements cut clearly out of the cooler northern sky. To the right of the Castle they noticed the wing which had not suffered in the conflagration — its sashes and windows and verandah shone very white in the sunlight. The boys began to marvel at the gateway — they had never seen such a gateway before. It was actually a dwelling-house, and out of this fairy-tale portal walked a fairy-tale old woman to laugh with them and at them, to welcome them and to wonder at them, to feel the texture of the blue cloth on their tunics, to finger their golden-coloured crosses, and now and again to stoop to discover what particular sample of sweating imp lurked beneath the blue toadstool of a hat. The old lady caught Christy Hickey's hand and showed no eagerness to release it as she talked of soda-bread and butter-scotch and mushrooms on the coals, and eggs as brown as . . . as brown as . . . here she tried heaven and earth and ocean for a suitable comparison and failed to find one. When at last the astonished youngsters estimated that there was a period to her clucking, she began her incoherencies over again just to show her delight at this, her new family.

BY THE SEA

Afterwards the white gates that showed blotches of rust screamed open: the boys began to shout, "Where? Where?" and to answer, "Over there! Over there!" They streamed across the grassy lawn and dumped their possessions beside the wall adjoining the road. Beyond the road was a short field that sloped down to a cliff above the sea. Above them the field lifted in gentle acclivity to the Castle. Below them stretched the fine span of the bay.

Bell-tents and bivouacs up, latrines, grease-traps and hip-hollows dug, flag hoisted; water-carriers, couriers and cooks appointed — all the dismal chores performed with new zest. The owner of the Castle came down to greet them. He was enormous, Irish, and friendly. He stood smiling at this ant-hill of activity on his land. He asked the Scoutmaster to bring the boys up to help him pick his gooseberries. He had many things that would interest them, he said.

The rest of the day was a great rush hither and thither in an effort to experience everything at the same time. They swam before dinner; after the swim they rushed here and there on the long strand marvelling at new wonders. They found three green glass balls and some huge chunks of cork. Also a battered wickerwork lobster pot. They walked along the tide's lip for the most of a mile and found things eloquent of the sea's mystery. On the high-water mark, clothed in seaweed, they saw the body of a marmoset — at least Jimmy Stephens said it was a marmoset, though the others considered it a plain monkey. Then there was the skeleton of what someone suggested was a bottle-nosed shark.

On the way back to the Castle they met the old parish priest — he examined them unbelievingly over his breviary before he addressed them. One of the younger Scouts stood on his hands to amuse the old man: the boy held his balance for a short time before sprawling backwards into the fuchsia. When they went up to the Castle they found marvel piled on marvel. The gooseberries were of two kinds, the red and hairy, and the amber and hairless. The man who owned the Castle had a trick gooseberry. It was as big as a small apple. He had grown it by removing all but one of the immature fruits on a branch. By allowing this single gooseberry to droop into a cup of water he had produced a freak fruit. He also had a hawk chained to a perch : when the youngsters threw pieces of stick to it the bird pounced on them ferociously. There was a fig tree growing in the open air near the garden door. As a final titbit their host made his Alsatian leap high to pull a bell-rope. Towards evening, with bulging pockets, the Scouts ambled down the lawn.

Night came upon the Scouts and heightened their sense of adventure. True, they sang around the fire, more to justify a cardinal principle in Scout literature than from motives of inward urgency, but they were more than satisfied with this simulacrum of enjoyment — they enjoyed the singing and the firelight because it would be a type of blasphemy to admit that they did not enjoy it. But the strongest perceptible emotion amongst the boys was a type of inarticulate fear which the lusty singing did its share to dispel. Afterwards a great beast of a moon clambered up the blue velvet sky — the boys struggled to the top of the mossy wall and saw what wonders it could work on the ballroom floor of the ocean. As the daylight seeped out of the heavens the reiterated complaint of the tide-edge impinged more and more upon the conscious ear. Insignificant sounds increased in portentousness ; the violent bugling of a cow from the shelter belt behind the Castle rocked the world ; a spurt of laughter from the village almost approximated to rifle fire ; a light flickering on the hills was a thing of great mystery. The boys crowded in on the dying fire. What remnants of cold the summer night held fastened its hooks in their backs. Christy Hickey watched them narrowly and was quick to recognise the sense of dwarfishness in their faces. The boys continued to shrill loudly in order to compensate for their inner cowardice.

Then the camp bugler stood up beyond the firelight and sounded "Taps". His instrument flung the separate notes out into the shining night sea. On leaving the bugle each note seemed to become a small silver globe that went bounding beautifully out to seek its fortune in a blue world. When he had finished, the echo of the music took a while to die.

Christy Hickey opened the end wall of his own white sleeping-tent and hung a large black crucifix within on the pole of the opposite tent-wall. Under the crucifix he suspended a lighting storm lantern. As he did so, he kept repeating softly to himself, "The tents of Israel, the tents of Israel." The boys crowded in on the mouth of the white tent, the surplus spilling out into the grassy dark. Then the Scoutmaster knelt beneath the crucifix and gave out the Rosary. Prayers never seemed so delightful before; all the old appellations flashed new lights from unsuspected facets of grandeur. The praying fused them warmly into one another, as if indeed this single act of communal moonlight prayer had the power to make them blood brothers. The drone of the praying made them sleepy, too; when the Rosary and Litany were ended each small head was fully loaded with sleep.

Eight boys in each bell-tent—seven and a patrol leader. Christy Hickey and Jimmy Stephens were to sleep in the white sleeping-tent. Christy walked around, warning the boys not to put their hand to the canvas if it rained and impressing on the patrol leaders the necessity for loosening the guy ropes in a shower. Before long he blew the whistle for lights out. Afterwards he stayed at the wall for a while.

He was looking out over the sea. He released breath through his nostrils in easy hisses of satisfaction. Now that the boys had retired and were safe, he found the knapsack of responsibility slipping from his shoulders. This was his first outing of this nature since his appointment as Scoutmaster, and, as the group was a new one, all but two of the boys had never been under canvas before. He looked across his shoulder. Just then Jimmy Stephens put his head out of the sleeping-tent that he and the Scoutmaster were to share, and looked expectantly towards the figure by the moonlit wall. Christy padded softly around the bell-tents. A snatch of eager narrative filtered through the canvas — ". . . a weeny rabbit that a weasel killed — an', man, he was hot!" He walked to the triangular doors of the tents and threw back the canvas so as to give the boys air. Within, the boys were lying like the spokes of a wheel, the recumbent bodies radiating from the tent-pole. As he rustled away he found the dammed-up tittering break softly behind him. He smiled contentedly at the sound. Then he blessed himself, slipped into the tent and stripped speedily. Jimmy Stephens and himself conversed softly for a while before they bade each other good night.

Christy found it difficult to sleep. The excitement of the day, more or less dormant during dusk, now began to gnaw in him as a wary mouse gnaws in a house that has grown silent. Tittering began in one of the tents — the patrol leader's voice was raised in muffled reproval. An inquisitive cow began to lumber down the lawn. With his ear to the ground Christy could hear the animal tearing at the grass as if it were paper. The noise became more determined as the cow approached the tent. Finally the animal's shadow lunged across the canvas. He could hear her breathing and snuffling close to his face but he made no movement; he tautened his body and hoped that she would not become entangled in the tent-ropes. Jimmy Stephens was breathing easily in sleep. Then the cow, satisfied with her scrutiny, bore away to the left and soon he heard the soft plopping of falling cow-dung. Christy smiled and dropped down into uneasy sleep.

It was two-fifty-five by the phosphorescent face of his wrist-watch when the patrol leader of one of the bell-tents roused him. "Christy! Christy!" he called agitatedly, shaking the Scoutmaster's shoulder. "Christy!" the boy said, "Richie Maloney is retching off his stomach all the time." Christy slipped on his shoes and scrambled into his overcoat. He felt in the pocket of his overcoat for his torch. Outside, the night was possessed of a surpassing brightness. The sky above the sea that was previously powder-blue had now become suffused with a delightful apple-green. He had scarcely time to appreciate its curiousness when the night-air tentatively laid its keen blade across his skin. He flashed his torch through the tent doorway, picked out the patrol leader and another boy holding the sick scout upright in a sitting position. He stepped carefully among the still forms and put his arm around the sick lad's shoulder. He flashed the light full into the pale face, and the boy's reaction to the light seemed so unusual that he immediately switched off the torch. "What is it, Richie?" he wheedled. Then, "Lift him up!" he whispered to the other two. "Perhaps he'd be better off out in the air." The boy made no effort to put his legs under him, so Christy carried him in his arms.

Out in the air the sick boy brightened momentarily; then his head lolled heavily. The Scoutmaster slipped off his overcoat and threw it across Richie Maloney's shoulders. He helped him to a sitting position on a little mound near the wall. "Richie! Richie!" he whispered again. Then to the other two, "Call Jimmy

Stephens and ask him to get the drop of brandy out of my case." One of the boys raced towards the white tent.

Christy began to speak softly to the sick lad: once again came the weary effort to raise the heavy head. The other Scout was whimpering with cold; Christy told him to put on some clothes. The boy went away into the bell-tent. When he was alone with the sick lad Christy slewed him around until the moon was shining into the wan face. Suddenly the Scoutmaster noticed that the boy's weak bulbous tongue was ballooning out through the opening of his mouth. Before the cold significance of this could reach Christy's consciousness, the boy had begun to snore stertorously. Christy cupped his mouth against the boy's ear and clearly crooned out the Act of Contrition. His maternal eyes kept holding the boy's profile as if seeking, by the power of animal fascination alone, to pin the soul to life. But Richie Maloney suddenly added two terrifying inches to his size, deflated all the air that was in him in the ultimate throe, squeaked like a wet palm on a bannister-rail, and died.

Christy held the boy for an unmoving minute after he knew that he had passed out. The moon froze the pair to a piece of statuary, the sight of which chilled the two returning Scouts. "What is it, Christy?" Jimmy Stephens began anxiously, crouching down to the moonlit pair. The other boy was just beyond Jimmy's shoulder. Christy let the body sag a little. "He's dead!" he said. "Sweet God above!" said Jimmy, "How could he be dead? Why do you say that? He might only have fainted!" Jimmy put his hand against the inert head — it was now the head of a broken doll. In the background the patrol leader began to blubber. It was a chittering type of blubber. Jimmy Stephens began to cross himself over and over again. "But what'll we do, Christy? How'll we face home with him? Didn't his mother warn you to watch him carefully ? We watched him, Christy, didn't we ? The two of us watched him, Christy, didn't we ? "

The morning was thrusting its great green fist into the sky. The inshore wavelets kept repeating " Lipsss — lipsss — lipsss ". A cock crowed from the fowl-runs behind the Castle.

Christy spoke to the patrol leader. " Val," he said, " get Tom Donnell's bike and ride for the priest. Ask the priest where the doctor lives and bring him too. Not that it's any use now, but . . . Hurry, Val, like a good boy."

Afterwards the affair became nightmarish. Christy carried the body into his own tent and covered it with a sheet. Jimmy Stephens and he took their clothes out into the dew-wet grass and dressed themselves. By now it was clear that the tragedy had communicated itself to the other Scouts. Heads appeared in the doorways of the bell-tents ; a chorus of whispering broke out. It was difficult to know how the news of death had spread. Perhaps the subconscious is always sharpening its ear to hear it, senses are sharpened to apprehend it, a further dole of smell is kept in reserve to sniff new-made clay even through sleep, an extra access of sight is held in reserve to visualise (even through two canvas walls) a taut blue face and the final grimace of stripped teeth.

The Scouts were up and dressed and about without reprimand. They huddled in little frightened schools well away from the tent where the dead boy lay. A light twinkled in one of the windows of the Castle. The inquisitive cow munched nearer and nearer to the tent of death. No one raised a hand to frighten her away. The animal put a truculent head against the canvas and snuffed loudly. Christy took a step or two in her direction and stamped suddenly on the grass. The cow heaved out with astonishing agility. A figure with a lighted candle in its hand came to a window of the Castle. Then the lights of the priest's car were shining through the bars of the gateway. The gate clanged open and the tyres roared on the gravel.

Morning was upon them almost before they realised it. The owner of the Castle came down with his wife and led away the boys for a phantom meal. When later they emerged into the strengthening sunlight the old woman of the gateway was walking around in the dew-wet grass. She was tying and untying her fingers and calling out the Holy Name. People began to knot outside the white-barred gate. Two vivid young women strolled east the road. Each was swinging a blue bathing costume. When they learned the news from the people at the gateway the pair were pricked of their splendour and became ordinary frightened people. The boys looked up at the sun mounting behind the sandhills. The holiday was over. They set about taking down the bell-tents and piling their belongings. The little white bivouac was left standing, and the disconsolate lads sat dismally on their gear. The sea had a great sleekness to it. The thin mist of morning was vanishing; the long revolving lip of the tide was increasing in whiteness. The boys looked wistfully at the sea, at the faint mountain-camps of the south, at the creamy flanks of the sandhills, at the long, attenuating scimitar of sand. Then they looked at the tent of death.

THE END OF THE WORLD

WE used to play games among ourselves in order to disturb the placidity of the place. Most of our games were games of pretence. That is to say, we started with tiny imaginative embers and kept blowing and blowing until we had a mythical conflagration. On rare occasions we had real flames, the annual race-meeting, the death of a prominent man, unexpected courtships, the downfall of a beautiful woman, first births and so on. But mostly the fires at which we warmed ourselves were imaginary fires, failing whose warmth and cheer some of us descended to the minor sadism of thumbing blackheads out of one another's cheekbones. That, or the brutality of direct address. For it is an article of faith with us that oblique commentary is a blessed thing, not unlike the shaft of sunshine striking through the church window, across which the man in the folk-story hung his jacket.

So, naturally, I was delighted when I spied the item tucked away at the bottom of a page in the newspaper. I slicked it out with a razor-blade and poked it away in my fob-pocket. When I reached the harness-maker's I took out the cutting and passed it around among the men. I gave it to the harness-maker first, as was his right as host.

The item in the newspaper said that a Rumanian (or a Hungarian or a Yugo-Slav, I forget which) had prophesied that the end of the world would come the following morning precisely at two o'clock.

Hereabouts the radio is common. And from our cousins in the States we get more than our share of American magazines. We also have a pair of picture-houses. All these amenities serve us highly: if we aren't

86

able to differentiate the seventy-seven different types of jealousy by this time, it isn't day yet. But in spite of the radio and the magazines and the cinema, the lacunae in us are both surprising and formidable — lacunae which astonish even ourselves in our solitary if infrequent contemplations.

As regards the end of the world I quickly discovered that I had green faggots for my kindling. Still, I counselled myself to patience and blew assiduously at the seed of my fire.

The saddler spoke first. He said it was all his bloody eye. I felt that the wrong keynote had been sounded. The man should have rung the middle C of pleasant pretence. But we had to humour the saddler, as he held us in the hollow of his hand, inasmuch as we were dependent on him to give us sanctuary against the weather and our loneliness. He spoke with high bravado as if a show of initial sternness would, once and for all, put a stop to this tomfoolery of an end to the grand world. When I saw that pretence had been jettisoned I grew peeved. In my heart I kept protesting that it wasn't fair, that the harness-maker should have been traditional, and should have thrust slyly and obliquely at the story. I had wished us to remain knaves manufacturing knavery. Sourly I withdrew from the men, put my shoulder against the jamb of the door and tried finitely if perversely to appreciate what the world's end would mean to our town.

On the opposite side of the roadway, at the entrance to the market, a fishwoman was standing behind an open box of fish which was set upon two empty boxes. As I watched her she viced a mackerel by the gills and ran it through the O of the thumb and forefinger. Well, for one thing, the end of the world would put a stop to that sleazy antic. In the midst of my resultant good humour my mind took the bit in its teeth and ran away. Suddenly

THE END OF THE WORLD

I found myself gigantic and wholly capable of ending the world myself. This I proceeded to do. I clawed down the scarlet-and-white ice-cream bannerols, banged the Mediterranean-blue whiskey signs, tangled up the old electric wires, beat immense caverns in the roadway, kicked over the steeples, disembowelled children playing hopscotch, smashed pigeons into sunny slates, shredded petunia posters, jangled plate-glass windows — finally I rammed my fist back Mick Meenihan's throat and, once and for all, set a period to his singing "Moon-*Wine* Shimmering in Your Hair". As a postscript I crashed down the high chittering blue hat-band in the cinema-operator's cabin.

Sated with destruction I turned back into the shop. Then Frankie Horan spoke up out of his wryness : whatever it was he said, brought me in among the others on the crest of a warm conversational wave. I twinkled with miniature happiness. I cast about for a simile and found it ready to my hand. Our humour, I thought, was like a little shrine-lamp with a weighted base that would topple and sway in an alarming fashion and then unaccountably right itself. I grew ashamed of my former peevishness. The twinkling spread among us. We booted the world around as if it were a football. I felt wondrously proud of myself for having brought up the matter — for having made this pleasant warmth in our ways.

Frankie Horan said : "You must admit that the Man Above put up with the thieves and ruffians for a long time."

Jack Donovan said : "I leave to anyone if that's fair talk in the presence of an honest tradesman. Twenty-five years I'm coming in that door and I never yet saw the saddler here put weak leather in a collar. Aye, or puttin' fibre in the linin' of a straddle an' tellin' the unfortunate farmers 'twas curled horse-hair."

Jim Sheehan said : "In the Hereafter if I find all of

ye in one place, I'm praying here and now that I find myself in the other."

Mickie Duv Larkin said : " It's comin' just in the nick o' time. I've a fishery prosecution hangin' over my head for Saturday's court."

The saddler laughed heartily. We began to enjoy ourselves prodigiously.

All through the evening the hocus-pocus spread. Man, 'twas great ! Those who weren't perturbed pretended to be perturbed. Some of the variants of the story I heard amazed even myself with the fine skin of truth they had on them. I had to show the cutting to several people who stopped me on the street. The cutting was out of an English paper I get specially for the horses. It gave the Rumanian's name down in black and white — also the things he had foretold already. Myself, now, I thought the man an honest sort of a fellow but a sort of a fool all the same. Whatever way things turned out he couldn't be much the gainer. If the end of the world didn't arrive his name would be a byword in the mouths of the people ; while if it did come, there would be none of us left to hang laurels on the prophet. But I'll give it up to him that I'd say he thought he was acting according to his lights. And besides, it's not right for any man to set himself up as a judge of another.

About eleven o'clock that night I was sauntering home for myself, intending to be in bed for once in my life at a respectable hour. Besides, I had promised Danny Sweeney to go flood-fishing with him early the following morning. Passing Louis Fitzmaurice's hall-door I saw that it was open — I sort of sensed Louis smoking inside in the dark. The devil pinched me — I flung him good night and passed on. I made a bet with myself that he'd call me. I gave him two intervals to do so. In the first interval he was to recognise the sound of my step, gait and voice. The second interval was for the plupping apart of his lips from around the pipe-stem preparatory to the calling of my name. I won my bet — suddenly I heard an unrehearsed "Vincent". I slowed down and forced him to call me a second time. As I came round the doorpost I adroitly switched my greeting into a yawn and did my best to muster up a counterfeit irritation. He drew slowly on his pipe. Now and again the pipelight on his face glowed and died. He smoked on, solemn as a mandarin.

" You're in a terrible hurry home, to-night," he said.

" Maybe I've cause," I said darkly.

" Seldom with you have cause," he said. " Move in for a few minutes. I won't take the head o' you."

By the light of the next pipe-brightness I examined his face. You would have known him anywhere for the publican he was. The standard mixture of solemnity and rascality. The pushed-out lugs made the face an isosceles triangle, his narrowing skull yielded a vertex in a lock of dark hair pomaded to the forehead. His finely waxed moustache fitted the geometrical verity of his face; the long slender moustache-ends bisected the base-angles at his lugs. His eyes were wonderful eyes. They were capable of the subtlest flattery by offering you their whites in exchange for your wonders.

" What's this I hear about the end of the world ? " he asked.

Now the pipe-brightnesses fell thick and fast upon me. My breast gladdened at the solution of a problem that had been pecking at me for many years. Now, for the first time, it was clear to me why Louis Fitz. smoked a pipe with a dropped bowl. I had always thought that it was because the weight of such a pipe was taken partly on the chin, but with a sudden access of clarity of vision I now realised that Louis Fitz. — and all the other millions of

Louis Fitzes throughout the world — were men inquisitive in the extreme, and hated having the range of their vision destroyed by a pipe-bowl and a fist clenched around it. I gained a new respect for Louis Fitzmaurice.

I handed him the cutting ; he cracked a match to read it. He didn't ask me to turn on the electric light although at that moment I happened to be itching a dying pimple on my cheek with the button of the switch. No publican in his normal vigour and senses lights his hall-light at eleven o'clock at night, unless, God save the hearers, it's a case of a sudden death or a homecoming after an operation. Louis and myself had a bout of wrestling trying to pronounce the Rumanian's name. With the pipe-stem venting the air between his cheeks he went off into hegs of laughter at the idea of anyone having a name like that. He gave me back my cutting ; I fingered it back into my fob-pocket. He took out his watch and concertinaed his chin into his chest as he tried to read the time by the light of his pipe. He made ribbons of the fine triangle of his face before he finally saw what o'clock it was.

" A quarter after eleven," he said. Then, with a sham gaiety : " That makes it two and three-quarter hours till the end of the world." I didn't laugh.

" Sit in ; sit in," he said arrogantly, " 'tis seldom I have a chat with you."

There were two mahogany chairs against the wall on each side of the small hall-table. On the table was a check oil-cloth, in the middle of which was a maidenhair fern in a *jardinière*. I sat on the chair farther from the door. Louis pulled his chair across from me in order to let me see my due portion of an up-ended rectangle of moon-bright street.

The people came out from the pictures, the gods thumping lustily along the pavement, whistling cheerily as they went, the tip-ups in long swaths mincing inhibitedly in mid-road. When the last of the people had flowed past us and things in the town were terribly silent, Louis turned the key in the shop-door and brought out two bottles of stout, a glass and an opener. He placed them on the table in front of me and partly behind the *jardinière*. " 'Tis mortal close to-night," he said.

Etiquette demanded that I say, " Tck-tck." I said it and added for good measure. " This is too much altogether."

We talked and talked. Now and again the apparition of a benevolent rosy face appeared from nowhere to encourage me. The old rascal pretended not to have heard stories I knew I had already told him. He made me tell them all over again. There was nothing left for me but to better the previous tellings. While we talked I nursed my two bottles of stout. I knew they'd have to last me till the end of the world. Times there were that the stream of my narrative was filtered through stout-froth and the maidenhair fern. By this time the street was like a deadhouse. The last noise was that of a pony and trap jigging into the country. We saw the flutter of a nurse's veil in it.

Louis and I held talking on everything and anything. We talked of heartburn, Jane Withers and the inbreeding of rabbits; of the County Council rates and dead Canons and the scarfing of welding-iron; of pewter and rock-salt and the bars in Montreal; of house-leek and ptomaine poisoning and old meadowing. But through all the trading of knowledge and the tongue-tossing of news, my brave Mr. Louis Fitzmaurice kept nibbling and nibbling at the end of the world.

At one o'clock I topped the second bottle : I squeezed that out till a quarter to two. About a quarter after one we heard a noising behind the stairs door. Louis got up quickly, stuck his head in the doorway and commenced whispering up the stairs. I dare say he was telling the wife what was keeping him in the hall. When he came back I made the decisive movements a person makes before breaking company, but Louis broached a fresh topic of conversation with over-zeal.

Two o'clock banged out from the steeple, and, indeed, the world didn't come to an end. Louis and I were side by side in the doorway when the hour rang. After the second stroke there came a great calm. Louis looked up at the stars. No crack appeared in the roof of the sky. I heard no trumpet and, curiously enough, I found myself undefinably disappointed. High up in a top room a child began to wail — we heard the mother's voice comforting it. The child's complaint became submerged in a reluctant wetness.

On the off-chance that the town clock was fast, Louis and myself gave the coming of doom an extra five minutes. But even after the extra five minutes everything stayed up. I left him and he closed the door softly behind me. When I found myself utterly alone in the moonlit street, I felt exhilarated beyond description, though deep in the exhilaration was the far gnaw of the disappointment that now I should never know whether the stars were merely stars or scales on the back of the Big Salmon. As I walked home I saw the walls silvered with snail tracks. At the corner of our street there was a steel electric pole. With the dint of the glee that was on me I struck it smartly with my open palm. The whole pole rang with the truth of a good bell.

When I reached home I closed the door softly behind me and tiptoed into the kitchen. Before I switched on the light I covered the switch with my two hands so as to smother the click of it. When the light went up I saw the clock-beetles that the turf had brought in to us, racing clean-mad all over the floor. I hopped quickly here and there among them and, selecting the bigger clocks, I cracked them under my boots. When the last beetle had reached sanctuary I was left with five or six flattened beetles. They looked like squashed chocolate sweets on the floor.

Then I heard the creak of old ankles over my head. Even before I raised my face I knew that my mother was leaning over the bannisters of the landing. We looked at one another for a while, each waiting for the other to begin. "Tell me, Vincent," she said at last, "what kept you out till this hour of the morning?" Defensively I reached for my fob-pocket and took out the newspaper cutting. I held it upwards in her direction. I said: "Look, mother, a Rumanian foretold the end of the world for to-night at two o'clock, and I was below in Louis Fitzmaurice's till this very minute keeping him company." She said: "And will you tell me what in the name of goodness were ye doing there till this time?" I said: "What were we doing, mother, but waiting for the end of the world."

Against this talk the poor woman was weaponless. Then, as we eyed one another, out from their cubby-holes sneaked two mighty rogueries: the roguery that was hers to bequeath and the roguery that I had inherited. I saw my soul in an old mirror. Never afterwards in my life did I come closer to my mother than at that moment. The laughter common to our blood lay between us like a red carpet with a rich pile. The set severity of her face was marred by the tears of her feeling for me. And as she turned from me and in her bare feet padded back along the landing, I sat down, clasped my hands between my knees, and, in spite of myself, I found myself rocked and rocked with the joy and the grandeur of it all.

THE EGOTISTS

ALL the while I had one eye closed and I was gauging the
sun with the other. I was endeavouring to set it in align-
ment with the unkeen edge of the Wall of the Green and
at the same time keep it sitting on the horizon. I kept on
saying to myself: The very instant that that red ball of
fire in the sky nestles into the required position, I'll ask
the Boy Hero to show me his wounds.

But my eyes grew heavy and betrayed me. I shrank
and shrank till I was too puny to uphold them. Wearier
and wearier and wearier. Once, indeed, exhaustion
sealed up my eyes in spite of me, and, in the resultant
absence of positive light, I saw four swimming suns,
merging, passing, looming, receding, idling out. Green
suns and crimson suns. Crimson suns edged with green
and green suns edged with crimson. Leaping, vaulting,
outspringing from one central constant sun. Opening and
squeezing my eyes, I tried the elasticity of the trick three
or four times. It pleased me well. It revealed to me a
new power of my eyes. It showed me that my eyes, of
themselves, utterly without recourse to cerebration, held
memory, a tiny finite memory, but memory just the same.

Suddenly, remembering my resolution, I strained my
eyes wide open and, oh glory! I was just in time to catch
the sun in my trap. Naturally I was delighted at my
success. So I treated the sun cautiously, holding it firmly
and raising my head slightly when it threatened to escape.
Then, without stirring hand or foot, I said to the Boy Hero
who was lying on the sun-warmed board beside me:

" You never showed me your wounds."

I wasn't really interested in his wounds. Honestly,

I was not. It was just that I had promised myself. On hearing my request the Boy Hero grew more important, more monastic, more secluded, more sham-unattainable. And I was quizzed to think that his mind was hurdling, hurdling, hurdling in a thin athletic hell. Hurdling all the time, back, back, back, '25, '24, '23, '22. Back to '22. Deflated, white as a sheet in his mind's face, his memory reached '22.

Silvo was above us, straddling the crossbeam of the stand of the swingboats. They were just children's swingboats, else, how could he take part in our conversation? Now and again, chink-a-chink, would fall the coin of his contribution into our hatful of talk. He ceased tightening a nut with a monkey-wrench, indicated the laager of caravans with a benevolent arc, and said: " Me? I painted 'em all; every single one of 'em."

And oh, boy, will you watch the sun? Unknown to myself, I had taken my eyes off it for one moment to ask the Boy Hero to show me his wounds. And will you just look at it now! It is fairly clattering down behind the horizon. That's what comes of taking your eyes off it for an instant. Then and there I resolved to watch it shrivel down to the faintest possible segment. After it had vanished from my sight it would be a circle tangential to the horizon on the invisible side.

Since the Boy Hero had made no move to show me his wounds I protested to him again: " No, you never showed *me* your wounds. Honest, I wasn't there when you showed them to the other lads." I didn't give a tinker's curse for his old wounds. It was just that I didn't like to break my promise to myself. I was really thinking of what I should make of myself. The first thing that scuttled into my head was a politician. So I said: I shall be a politician. So I cross-hackled myself without mercy in this fashion: What qualifications do you possess that

you imagine you would make an adequate politician ?
And I said : Cuteness in small things ; reluctance disguised like a wren-boy ; also lip-pursing acceptance of
unpopular responsibility. And then ? The phrase, " In
the final analysis." Yes, indeed, I vouchsafed myself, not
a bad start as a politician. But . . . But what ? But
won't it be intolerable never to be able to snarl at people,
never to be able to show your teeth at people, never to be
able to tighten your fist at people ? So I raised my hat to
myself, very politely indeed, and said : No, thank you,
on more mature reflection I will not be a politician.

The Boy Hero began bumbling on my right : " Didn't
I show you my wounds an' we swimmin' above in Poul-
coppal ? I'm certain I did. I showed 'em to all the lads
that day. They said they'd never seen anythin' like 'em."

Silvo was riding along the stout crossbeam. The crossbeam was arbitrarily chamfered and the short chamfers
had been painted crimson. It was as if they had been
licked into it by a tongue dipped in crimson paint. Silvo
indicated the presence of the merry-go-round with a
deprecatory thumb and said : " The gadget here broke
down in Kilkieran in Connemara. I said to the Boss,
' Boss,' I said, ' I'll do up the whole joint if you get the
paint out from Galway. What I mean to say, Boss, is
that it'd be a sort of pleasant job for me seein' as I have
a taste for the thing. But, Boss,' I said again, ' you've got
to understand this. I've got to do it my own way or no
way. See, Boss ? My own way or no way in the wide
earthly.' What I meant to have him understand was . . ."

Dwindle, dwindle, dwindle. That's the sun, that large
sanguinary coin that's slipping into the slot of the west.
Then I said to myself : No politician ! What then ? And
I said : I'll be a poet. And I said : What qualifications
do you possess that you imagine you would make an adequate poet ? So I emptied my mind's pockets and found

97

the curious word " unbrave " and some few disconcerting phrases like " the chagrined greyhounds and the gonfalons " and " milk me, O cedars of the priory gate ". To tell you the plain honest truth, I wasn't extra proud of these contributions, but if anyone was going around the country collecting disciples of the esoteric, I was determined to stand up and be counted.

The Boy Hero took off his jacket in three brisk snaps. He plucked up tufts of shirt from inside his trousers-belt and fiddled the garment over his head. Proudly he put his finger on each of the five mathematically spaced dots on his stomach. One of the dots took my fancy. His finger had lingered at it lovingly. It was a delicately formed aperture glazed with pale-blue skin-glass. While his finger was still demonstrating its rarity the Boy Hero said : " Bfff ! There's the one that nearly gattled me."

The Hero continued without let : " I was on the flat of my back in the Mater when Collins came to see me. ' What age are you ? ' he says to me. ' Eighteen, sir,' says I to him. I showed him my wounds as best I could with the bandages. ' 'Tisn't one in fifty'd live with five machine-gun bullets in his breadbasket,' Collins said again. ' I know that, sir,' said I. ' You're a tough kid,' Collins says to me. ' I'm goin' to christen you the Boy Hero.' So they had a man there to take my photograph an' I propped up in bed shakin' hands with Collins. It came out in the newspapers a few days after. I had it above in the gods of the cinema one night an' didn't Paddy the Taypot snap it out o' my hand an' make pieces of it. I was fit to be tied. I tried to get another copy of it from the newspapers but it couldn't be got for love or money. . . ."

Silvo swung down out of the sky and loomed over us. To us he was an angle-snap of a player in an All-Ireland. " Yes," he said, " the fellah brought his message all right.

He had 'em all. White lead an' boiled oil an' turps an'
umber an' ochre an' burnt sienna an' primrose yellow.
An' half a dozen big tins of Seagull brand white paint.
An' half a dozen lovely lively brushes. Be the Boss as he
may, I'll say this much for him, he's no way mean. So
on the first wagon I painted businesses off a Celtic
Christmas card, dragons and lizards and snakes chewin'
their own tails. I had only one side of the wagon done
when the Boss seen it. 'Hey!' he said, 'I don't go in
much for this dragon stuff.' So I said, 'But it's good,
Boss, honest it's good!' An' he said: 'Oh hell! I know
it's good. Don't go on tellin' me it's good. But once
an' for all, I'm not goin' to have this joint shiftin' around
the country like the Book of Kells on castors.' You see,
he had to admit my stuff was good. But the Boss is a
stickler for the old stuff, the scrolls and the leafy fakieme-
jigs at the wagon corners. So I gave him what he wanted,
didn't I? Look around you! The proof of the pudden
is in the eatin'. "

Someone threw the scaldings of a teapot out through
the open upper-half of a living-wagon door. I glimpsed
the white hands and the bright brown earthen teapot. A
dog mooched out from under the wagon and put his nose
remotely in the direction of the steamy spilth.

Low in the west the blood had clotted over a large
area of evening sky.

So I said: Yes, I shall be a poet. I shall roll bones
over stones on lonely acres. That is, of course, on the days
on which I feel the sap of traditionalism high in me.
After all, it is a good bet to wager one tiny lyric against
the *Encyclopaedia Britannica*. That's it, I shall be a poet!
I shall speak in candlelight. And then, remember, oh,
please, please remember. For one's grandchildren to be
wryly proud of one, that indeed is grandeur.

The absence of lustre in my face left the Boy Hero no

alternative but to pull on his shirt. He made a gambler's throw. " I bet you never seen a fellow with wounds like that before. I was sorry I didn't keep the photo of myself an' Collins. 'Twas he called me ' The Boy Hero ' first, d'you see ? " Puff-puff went the little bellows of his pride at the feeble spark of his unshared glee.

The lower jaw of Silvo's wrench started walking up to meet its mate. Silvo's fingers brought the wrench's mouth from a geometrical yawn to a geometrical grin ; thence to a death-clench. He began again : " There was a schoolmaster in a place near Kilfenora in the County Clare. He's the fellow I was tellin' ye about. I got a loan of a big thick book from him. It was called *The Amateur Decorator*. He seen the work I done on the wagons — that's why he gave me this book. But I couldn't make hog, dog or divil of it. No, I'm a liar ! I learned how to stipple out of it. See the two bottom panels on the door of that far-over living-wagon. That's what they call stipplin'. I done it after readin' this fellow's book. With a sponge I done it. . . ."

The houses beyond the Green were taking all the sun. I saw one chimney-pot in particular. It had gathered to itself all the crimson the west could spare. Finally this pot was so orange-bright that it pensioned off all the grey walls below it.

To myself, within myself, I was debating : My elbows would not be so cramped-up in the short story. After all, what is the poem but a literary corset ? Form plus figure minus comfort. Pink, pretty but constricting. I should detest having the basket of my fancy so completely encased. But the short story ? The short story is no sop on the road ! All very fine for Flaubert to say to Maupassant : " Look at that tree ! " All very fine for Virginia Woolf to say, " Young man, look out of your window." If I looked out of my window I should see the Boy Hero here putting on his shirt after showing two idlers his wounds, and I should see this blockhead Silvo with his monkey-wrench. All the same I confessed myself tempted. I said: I can utilise the expressions I've filched from the people's mouths, juggle them with a few of my own composition and who'll be the wiser? So as a beginning I strung the daisy-chain of my pet comparisons, saying: As good as bread; as fat as a parsnip; as quaint as a cowbell; as barren as a jennet; as bald as a bladder; as dramatic as . . . as dramatic as a woman.

The Boy Hero was still talking: " I was in the Fianna down in South Cork the first Trouble. I'm tellin' you I served my time there in a hot shop. I was put mindin' a trap-mine in the middle of the road one day, myself an' a young fellow called Driscoll. Nothin' would satisfy this Driscoll but that he'd disconnect the mine in order to let his sister into Drimoleague in the ass an' car. I kept well up the fields while he was disconnectin' it. The ass an' car came in mighty handy — for carryin' the pieces of him home! I was a lucky man I kept well up the fields."

On hearing this Silvo became a different person. He whined, actually whined. " Easy, easy, easy," he said, " for God's sake, easy. That fellow was a brother o' mine. My own name is Driscoll. Honest to the beautiful an' good God he was a brother o' mine. Honest to God, as sure as I'm standin' here, he was a brother o' mine."

The walls between me and the sun were jet black but they had rims of fire. I said: Indeed and indeed, it's all very fine for Flaubert and Virginia Woolf. Now if I only could travel. I knew a fellow who was on a holiday in St. Malo. He used to tell of the tawny sand outside the thick walls of the town. I knew another fellow who spent a month in Bornholm in the Baltic. Me? Hell! I never got a chance to travel.

The Boy Hero readily disposed of Silvo's agitation.

" I know," he said, " that was tough about *your* brother. Let me tell you about *my* brother. My mother was left a widow on a small holding outside Skeheenarinka in South Tipperary. There were only two of us in it, my brother and myself. My father and my mother weren't natives of that place at all, they came from the Urlingford direction. So this morning I'm telling you of, my brother died of typhoid fever. Ah! we were lone birds. When it was time to coffin the brother there was no one in the house. There was no one at the wake but as little. All the neighbours were in dread of the fever. This is Gospel truth I'm tellin' you. So my mother says to me, ' Go to the door an' see would you get anyone to help you coffin your brother.' I went out in the yard. There were people down at the mouth of the boreen. I saw they were keepin' on the wind-side of the house. Then I saw a crowd o' men hidin' in an outhouse. I stood there with my two hands as long as one another. I stood there for a good while. Then a Sullivan boy stepped out of a cowhouse. He called out to his two first cousins. They were Sullivans too. The Sullivans coffined my brother. They got under the coffin with me and they gave it the first shoulder. I never forgot it for the Sullivans. I'd go up to my neck in the river for a Sullivan. I'd give my heart's blood for a man of the name! "

Up in the sky Silvo was saying: " God help us, but they were terrible times. Myself an' my father tryin' to fit the pieces of poor Florry together, an' my sister screamin' below in the room. . . ."

I said to myself: If only I could remember the story that fellow told me about the theatre in Alexandria. I mean to say, if I only had the sense to take it down after I heard it. I bet I could write plenty short stories if I only travelled. How can a man write short stories if he doesn't get a chance of travelling ?

THE EGOTISTS

We had our problems, the three of us, so we fell silent. The problems eddied in us, steamed in us. Then, all at the same time, the three of us said " I " together.

Instantaneously I realised that the three " I's " were three tiny glass balls, painted silver on the outside, much like the ornamental balls one sees in the Christmas Crib. And the three silver glass balls banged together and fell to pieces on the ground. I saw by the pieces that the balls were gilt inside. I kept looking at the pieces of the three silver glass balls. I should have liked to be in a position to call the pieces shards, but, honestly, they weren't shards. They weren't quite thick enough for shards. These were merely miserable bits of trumpery silver and trumpery gold — sorry pieces of concave silver and convex gold.

Then somebody inconsiderately quenched the light in the western world. I was suddenly aware of the widening cold.

SUNDAY MORNING

THE girl came skipping down the sunny pavement. At her shoulder-points the scarlet globes of the skipping-rope handles were describing small scarlet circles. Each time her shoe-soles touched the brownish flagstones a soft welcome was shot through her thirteen-year-old body. She skipped down into the short narrow street; thence to the braver and more open street. She skipped past the little club. Behind the glass and the perforated painted tin in the club-window two dim men were dreaming out Sunday morning. The men were smoking pipes; over their hats the sunlight was busy tinting the pipe-smoke with off-purple. The girl raced past the shuttered pork-butcher's, past the intimidating frontage of Hogan's the draper's where the twenty-six letters on the fascia board glittered like the possessions of a king. Speeding thus, the whole of the girl's body was singing a song of Sunday. Sunday was a brave day. Sunday was a great day. There were times on Sunday when you owned the whole town. Now, for instance, there was no one to usurp her authority over the sunny streets. True, there was some statuary in odd doorways. Those were people lying in waiting for the pageant of the congregation emerging from the ten o'clock Mass.

Then suddenly the chimes were about and around, banging and clanging everywhere. A quarter-past. A quarter-past ten.

Henebry's the jeweller's had been closed for close on twelve months. Henebry's had black shutters. Passing the place Kitty Connors saw her name chalked up on the black shutters. Her name put out a hook and the hook gained purchase on her plaid skirt. For a moment the sunlight played tig with her and would not reveal the remainder of the inscription. Like school, she thought, when a blade of window-light taunts you with a problem on the blackboard and then puts its white hand over the solution. The girl walked on two steps and cheated the tricking sun. The inscription read: " Kitty Connors loves Martin Mongan."

On the instant she experienced the roping and churning and flaying of terror. Terror had all that sunny Sunday by the throat. She felt her strength leak away from her as if it were brilliant arterial blood walking out through a wide wound. True, a remnant of her valiance compelled her to try two further skips, but indeed they proved to be a pair of laughable lustreless hops. She choked with the idea of making a great breach between herself and the shutters. The breach made, to hide. To hide in a dozen blankets in a cupboard within a cupboard. To hide in the heart of the pampas-clump on the verge of the laurels at midnight. And then her heart, hitherto faithful to her, became an ill-killed trout in her breast-pocket.

But the writing held her as it watched her disintegrate. Slowly she put the red handles of the skipping-rope together and wound the rope around them. Her flaming face turned and surveyed the street. There were people in doorways — watching her, it seemed to her. Then she began running. Back up the wide street she skeltered, into the narrow street, and again into her own wide street on the fringe of the town. High on the terrace to her right the children of her street were chittering like sparrows. One of them sang out after her as she ran. Then they all came to the grey wall over and above her and called her. But all the time the bellman in her head was continuing his declamation. " Kitty Connors loves Martin Mongan. Oh, Kitty Connors loves Martin Mongan. Oh, Kitty

Connors loves Martin Mongan."

All through the race she was defending and accusing
herself: oh, but it isn't true, it isn't true. He walked up
as far as your door with you the evening of the music
exam., didn't he? Didn't he? Answer me out, didn't
he? He did, he did! All right, he did! But I tell you
it isn't true. Didn't he offer you a bar o' chocolate at
Murphy's o' the Corner, Christmas Eve Night? Didn't
he? Didn't he? Answer me out! But it isn't true! It
isn't true! I tell you, it isn't true! Didn't Sister Regius
tell you a Wednesday that you were getting very forward
in yourself? Didn't she tell you that? Answer me out!
Answer me out! Kitty Connors loves Martin Mongan.
Oh, Kitty Connors loves Martin Mongan. Oh, Kitty
Connors loves Martin Mongan.

'Less the mercy o' God the whole town had it. They
all had it; gentle and simple had it. Dinny the Club
had it. The Corcorans o' the Mile Gate had it. Nell
Sweeney and Andy Sweeney of Upper Street had it. The
Donoghues had it. The whole town had it! Kitty
Connors loves Martin Mongan. 'Less the mercy o' God
alone, the whole town had it!

Panting, she reached her own house. She set her
hand to the rolling gate leading to the yard and, steadying
her feet, thrust suddenly against the gate. The gate rolled
easily on its greased rollers. The sheep-dog in the yard
offered her his perfunctory tribute of two family barks.
She crashed the gate to behind her and set her back
against it.

Now she was free to grapple with the main terror.
Her father was at the ten o'clock Mass. He'd be certain
to see it on Henebry's shutters. He could hardly have
seen it going down with the light against him. But he'd
be certain to see it coming back!

She heard the tines of the pitchfork clacking on the

stall cobbles. Then she saw Tom Dunne's new navy-blue coat hanging on the edge of the stall-door. She went into the kitchen and presently came out. Then she sidled down to the stall-door with something hidden in her hands behind her back.

The gloom of the cow-stall was sea-blue in colour. From the doorway she looked into the deep cave of the place: in a remote part of it she saw the white breakers of Tom Dunne's shirt-sleeves. The prongs were noising superfluously on the cleaned quoins. Sunday was affording Tom Dunne the privilege and the luxury of gathering ungatherables.

She called to him:

" Tom!   Tom Dunne!   Tom Dunne! "

The urgency in her tone of voice sucked Tom Dunne out into the sunlight. Discovered, indeed, he proved to be a plump-faced fellow with the powdered quartz of perspiration under the dark cliff-top of his hair. One had barely caught the contours of his features when the sun shrivelled his face till it became a desiccated balloon.

" Well," he said, with a spit, " if it isn't Pigtails! "

He began to upbraid her. " Your shoes! Your two lovely Sunday shoes! Tck-tck! In the middle of the dung. In the middle of the dung. Tck-tck! That's it! Stamp on 'em well! That's it! Oh, your lovely Sunday shoes."

She remained silent. " Well, Pigtails," he asked, " what is it ? "

She stamped her shoes and carefully watched the stamping. Then, with her eyes still on her shoes, " Something I want you to do for me, Tom Dunne." All the while she had her hands behind her back. (I'm going to get an apple, thought Tom Dunne. She has me like Adam in the Garden, thought Tom Dunne. And then he laughed outright at his own wit.)

Before replying the servant-boy gave a deferential gesture that his forebears had miraculously rescued from the middenheap of mediaeval manners. " What is it, my little woman ? "

" 'Tis how . . . 'tis how my name is written up on Henebry's shutters."

" Up on Henebry's shutters ? "

" Yes, with chalk."

" With chalk ? "

" Yes, with white chalk on Henebry's black shutters."

" Black shutters ? So they are, indeed, black shutters."

" Yes."

" *Your* name? "

" Yes, *my* name ! "

Judicially, " Well, I wouldn't call that the height o' treason, Pigtails. The Henebrys are all dead and buried for themselves for the past twelve months and more."

" But 'tis how . . . 'tis how there's a boy's name up on the shutters as well."

" Oho ! Oho, Pigtails ! A boy's name, faith ! " Tom Dunne pummelled his nose to provide an alibi for his already incriminated and smiling mouth.

Then the banging chimes of half-past ten broke out from the steeple. The clangour ripped the cloak of her poise from her back.

" You must hurry, Tom Dunne. My father ! He's at the ten Mass. My father is at the ten Mass, I tell you. The people'll be out in a minute. You must hurry, Tom Dunne. You must hurry."

Tom Dunne drove the fork full into the manure heap and reached for his jacket. When he turned again she was holding out a damp cloth. " Here, Tom, rub it out with that," she said.

" Cloth ? Shah cloth, Pigtails. Haven't I me red handkerchief an' me spit ? "

"Ah, take the cloth, Tom. Do! Do it good, Tom Dunne. Won't you promise me you'll do it good?"

"All right, sure, I'll take the damp cloth. Just to please you. Look, can't I put it in me pocket and pretend it's me handkerchief?"

"Do it good, Tom. Be sure you do it good."

She followed him as far as Collopy's corner. Here she waited, a palpitating sentinel, and watched him efface the inscription. He did it competently with a bold swing from right to left followed by some energetic zigzags. He gave the whole a last cheery lick, after which he half raised his victorious hand to the far flicker of his sentry's dress.

Then the first spillings of people from the Mass came around the corner. Suddenly the street grew replete with the genteel roar of Sunday shoes.

Kitty was waiting for Tom Dunne in the yard. When he came in she gave him a florin she had taken from her store in the wicker casket in her room. Taking the coin he spat on it and then the pleasure of acceptance broke down his face into the tired red balloon. "Now I can go out to Cloonalla, Pigtails," he said.

Moving away from him her gait became queenly. At last she was mistress of her small heart.

Behind her the garden door stole open without creaking and her young brother Paddy padded softly into the yard. He crouched behind the water-butt, his highwayman's slouch weighing him down as if it were a man's frieze overcoat. Tom Dunne saw him and kept his smile a constant, lest it should play informer. Paddy crept after his sister, all the while pointing his ponderous gun-of-air at her. Then he pulled the trigger-of-air of his gun-of-air and said "Krrck! Krrck! Krrck!" The sounds seemed to come from his crinkled eye rather than from his mouth. Then he gave a blood-curdling boyish yell and shouted, " You're dead, Kitty; you're dead, Kitty; you're dead ! "

Instead of clutching her breast in the mimicry of murder, she rushed at him and attacked him with all her kisses.   She kept crushing him violently till he commenced to claw her out from his redness.   Then, grabbing him by the wrist, she bustled him out through the rolling door and with a competent forearm sent it home behind her.   The pair of them went clippety-cloppety-clip on the pavement.   Upstreet a white and orange ice-cream pennant spied them approaching and, in an access of Sunday joyousness, it called, " Come ! come ! come ! "

THE WILL

BIG Mick Kinsella was dying. He refused to admit the fact, but he was dying just the same. Priest and doctor had come and gone. The doctor hadn't put a tooth under it — he had told Big Mick plump and plain that he was for the road. And all Big Mick could proffer in place of reply was, " Pssssh, wssssh, hsssh."

When the noise of the doctor's car had died away, the sick man kept reassuring himself with similar deprecatory sibilant noises. Nora Hallissey came into the room and started to cajole Mick in her simple fashion. She was a first cousin of his and had been keeping house for him since his wife had left him after a trial of childless marriage. Nora wanted him to settle up his affairs, and she kept saying, " Sure, 'twon't make you an hour older nor a whit the worse," or " Younger and livelier you'll be, if anything, with that load off your back." Big Mick hushed her, saying, " To-morrow, please God, I'll have all this rubbed out," and, " Faith, the time hasn't yet come for Mick Kinsella to hand in his gun."

His poorer brother, Ned Kinsella, who lived on poorer land down the road, came scuttling up to reason with the sick man. Ned kept hopping in and out of the room like a fiddler's elbow before God gave him the strength to broach the subject that was troubling him. Before that, he was one moment at the kitchen fire and the next at the bedside. When finally he spoke up he kept crackling his fingers with the terror that the farm would go from himself and his son Jim. His words were broken, and quavered. " Settle your affairs, Mick. Sure nobody has a lease of life. Can't you tear up your writing when you get better?"

But all his brother Mick answered was, " I'll battle it out, I tell you, Ned. So I will, with the help of God. See now if I don't. Don't let ye be bothering me now an' I not so well."

Then, in desperation, Ned Kinsella blurted out that which was most secret within him. " Your wife will have it all, Mick. The farm will leave the name. You wouldn't like that, Mick ? " Then, pressing home the point when he saw it was not resented, " This was the Kinsellas' ground ever and always. If she gets a hoult of it, she'll divide it among a pack of hungry griping nephews and nieces. There's a parcel of them with their mouths open ready to swallow it like gearrcachs in a nest. They'll have it all, seed, stick, an' stone." Then, wheedlingly, " You're not forgetting my son Jimmy, are you, Mick, nor Nora here who minded you and tended you hand and foot all these years back ? Jimmy Kinsella worked well for you, Mick. Slaved himself to the bone, day in, day out. You won't deny that, Mick ? Speak up for my son, Nora Hallissey. A good right you have to speak up. Your mother was a Kinsella. Talk up for him, I tell you, Nora Hallissey ! " Then, turning from the two of them in mock despair, " Ah ! if only my poor father that's in his grave could see the land he'd give his heart's blood for and it going out of the name ! "

Big Mick grew very quiet and thoughtful in himself. " True ! True ! Very true ! " he pondered aloud. " Maybe ye have the right of it. 'Tis a bad thing to be too stubborn. 'Tis kind land, 'tis good land, 'tis warm land. 'Twould be a sin if it left the name. Ye're my own, I can say what I like to ye." Then, as the far flame of anger overcame the twin evils of illness and obesity, " No ! she'll never put a foot in it ! No ! No ! Nor anyone of her seed and breed ! " The sick man drew a racking breath and, in exhaling, said petulantly,

THE WILL

"Yes! yes! ye can send for Andy."

There was a notable elation in Ned Kinsella's voice as he told the servant-girl to go for Andy Reynolds. The girl had ungovernable bleached-straw hair and a soiled, tattered, blue smock. Huge ABCs with meshes as big as pennies patterned her collops. A pair of cut-down Wellingtons flup-flopped around her heels as she walked. It took her a long time to grasp the purport of the message. When finally she got it right she made off across the fields to Andy Reynolds's cottage. And scarcely was she across the dry-wall than Big Mick heaved high in the bed, became cyanosed and died.

Andy Reynolds was diminutive, alert and old. Turn and turn about his face was corvine and vulpine. A battalion of lawyers had failed to pick a hole in one of his home-made wills and this had gained him a wholesome legal reputation in the neighbourhood. Andy showed surprising agility as he moved up the path in the Long Meadow. The servant-girl moved fearfully before him.

When Andy entered the farmhouse he took in the situation at a glance. Ned Kinsella was sitting disconsolately at the hearth, crumbling his fingers like broken bread. Nora Hallissey was on a small stool under the chimney — she was gathered in a ball like a hedgehog. Ned gave a broken-hearted look at Andy and changed from crumbling to a rhythmic in-and-out movement of his hands as if he were playing a concertina. Andy's keen eyes saw that the room door was shut. Noting this confirmation, he became more alert, more cruel; then unaccountably he grew buoyant and cheerful. For a moment the whimsicality of the crow in him overcame the cleverness of the fox. Not for long, however. He turned on the servant-girl who had taken refuge in the darker portion of the kitchen. "Get out!" he snarled at her.

THE WILL

The girl gathered her ungainly body to her and ran out the door.

" Lord have mercy on the dead ! " said Ned Kinsella to the fire. The hedgehog squirmed, showed some portion of its body that was light in colour and rolled up again.

Andy Reynolds did not " amen " the prayer. He chuckled as he sat at the head of the table and perched his steel-rimmed spectacles on his nose.

" Hush ! man, hush ! " he chided obliquely. " Sure you're not going to let it go with her ? "

Ned and Nora were dumb.

" Lovely warm ground," he taunted, " the loveliest and the warmest of ground. I've heard tell of men did murder for a-deal-sight colder ground than this ! "

Ned Kinsella bitterly swung his head this way and that, as if he were telling his troubles to the flames. " Vo ! vo ! vo ! vo ! vo ! " he complained.

" Ah ! hush your psalmin' for yourself an' have a spark of courage in your four bones," spat Andy.

" Courage ? Courage ? Errah, man, what use is courage now ? "

Andy laughed. " I'll shortly be showing ye. Where here do ye keep the pen and ink ? "

A harsh bout of echoing laughter came from Ned. Then, " 'Tis on the ledge o' the window — for all the good 'tis to you."

Old Andy drew a long envelope from his inside pocket. He fondled it. He took out the will-form and studied the precedent will that was attached to it. The specimen will was written sprawlingly in red ink. Andy pounded the recalcitrant parchment in order to flatten it. Then he dipped his pen with the far-away grandeur of the barely literate and began to write. He leaned savagely on the downstrokes and jerked frightfully on the upstrokes. His mouth was working as he wrote.

THE WILL

". . . To my nephew James Kinsella . . ." — articulating, he placed a hyphen between each syllable — ". . . in the townland of . . ." Then, half to himself, " I'd better leave the other one a hundred to make it sensible like."

Ned Kinsella turned his head as if he were peeping round a corner. " What the hell game is this you're at ? " he queried.

Nora Hallissey uncoiled herself. " I'll not witness it for you," she said, " the man is stone cold dead."

The servant-girl ventured to show her nose to the door. She had a peck in her hand. Andy gripped the pen as if it were a foreign dagger. " Get out, you meddlesome strap, you ! " he pounded. The girl reddened up to the two ears and disappeared.

Andy finished his drafting and stood up. He became as sweet as pie as he looked out over his glasses at the woman. " Mick is leaving you nothing, Nora," he said. " You see, there's a point of law in a ben-ef-ic-iary bein' a witness. But Ned here'll see to it that you'll never want for a bit, bite or sup, nor a roof over your head." Turning towards Ned, " I'll have your word for that, Ned Kinsella ? "

" The devil himself out of hell won't get me to put my name to that," broke in the woman.

" Faith, you will, girl," said Andy patronisingly, cocking his head spryly on one side. " You see, when all is said an' done, Nora, you're a woman, and it's no difficult matter to ease a woman's conscience." Then, in a more subtle tone, " Come now, your mother was a Kinsella, Nora Hallissey. Are you going to sit idle and see the Kinsellas' ground go among strangers ? And remember this, my good woman, he sent for me, didn't he ? Answer me fair, woman, did he send for me or not ? And tell me this much, Nora Hallissey, are you going to go against a dyin' man's wishes for the sake of a tick or two of the clock one way or the other ? "

" He sent for you," said the woman slowly. Already her tone of voice showed that she had begun to justify herself.

" What more is there to be said ? " trumped Andy. Then, abusively, " Get up out of the corner, woman, and do the right thing by one of your own blood."

Nora stood up, in terror. She looked into Ned Kinsella's face for a sign. Ned nodded a dubious yet eager affirmative. Then he, too, stood up.

Andy crowed again. " Shah ! " he said, " 'tis easy ease a woman's conscience. I promised that I'd settle it — and I will ! "

The alert old man first went to the kitchen window and peered narrowly at the corners of the panes. Disappointed, he turned and looked closely at the back window. " Hijay ! " he said, " if you didn't want them they'd eat you out of house and home."

When he looked again at the front window there was a fly drumming against the glass. " There you are ! " gloated Andy Reynolds.

He pulled out the kitchen table, and caught the fly with a quick flick of his cupped hand. " A fine fat lively laddo, too," he commented. The woman was frozen in the wonder that he had not skinned his knuckles on the window frame.

Andy stood in mid-kitchen and, holding his hand on high, pivoted his fist from the wrist. Through a crevice in the fist-prison a weak jet of buzzing escaped. " Open the room door, woman," he said.

The dead man's mouth had sagged open. With his left hand Andy laid the will-form, together with the pen and ink, on a small bedside table. Then, gauging his distance carefully, he clapped his right hand over the mouth of the corpse. He flattened out the hand and then slid the jaw up under his palm. Saliva greased the jaw's movement. He whipped off his scarf and bound it around the head, effectively closing the mouth. Turning towards the door, he saw Ned Kinsella watching him in astonishment.

" Don't let you be standing there, Ned," he said. " You being present, and your son a ben-ef-ic-iary — there might be a point o' law in that. Go up to the fire for yourself."

The room door closed. Andy was alone with the woman and the corpse. He placed the pen in the dead man's hand and, moving it as one would when teaching a child to write, he traced the name, " Michael Kinsella," on the paper.

Next he placed the will on the table and signed " Andrew Reynolds " as witness. He handed the woman the pen, and his expression was intimidating when he brought her to his wish. There was a tremor in her hand as she signed " Nora Hallissey ".

Andy seemed overwhelmed by an access of legal glee. " Now ! " he said, " the land won't leave the name." Then, rounding fiercely but elatedly on the woman, he said, " And, Nora Hallissey, if they put you in the box, remember that when he signed the will — *there was life in him* ! "

GENTLEMEN, THIS IS ARMAGEDDON !

THREE brightly dressed persons walked down the main street of a small Irish country town. Their brilliant attire offended the beige ground, the colourless stone walls and the faded paint-work of the sun-blistered shop-fronts.

The three persons — two women and a man — were concert folk : they were members of a variety troupe that was playing at the local hall. The hall itself — an awkward galvanised structure — stood on the higher ground at one end of the town.

The man was walking in the middle. He was extremely small of stature. Nature had most unfairly branded a scowl on his face when sending him out on the important errand of his life. His face could fairly be termed cadaverous : the tambourine-skin that covered it was chocolate-brown in colour. His out-thrust nether lip was half tremulous, half ferocious. But his eyes held the seed of his features' redemption — year in, year out, they cried " I spy ! " on his gimcrack ferocity. They were the honest, sincere eyes of a spaniel. His hair was a brush of silver wire : his chest was large enough to suggest deformity. One postman-ish shoulder was tilted to northeast. He was dressed in a threadbare green suit with a trailing red tie falling out over the junction of the coat-lapels.

The two women carried on a loud vivid conversation across the man's silver hair. If, in the course of their talk, they had occasion to address him, they called him Nicholas.

The woman walking on the man's right was fortyish. Though her complexion had been savaged by the continual use of inferior face-cream and grease paint, yet her face still held certain remnants of beauty. It was a sound-boned face under the bare jut of jet hair. Her movements were delightful. The tilt of her head was a treasure, and her bosom was ideally poised. Every time her shoe soles found firm purchase on the pavements, her silk-sheathed calves shuddered. She wore a short coat of imitation leopard skin over a moss-green frock. She contrasted strangely with the woman on the man's left who was large and flushed. This woman walked with the agitated jerky movements of the comedienne. Her bust and buttocks and legs had been ordained to provoke laughter. Coarse spikes of blonde hair protruded from beneath her ridiculous toque. Her mouth, which showed ranks of false teeth, was the mouth of a ventriloquist's doll. A white linen frock made her figure more elephantine than it really was; the navy-blue cardigan fastened about her middle by its lowest button gave her the appearance of a moored balloon. Now and again, in the course of their conversation, the women threw Nicholas the bare bone of a phrase, whereat he growled contentedly and ploughed ahead through the town. The trim black woman was addressed as July, the inflated comedienne as Vonny.

As Nicholas, July, and Vonny walked down the street they left a wide furrow of interest in their wake. Men idled carefully to the door-jambs and watched them intently. These men's reactions to each of the walkers was interesting. They scowled when their eyes lighted on the crouched Nicholas (what an injustice that they could not see his splendid eyes — his suffering eyes); the onlookers' eyes narrowed to red kernels as they fell on July, but the wind of laughter was up and about them, blowing and bellowing, when the eyes fell on the waddling Vonny.

GENTLEMEN, THIS IS ARMAGEDDON!

At the long street's end the flagged pavement petered out: a gravelled path and the disconsolate shop-fronts yielded place to a file of fairly trim cottages abutting on the pathway. One or two of the cottages boasted small lawns; some of the remaining cottages sported windows chock-full of geranium plants. These incarcerated blooms pressed their pathetic brick-red faces against the cob-webbed glass.

Paddy McKenna, the hackney driver, was sitting on the sill of his geranium window when he noticed the concert folk approaching. Behind his head, affixed to the glass of the window, a notice stated that Patrick McKenna had motors for hire. The use of the plural of motor was a business exaggeration — Paddy owned but one motor and that was a most unpredictable vehicle. He was not wearing his jacket; his shirt sleeves were furled around his flabby biceps and the forearms showed smudges of axle-grease. Paddy had a huge harvest-moon for a face; his dolly-blue eyes held more than their due share of electricity.

As soon as Paddy realised that the persons approaching him were concert-folk, he made haste to put himself in suitable trim. He hurriedly took out a crumpled cigarette from his fob-pocket, lighted it and settled himself firmly on the sill. Nicholas and July and Vonny approached; they were moving rather slowly and were examining the windows of the cottages.

Arrived level with Paddy McKenna the trio stopped. Vonny saw the card nestling among the geraniums and addressed Paddy:

" Are you the man who has the car for hire ? "

" Yes, miss, I am." Paddy obsequiously topped his cigarette and stood up whilst tucking it away.

" Can you drive us to Leithmore ? "

" I can indeed, miss."

GENTLEMEN, THIS IS ARMAGEDDON!

"How far is it from here?" queried Nicholas mildly.

"A matter of about eight or nine Irish mile of ground," said Paddy. Then, after a short inspection of the three, "A part where they do little else besides torch salmon and clift goats. Of course there are a few warm farms o' land there, too."

"What direction is it in?" This again from Nicholas.

"Layd-mu-ar, where are ye?" said Paddy, looking at the horizon. "D'you see that lump of the blue hills beyond the last of the houses? Up there is ye'er Layd-mu-ar."

Vonny took command. "Can you drive us there now?"

"This very minute, is it?"

"Yes, immediately."

"Right you are, ma'am. I'll be with you in a minute. I'll stick on me coat and pull round the car." Then, belatedly, "Where in Laydmuar are ye intendin' goin', if I might ask?"

"Do you know a farmer there by the name of . . ." July fumbled in her handbag for a letter. ". . . Deegan? Jack Deegan I think the name is."

"Well, I couldn't be rightly sure. But there's Deegans there all right. There are a couple of Deegans there with tidy holdin's. The name is there all right, I'm certain of that."

The car was driven around to the door. Paddy had his Sunday jacket pulled on above his workday pants. Nicholas sat in front with the driver: July and Vonny sat in the rear seat. As the car moved forwards, Paddy ventured a quick glance backwards at his window and spied his wife's face nestling in the geraniums.

During the journey there was little conversation. Nicholas kept his brown eyes devotedly fixed on the road. Vonny began complaining bitterly of the pianist in the variety company, and July threw her an occasional word of agreement.

An ivy-covered house stood at a cross-roads. Paddy changed gear, swung around by the house, and the car churned forward uphill. The road was now rutted and damp under roadside trees. Vonny's complaints about the pianist were throttled by the pitching and lurching of the car. Her complexion increased in redness. Nicholas turned in his seat, blinked his eyes and said, in an unexpected falsetto of mimicry, " Gentlemen, this is Armageddon! " The women began to laugh immoderately. Paddy dutifully gave a little neigh of laughter.

It was September. Autumn had just set her torch to the beech trees. Plumes of yellow shot through them from the first branches above the boles to the very topmost crests. The car left the trees behind and the country grew more rugged. Here and there the stony bones of the world gaped out of dead pastures. The hill-road rose in the undulations of bogland. Above the immediate hilltop the sky had gone pewter grey. The smell and chill of thunder were in the air. The hedges were of black- and whitethorn. The whitethorn was wind-whipt and tormented by the bog-blast; it had writhed away from its tormentor, sometimes becoming unduly elongated or top-heavy. Here and there on the roadside a great bush of fuchsia hung out its blue and crimson bells among the dark leaves — the whole bush seemed a lamp set against the livid heavens. The hidden sun had edged the great thunderclouds with murky gold. Sheep clustered in the field-corners stopped cropping to watch the car pass. The car frightened a turkey in a bush-top. Goats tied together with bucket-handles clanked away from mid-road as the car approached. The cottages on the roadside were roofed with materials that were half slate, half flagstone, and the joints were pointed with cement. The little houses all had an attitude of crouching.

The car reached the crest of the hill; away beyond they saw a jumble of hilltops with brown bog-land between. The women were now sitting erect in their seats. They were looking through the windscreen and had grown thoughtful and silent. Before them stretched the rutted hopeless road. Nicholas's eyes were unspeakably sad. Vonny suddenly asked, " Have we much farther to go ? " Her voice was the voice of a tragedienne.

" Across this hill, near the second townland and we're there," said Paddy.

Far away in the west the rain drew its white muslin scarf along a skyline that was serrated by turf-ricks. Objects in the middle distance grew extraordinarily clear. A hare walked up the road towards the car. " A hare, bigod ! " said Paddy ; Nicholas and the women squeaked with interest. The hare looked at the approaching motor for a moment ; then, as Paddy accelerated, the little animal strummed the road with his hind legs and moved gracefully away, still keeping to the roadway. After a hundred yards or so he dodged down off the raised road and weaved in and out among the beds of heather. Watching him eagerly from the car the four saw him, then lost him, then glimpsed him before he vanished utterly into the high uncut bog-land. A group of men cutting turf on a bank ceased work and watched the hare fleeing from the car.

After a mile or so Paddy stopped the car beside a youngster who was clamping turf on the side of the road. " Where does Jack Deegan live, sonny ? " he asked.

The lad was both stupid and suspicious. He seemed reluctant to reply.

" Is it ' Jacky Bawn ' or ' Jacky the Thistle ' ye want ? " he asked after a time.

Paddy spoke, " ' Thistle ' is an ould fellow, isn't he, and ' Bawn ' is a young married man ? "

" That's right," the boy agreed.

Vonny intervened. " It's the young married man we want."

The boy pointed. " That's Jacky Bawn's in there in that clump of trees. Ye go in by the passage beyond the cutaway and keep on up to the house. Ye'll pass in by the cottage with the white gate-piers."

The passage from the road to the house was alternately soft and stony. At last the car slithered into the farm-yard. As Paddy hastened out to help the women alight he saw a curtain drop in one of the windows. The in-evitable sheep-dog came rushing out and began raising hell. Mud and cow-dung were inches deep in the yard. The house itself was long, low, and thatched, with small windows. It sorely needed whitewash and the thatch was green and rotten. As the women and Nicholas stepped down large drops of rain began to fall.

" Well, good sweet hell ! " said Vonny. Balancing herself on the higher cobbles of the yard, she looked at the tiny windows, at the ochreous door, at the green-tufted thatch. She saw the dismal elder hedge and the sick-looking apple trees beyond it. A delicate turkey piped five miserable young turkeys down the yard. House, hedge, trees, dog, turkeys — all seemed ineffably decayed.

Just then a young woman came around the corner of the building. She had on a bottle-green soiled jumper : a packing apron was hitched awkwardly around her middle. In her hand was a rusty bucket to the sides of which yellow meal clots were adhering. The woman was sweating. The sweat stood out on a vivid face which held live-coal eyes and unusually red lips. The hair was as black as black could be. She was wearing two earrings that looked like two large drops of congealed blood. When she saw the newcomers standing in the first of the rain she rushed forward screaming breathlessly, " Oh,

Vonny!" "Oh, July!" Then, "Oh, Nicholas!"

Vonny and July forgot the dung on the cobbles: they rushed forward and fell upon the woman. "Nanette! Nanette!" they shrilled. They caressed her in the demonstrative way that showfolk have. When they released her to arm's length, the better to view her, Nanette escaped and rushed forward to clasp Nicholas. Nicholas kept murmuring her name fondly. Now all three women were crying. Then Nicholas struck a grotesque attitude and spouted, "Gentlemen, this is Armageddon!" Nanette laughed hysterically at this. Paddy McKenna was leaning across the bonnet of the car watching all four intently.

A young man moved in the orchard trees. He looked into the farmyard for a moment. Then he sidled back out of sight behind an apple tree and disappeared. Paddy watched him go. The loose cross-curtain of the kitchen window was lifted slowly; then it dropped abruptly.

"I must show you my baby," said Nanette. The three followed her indoors. An old woman was seated in the cavernous hearth by the white ashes of the fire. A red knitted shawl was thrown across her shoulders. The eyes in her head were unusually keen. "My mother-in-law," Nanette said left-handedly. The old woman smiled grimly in their direction and bobbed in her chair. Her eyes slashed at them fiercely. She gave no intention of rising to welcome them, nor of extending her hand in greeting. There was an awkward moment. "My baby," said Nanette, and moved towards the crib which was beside the old woman.

The cradle was crudely made. The child was asleep, and Vonny and July protested vehemently against Nanette's waking it. Nanette thrust her face down to the crib; her lips were pursing and opening. She placed her

finger on the plump knob of the infant's chin and moved
the knob with a circular motion of the finger. The baby
grumbled up out of sleep. At first it grimaced. Then
it smiled sheepishly, showing its gums. Its eyes were a
good bright blue. Vonny and July cooed and jockeyed
for places at the cribside. Nanette lifted the child to a
sitting position and all the women kissed it in turn. The
old woman spat into the ashes. Nicholas was in the background: he was embarrassed at being, as it were, left
alone with the old woman, so he moved around to the
leeside of the group. When he looked down into the crib
he saw the infant's face under one of Nanette's blood-red
earrings.

By now the child was fully awake; Nanette took it up
out of the blankets and danced it up and down lovingly.
The old woman clucked disapprovingly. Then the mother
clasped the baby and pirouetted lightly around the floor,
finally stopping with the baby's face close to Nicholas's.
" Come," she laughed, " a kiss from Old Nick ! " Nicholas
put his face against the child's; his distorted features, his
narrowed eyes, his drawn nostrils, his tautened neck-
cords, the crude set of his kissing mouth gave him an
almost simian appearance. The old woman dragged her
chair harshly on the hearthstone.

A hulking red-complexioned girl of about eighteen
came in by the back-door. She had an armful of turf
which she threw at the old woman's feet. As she moved
across the kitchen her stupefied eyes never left the visitors.
Nanette spoke to her, " Hang the kettle on the fire, Moll,
and go out and see would you find himself." The girl
moved dreamily on her errand.

Nanette replaced the child in the cradle and placed
the teat of the bottle in its mouth. The baby began to
suck lustily. With Nanette leading the way the four
moved up to the upper room. There was only a faint

smell of sourness in the darkened parlour until they sat on the chairs. Then the odour of disuse — even of decay — filled the narrow space. Nanette took down photographs from the overmantel and passed them around for inspection. In one of the photographs was a lissom soubrette in tights and spangles. Nicholas's eyes kept wandering from the photograph to Nanette and back again.

Nanette went down to the kitchen to get ready the tea-things. She found the driver sitting on a chair opposite the old woman. He was drinking buttermilk out of a large blue mug. As the young woman moved in to make up the fire around the kettle, Paddy drew back saying, " Excuse me, ma'am, I'm in your way." Nanette protested that he was not and forced him to occupy his seat again. The old woman addressed Paddy directly : " You're a son of Jim McKenna's of the Graigue, aren't you ? " and when he agreed, she added, " You married a daughter of Dinny Keane the Pond, didn't you ? " and when Paddy again agreed, the old woman added venomously, " You did well, sensible man! Any man but a fool'd marry a girl from his own ground. To say the least of it he knows what he's getting." Nanette's sudden flush showed that the arrow had gone home. Paddy shifted uneasily in his chair.

The first flames sent scarlet prongs around the great iron kettle. Nanette was scooping out air-caves from under the fire with the tongs, and as the firelight caught the earrings they became glowing coals.

The lumpish servant girl came in by the back door and Nanette turned away from the fire to ask, " Did you find himself, Moll ? " " No, ma'am," said the girl. The old woman made a noise in her nose. The girl was no dullard ; she glanced quickly from face to face ; when she spoke again she did so over-speedily, over-glibly,

" There isn't a trace of him anywhere about, ma'am. I think unless I'm greatly mistaken that I see him goin' up the road to the forge an' the motor-car comin' in. If you like ma'am, I'll go up an' see."

Nanette looked at her coldly. " You needn't bother," she said. " Wash your hands and get a small jug of cream out of the dairy."

The old woman began to hum irritatingly in time with her rocking of the cradle. She leaned forward towards Paddy. " Will I get you another cup of buttermilk, decent boy ? " Paddy protested his inability to drink any more. He squirmed a little in his seat. Nanette returned to her visitors.

Soon there was a jingle of tea-cups in the parlour; loud laughing was heard as anecdotes were told and enjoyed hysterically. The soft barking of Nicholas mingled intermittently with the shrill yelping of the women. Then Vonny and July stood at the fireplace and did their new act.

VONNY : My sister Gladys went to sea in a schooner.

JULY : Your sister Gladys went to sea in a schooner ?

VONNY : Please don't interrupt ! I was just saying that my sister Gladys went to sea in a schooner.

JULY : But I distinctly understood that you were going to tell the story about the gentleman who sold locomotives.

VONNY : Please don't interrupt ! My sister Gladys went to sea in a schooner.

Then came an interruption from Nicholas : " Gentlemen, this is Armageddon ! " All four crashed into uncontrolled laughter.

Down at the kitchen fire, Mrs. Deegan transfixed Paddy with her hawk's eye. Paddy buried his nose in the dregs of the buttermilk. He had reserved these dregs for precisely such an emergency.

Nanette went to the back-door and looked out over the

fields. It was raining softly in large drops. She went down to the orchard wall. As she walked she kept by the walls so as to avoid the rain-drops. She looked over her shoulder once or twice. When she reached the orchard wall she called " Jack ! " into the trees. " Jack ! " she called again, urgently, pleadingly. There was no answer, only the reiterated phut-phut of the falling drops. She drooped and returned to the house.

When the three visitors were departing Nanette loaded them with eggs and butter and apples. She placed a pint bottle of cream on the floor of the car. All four embraced boisterously again and again. As they were leaving the kitchen Nicholas padded back to say good-bye to the old woman ; Vonny and July reluctantly followed his example. At first it seemed as if she would ignore Nicholas's out-stretched hand, but her innate courtesy overcame her prejudices and she shook hands with each of them in turn.

Paddy had the car started in the farmyard. A cohort of geese marched across the yard. One of them broke from file and rushed hissing in Vonny's direction. Screams and laughter came shriller than ever. " Jack will be sorry he missed you when he returns from the forge," Nanette kept saying limply. In the kitchen the child began to cry bitterly. The strange thought crossed Paddy's mind that the old woman was pinching it. Then the boisterousness of farewell began again, but it died suddenly without any appreciable cause. Paddy felt sadness seep into him. He was loath to slam the doors of the motor. Finally the car roared away, leaving behind a disconsolate figure with an arm raised in farewell.

A heavy silence fell upon the travellers as they rode back in the car. Nicholas continued to contemplate the dashboard with a hopeless gravity while Vonny sniffed into her handkerchief. July had taken refuge in a cigarette, and the strong sudden exhalations of smoke through her nostrils were indicative of inner struggle. Speech was superfluous; each of the four had made a self-contained world of thought that was intensely personal. Paddy's face was set in a type of infantile wisdom; when eventually he did blurt out into speech he realised too late that he had sinned unforgivably. "God!" he said, "and she's still wearing her red earrings." He shrivelled when he realised the enormity of his lips' offence. But it was too late. As they rode onwards towards the town Vonny and July and Nicholas kept stabbing him with the long knives of their eyes.

CHESTNUT AND JET

When April came, Joe Morrissey the farmer took down the nail-box from the top of the dresser and rummaged in it to discover the sire-horse's ribbons and rosettes. When at last he found them, they were in sorry over-winter trim. Each year it was the same. Each year he had to ask the milliner in town to make him a new set so that his stallion should look his best as he paraded the town on market day.

The black stallion was taken from the drudgery of the spring work and petted. Jack Donnell the young-old groom gladly abandoned the ploughing of furzy uplands and began to give the horse his April delicacies : porridge and new milk and beaten eggs and oats. There was also a mash, the ingredients of which he kept a tight-fisted secret. Dandruff-brush and curry-comb were unearthed and plied. Gradually the camouflaged splendour and dignity and terror of the animal emerged. Out in the farmyard the as yet white sunlight caught him in swaths on flank and haunch and chest and heliographed his power to the awakening countryside. The horse sloughed winter, welcomed summer, and trumpeted the indignities of his spring. He seemed to find the touch of the cobbles in-tolerable. He began to whistle and bell. His challenge was the blending of a cluster of four handbells in four different tones mingled with the far-away whistle of a railway engine. This extraordinary noise was the over-ture of his chaotic blood : making the noise his nostrils were two pouches lined with a terrifying red velvet.

Out in the farmyard the black farmer walked round and round the black stallion. Joe Morrissey was smiling

as he watched the cajolings and wheedlings and bullyings
of the groom. As day followed day the farmer began to
reflect the animal. The man's gait grew to have something of the strut in it. Watching him covertly from the
kitchen window, his wife Nora broke into a warm smile
as she measured the capers of her man. She threw back
her chestnut head as her nose emitted a hiss of humorous
tolerance. Her hands automatically kneaded dough while
her smiling eyes were busy loving her man. Suddenly she
was aware that her daughter Nonie was nuzzling at
her dress.

" Mam ! " The chestnut child of five was her mother's
image.

" Well ? "

Out of a crinkling face : " Can I go to town a Wednesday
with my Dad ? "

" No, my little filly. Not Wednesday. Some other
day, maybe."

" Mam ! "

" Well, child ? "

" I'm not a filly. I'm a lev-er-et."

The woman shook out the scarf of her red rich laughter.
" In the spring a filly, in the winter a leveret. Isn't that
fair ? "

" That's fair . . . an' Mam ! "

" Well, Nonie girl ? "

" If you go to town a Wednesday with my Dad will
you bring me back Queen cakes ? "

" I will, of course. I'll bring you back a big white bag
of Queen cakes. Isn't that fair, Nonie ? "

" That's fair, Mam."

Wednesday was market-day in town. That was the
day the stallion stood at Treanor's Yard. Joe Morrissey
had the terra-cotta-coloured posters posted on the walls

of the fair green and on the pillars of the weighbridge. "Royal Splendour," they bragged, "by Royal Musician out of Splendid Stream. . . . This sire is getting extra well . . . his stock is well known . . . terms . . . groom's fees . . . no responsibility . . . particulars from . . ."

Each Wednesday morning Jack Donnell and another groom danced the great jet Irish Draught up the long street of the town. About midday Joe Morrissey and his wife drummed into town in the tub-trap. Nora Morrissey generally shopped at a store on the outskirts; rarely did she penetrate into the town proper. Her husband saw to it that everything was right in Treanor's Yard. He stood a few drinks to the farmers who had brought their mares. In the evening he himself paraded the stallion down the street and then handed the animal over to the grooms who had been walking some distance behind him. Afterwards he sat into the trap with his wife and returned home. Speaking through the hoof-beats he told his wife how the day had gone with him, with whom he had been drinking, what price one of the stallion's foals had made. His wife listened with tranquillity and understanding.

Mary Sullivan was a neighbour of the Morrisseys. She came into Morrissey's one evening when the man of the house was out. Crouching over the open hearth, Mary whined more to herself than to Nora Morrissey: "Your husband, your grand black husband. God bless you, Big Joe! God in his infinite goodness saw fit to make Mary Sullivan an ould maid. I was in town a Wednesday when he led the sire-horse down the length of the main street. An' all the people came out of their houses to see the grand man and the grand stallion."

Minnie McNaughton was another neighbour. She was a labouring man's widow. She was childless. Speaking to Nora Morrissey, she said : " Fine and fine for you, Mrs. Morrissey. God loves the ground you walk on. I was inside in town on market day getting my commands and I heard the townspeople giving the height of splendour to your upstanding man. God spare him long to you and to your lovely children. When he passes down the street on Wednesday, gentle and simple stand up to see the grand man and the grand stallion. Fine and fine for you, Mrs. Morrissey. Fine again for you. . . ." The woman's voice grumbled on in lonely envy.

Gradually this became Nora Morrissey's problem — to picture her husband and the stallion through alien eyes. But try as she would, her eyes remained unalterably her own. In this effort of imagination she apprehended herself shaking her head suddenly as if to clear her head after a blow. The full consciousness of her antic inevitably flooding her, she would begin to upbraid herself for her foolishness. And to crown her discomfiture there was her little chestnut daughter at the table's head tossing her head and smiling as she mimicked her chestnut mother. On the instant their two laughters were blended in the sunny kitchen.

When next market day came Nora Morrissey went into the centre of the town. The market was a busy one and the streets were thronged. The woman bore herself over-bravely, as if expecting battle and experiencing sharp disappointment in its failure to come upon her. She went in and out of shops on the thinnest pretexts. She offered an excellent pretence of interest in the affairs of acquaintances she met on the pavements. But always she took care to stand where her eyes could command the higher end of the street. There she expected the man and the stallion to appear above the swirl of the people. As evening came an access of excitement compelled her to throw back her Paisley shawl from her forehead and display the light mahogany depths of her hair and the clean-cut outlines of her features. As time passed without her husband's appearance, an insane impatience began to have its way with her : What was keeping him ? Will the people have gone home ? What on earth am I doing here ? The whole side of the country will hear about me. What's delaying you, Joe Morrissey ? What's delaying you, I say ?

Then the two black dancers were out above at the street's end. Excitement tightened in the woman's chest. Now man and horse had moved well on to the stage of the town. Nora appreciated the strangeness of the as yet silent hooves whose tappeta-tappeta would presently carry their rhythm into her blood. Dark stallion and dark man were now dancing into audibility. Now she could see the ribbons and the rosettes. The animal seemed endowed with a deeper darkness than the man. There was a contrast in the lead of tubular white web which the farmer was holding lightly in his guiding hand and also in the pipe-clayed surcingle which circled the stallion's belly. The surcingle bisected the arc in the animal's back — to the rear of the white band was the treasured violence of the haunches. Man and stallion were completely confident, completely arrogant, completely male.

Nora Morrissey suddenly remembered the town and swung to view it. True for the tellers, the whole place had come out to see the man and the stallion. An old man displaying the last cheap remnants of vigour ; a rusty old woman finding herself being revolved like an old loco-motive on a turntable ; a shop assistant remembering hills and the beat of the tide ; a motor mechanic dreaming himself white as a hound's tooth ; a hobbledehoy finding a decade of years flung unbearably at his bewildered head ; a butcher pausing in the analysis of a belch to recall roses and the scent of roses ; six canker-eared corner-boys disinterring bones of buried manhood — the whole spring-throttled town was out to see the jet stallion and the jet man.

As they drew near her Nora Morrissey found herself instinctively withdrawing towards the wall of the shops. She made as if to cover her face with her shawl. Then, as a flame grows tall in a windless moment, she straightened herself, and throwing the shawl back from her hair and face she came out to the pavement's edge and began to glory in their coming. Lifting her head she made ready to greet her Emperor. Slow enough he was in seeing her. His face was as yet rigid with a high urban pride; his air was that of one who had delivered himself up to the reverence of the people. His set mouth disdained domesticities. For a terrifying moment she thought he would fail to see her. Then, being a woman, she made an unwarranted movement of her shawl. His processional eyes rested on her, abandoned her, recaptured her — then his face blazed up into recognition and dear emotion. The woman came close to sobbing in the sweetness of this public statement of ownership. For a moment the farmer relaxed his strain on the lead. Sensing this the horse raised his head and rang his great cluster of bells.

THE GOOD DEAD IN THE GREEN HILLS

EVERY night it was our custom in Friary Lane to gather into Tommyo's to talk over the many little happenings of the day, piling tiny incident on incident until even such a commonplace thing as a man's crossing from one side of the road to the other could assume an immoderate importance. Tommyo himself was as old as an eagle. He was stone-blind into the bargain. He was also as cross as the bees, but we were inclined to overlook his crossness, especially from the time he bought the beautiful radio.

A wireless, we found, was a great background to our conversation, even if we never gave it the slightest heed. Before the radio arrived our only way of passing the nights was listening to Peadar Feeney telling stories of Ireland long ago. Peadar was old too, a proper crow in clothes he was, but he was a great warrant to eke out his tales — he made " The King of Ireland's Son " last for a full fortnight of nights. I don't know how on earth such a comparison can be relevant, but that tale always made me think of Ireland as a bright, tattered, patched shirt. Three other stories of his I can partly recall: " The Loaf in the Mare's Ear ", " The Earl of Banemore " and the " Shower of Old Hags ". Those were sound stories enough, with good blood and body to them, but they couldn't hold candlelight to " The King of Ireland's Son ". His tales for the most part were reeking with anachronisms, but the skeletons had the authenticity of immemorial age.

We made him tell the stories over and over again, pressing him until such time as he could speak no more for want of spittle. In those days we were very proud of Peadar Feeney.

I'm behind a desk to-day with all the cleverness and the finality of printed papers to buttress me, but the time I'm speaking of, I was a poor perished creature, the blades of my naked shins honeycombed with ABCs, my two knees like two fingers of a mowing machine, my hair cut to the honest glib, and the two brown eyes deep in my skull draining my body of its vitality. Time and again I find myself thinking of Peadar Feeney. He was the man who stuffed my brain with fantasies. Even in this prosaic office I am occasionally horrified to find myself flattening hills and mountains with Iron Buttocks and draining rivers with Denis of the Drought. Those were the characters in the stories we heard from Peadar Feeney in Tommyo's thatched cottage long ago.

But the radio and the story-teller made sorry bedmates. I remember the night the man came to instal the set. I well remember the instant the machine or set or contrivance — we scarcely knew what to call it — leaped to light and life under his deft fingers. Old Peadar listened in stupefaction for a minute or two, then without speaking he rose and went out the door. At the doorpost he looked back at the ring of bewitched neighbours. A strange assortment of ingredients went to the making of that final glance — malevolence and dignity and fierceness and bewilderment and sorrow and enmity and pride. Small as I was on my stool under the cavernous chimney-piece, I had the good grace to appreciate that I had been witness to the end of an epoch.

After that, Peadar never came near Tommyo's any more. God's Gospel — but we didn't miss the man — hadn't we our wonderful versatile radio? At first blind Tommyo was inclined to chafe at Peadar's non-arrival, for the two men were distantly related. Once indeed

Tommyo's conscience pricked him to the extent of sending me back the Lane to Feeney's to invite the old story-teller to come down to listen to the radio. It was dark when I went into Peadar's house. The thatched roof was held up by a series of props, and the place was shrouded in the biting smoke of wet turf, so that I had great difficulty in seeing who was in the kitchen at all. Then, as fortune would have it, the fire yielded a sudden blink of flame, and in the brief moment allowed me I discerned Peadar squatting over the fire — I also saw his queer sister in the corner. She was down on her hands and knees and she was quietly attacking the wall. In common with everyone in the Lane I knew what she was at; she was clawing her way out through the mud wall, striving to break through to the neighbour's fireplace. Each bit of mud she scraped from the wall she placed in her mouth, chewed it until it was thoroughly moistened, then kneaded it with her fingers as children in the kindergarten knead Plasticine. When she had made a substantial pellet she presently threw it away. In the few steps I walked across the mud floor, my bare soles broke numbers of these marbles.

Into the murk went my message. " Peadar," I said, " Tommyo says to have you come down to listen to the radio." His sister stayed at her scraping, but Peadar's head revolved upon his unmoving body until his face was resting squarely on his shoulder. Over this face was the mockery of a wideawake hat.

" Spell Constantinople," he asked me.

" I couldn't, man," I said.

" There you are, see ! There you are ! "

I did not break the puzzling silence which followed.

" Who's right now ? " asked Peadar.

" You're right, of course," said I, " but what'll I tell Tommyo ? "

" First tell him that if the messenger is cold the answer

is cold, and secondly tell him that under the watchful eye of the Sweet Man Above " (here Peadar raised his hat) " the Good Dead are alive in the Green Hills. Will you remember that ? " he asked.

" I will indeed ! " Then he made me repeat the message.

I went back to Tommyo's. " What did he say ? " asked Tommyo.

" He said that if the messenger is cold the answer is cold, and that under the watchful eye of the Sweet Man Above the Good Dead are alive in the Green Hills."

Tommyo took the strange message with considerable gravity. He raised his eyes and said, " A bed in Heaven to them that are gone before us all, and let Him who made us unmake us." He sent for Peadar no more.

In the running of time Peadar's queer sister died and Peadar himself was removed to the County Home which was in a town about twenty-five miles away from us. The poor man was whipped away almost before we knew it ; he hadn't made any ins or outs on us for a considerable time previous, and for our part of it we were too much taken up with our beautiful radio to be bothered with him. But after his departure the memory of Peadar gradually achieved the proportions of a legend. An odd night, if our consciences happened to be extra-sensitive, or if the programme on the radio were not to our liking, we'd turn off the knob altogether and sit there by the fire with our two arms as long as one another, for we had lost the fine art of chaffing and conversation. Then, as naturally as anything, in the resultant silence, each person's thoughts would turn on Peadar and we were restless until such time as the blind man mentioned his name. After that it was Peadar this, Peadar that and Peadar the other thing, until we grew astonished at the immensity of his stature in our affection and pride. We began to regret the belatedness of our appreciation and made curious restitution by agreeing that in his day he had been a source of great glory to Friary Lane.

I was sitting at the fire in Tommyo's on the night that we heard that Peadar was dead in the County Home. It was early on a winter's night, about half-past six or so, and there were four or five of us around the great turf fire. Now and again the thunder of workmen's boots went west the Lane. The radio was turned off out of respect for poor dead Peadar, and now and again the dark man raised his hat (the old people always wore their hats inside or out) and spoke softly through the wintry rosebud lips in his beard, " The light of Heaven's candles be on you, Peadar Feeney," and we all chimed in with the Amen. Suddenly the blind man laughed harshly and said, " D'ye remember his message to me ? The Good Dead are alive in the Green Hills ! " Then all those present began to speak wryly and proudly of Peadar. For once I made bold enough to tell that he had asked me to spell Constantinople. This drew a short laugh from the men which the blind man killed at once. " He was a noted speller," said Tommyo with pride.

Then in ones and twos the men of the Lane began to drop in, and the conversation was all about Peadar Feeney. About seven o'clock Big Jim Bruadar pushed his head in across the half-door. He stared at us all for a fierce moment until he was certain that he had the full attention of the gathering. Then, " God's curse on you, Friary Lane," said Big Jim, " to let poor Peadar lie on the slab of the deadhouse for three days without a sinner's soul belonging to him to claim his four bones ! "

" Is that true for you ? " shouted the blind man.

" The Relieving Officer will tell you whether I'm a liar or no."

" And do you tell me he's not buried yet ? "

" He'll be buried to-morrow unless some one claims him and buries him in his own ground." Here Big Jim swore horribly and added, " And if it's a thing he's not buried at home may God's bitter curse fall on you, Friary Lane."

The blind man stood up. Oh, but it's a dreadful thing to see a blind man and he in his anger. " While I have a red penny," he roared, " I'll see that the man is buried in his own ground."

They sent down town for a hackney driver to arrange about bringing the body home. The hackney driver's father was a native of Friary Lane who had improved himself and gone down into the big street to better himself and his family. The driver himself had inherited the violence and the aggression of the Lane. He strode among the people in the kitchen like a minor king, but I gathered that by inversion he was secretly proud of his connection with the place. Moreover, that he was pleased that by the mere fact of asking him for his car, the people of the Lane had acknowledged the kinship. We all knew that his haggling over the price was perfunctory. When the ritual was at an end it was agreed that Big Jim Bruadar and Jack the Turkey should travel in the car to coffin the corpse and tie it on to the roof of the motor. Big Jim and Jack put on their Sunday coats and went off down town with the driver. Before they went the blind man spoke to them. " Pass up the chapel," said he, " and bring him west the Lane for the last time before ye put him in the deadhouse."

That was about half-past seven. When they were gone we began to estimate how long it would take them to get there and back. We reckoned they should be back for ten o'clock — a good hour to go, a half-hour to coffin him and get a few drinks, and an hour to return. The kitchen was well crowded by this time but the conversation was very poor indeed. You see, we had learned to rely on the radio for topics to discuss, and in its absence we felt wholly lost. After a time we began to speak on pigeons — why pigeons I do not know, but that was what we discussed. Then the blind man suddenly remembered the parish clerk (the pigeons in the church belfry must have reminded him), so he sent me down to warn him to leave the deadhouse open till ten o'clock or so and to be ready to receive the corpse. The clerk's name was Robby D'Arcy, and he was a man who was easily terrified. " Tck-tck-tck ! " he said when I delivered my message. " Such an hour of the night ! "

It was fully half-past ten before the coffin arrived. Every motor-car that went east or west the Lane before that brought the younger people among us spilling to the doors in excitement. At last we saw the lamplight gleam in straight lines on the coffin which was tied to the top of the motor-car. We all tumbled out into the street. Immediately it had passed the big three-storeyed houses of Bank Place the vehicle ground down to second gear, and then it purred reverently up the Lane. People began to emerge from all the houses right back along the length of the Lane, men adjusting their old smoky hats and caps and women hurriedly donning their black shawls. As the coffin passed slowly west each person made the Sign of the Cross and threw the dead man a prayer.

As was only natural, the car stopped in mid-road outside Tommyo's and waited for the dark man to come out. When he did so he was bareheaded. His head was cocked up for height and his beard was a proud jut under the street lights. We ringed the car, closing in around the dark man. He groped forward to the motor, then ran trembling fingers up along the polished bodywork until they reached the coffin. One by one the men took off their hats. Tommyo faltered around the car, his fingers all the while flickering on the coffin. That was the loneliness for you. A blind man's fingers on a coffin and a bareheaded ring of poor people underneath the lamplight.

Then Tommyo raised his voice loudly and protestingly, " The disrespect of it ! His coffin to have no mountings ! "

The circle of people repeated the word " mountings " as if it had magic and terror in it. Indeed, that was the very first thing we had noticed about the coffin — its nakedness — but no one had dared to put the common thought into words until the dark man had given us a lead. We had chosen the pretence that everything was satisfactory. But the blind man was the wrong man to shield a disgrace. " Take it back to Harrington's," he said, " and tell him put mountings on poor Peadar's coffin."

The car drove up a lane-way off the Lane ; the ropes on the coffin were loosened and the coffin itself borne in and placed on the carpenter's bench. Old Harrington worked by candlelight. He drove the mountings in without raising the lid. As he worked he kept repeating, " Poor wood ! Poor wood ! Poor wood ! " The crowd stood dumbly about him in the half-light, and whenever they moved, their boots brought up the stored smells of the shavings. The rest of the men and women were out on the passage-way leading to the workshop.

Afterwards the men shouldered the coffin down to the dead-house. There was no further need for the motor-car, yet it purred after the people out of respect so as not to leave the little funeral bare and naked in the eyes of the townspeople. The town itself was half asleep as we passed through, and since it was long past the hour for funerals, we must have made a ghostly procession. People out late stopped to cross and gape at our passing. " There's a Laner dead," they said as they recognised the mourners.

THE GOOD DEAD IN THE GREEN HILLS

The chapel itself was closed, but the dead-house was still open. The parish clerk lived at the chapel gate ; he rushed out and lighted the candles as soon as he heard the crunch of the people's boots. He handled the coffin and placed it properly on the trestles. Then he gave out a decade of the Rosary which we all answered. The tiles under my knees were snow-cold. While the prayers were going on I read the legend which ran around the walls. It was difficult to read as it was painted in an old churchy lettering, and its sense was broken by the hiatuses of the windows.

After the funeral, as by common instinct, we mustered into Tommyo's. Since Jack the Turkey and Big Jim had brought back the body they were given places of honour at the fireside. They were urged and lured to tell all about their journey, and despite the fact that they had some drink taken, they narrated every little incident with a thoroughness that was, and still is, a characteristic of the people of the Lane. What the sister-in-charge had said to them ; where the coffin had shifted slightly on the roof of the car ; the cross-roads where the people had lifted their caps to the passing coffin and the cross-roads where the unlettered boors had ignored it ; the condition of the porter in the various public-houses they had visited, and so on and so on.

Suddenly the blind man leaned forward and asked them : " What kind of a corpse did he make ? " This we all knew was a very important question, since families take an especial pride in the appearance of their dead. We were surprised the blind man hadn't asked it long before. At once we noted fumbling on the part of Big Jim, who looked across at Jack the Turkey, but Jack the Turkey made no move towards answering. Big Jim spoke himself when the silence had grown oppressive.

" We didn't see him at all. He was coffined when we

got there. They went within the black o' your nail o' buryin' him."

"Bad messengers! Bad messengers!" said the blind man. "You should have asked to see his face."

Jack the Turkey was porter-valiant. "Admittin' we didn't see him — an' what did that signify?"

Up blazed the ready anger of the blind man. "What did that signify? In God's name are ye stumps of fools? How do we know that it isn't an old fisherman from the west ye brought home to us instead of our own Peadar Feeney?"

"Oh!" said all the men in the kitchen, and recovering themselves quickly they tore in like dogs on Big Jim and Jack the Turkey.

"Aye, or an old army pensioner with tattoos on his chest and hands and feet."

"Or maybe a rotten rope of a horse-coper."

"Or a tinker-man after his dirty years in the ditches."

Big Jim and Jack puffed down into a solemn contemplative silence. They would have rebelled, but it was never given down in the story of the Lane that there had ever been a rebellion against the blind man.

The sightless face swung around us pouring scorn on the messengers. "Before God, I'm blind," he said, "but these here are blinder!"

Nobody spoke for a while. Then, "It isn't too late yet," said Tommyo. "I'll tell you what we'll do. We'll rap up Robby D'Arcy and we'll ask him to open the dead-house and give us one look at the face of the corpse." The way the dark man said it, it seemed the most natural thing in the world.

The blind man had his hand on my shoulder as we trooped through the sleeping streets. He never had need of a stick or a dog while there was a boy to be whistled for in Friary Lane. We came out into the open area before the chapel. There was the spire reaching up into the moonlit sky. Glancing over my shoulder now and again I could see Tommyo's face and chest. For all the world it looked like the figurehead of a ship. The men were clumping steadily behind him.

Robby D'Arcy was a long time coming to the door. When he saw who was there, his white face hadn't the courage of saying " Tck-tck ! " He looked out of his hallway at the cluster of faces. He was in his shirt and pants and his feet were bare. The knocking must have dragged him out of bed. Robby was an early riser because he had to ring the Angelus in the morning.

" In the name of the Good God, what is it ye want now ? "

Tommyo was stern. " It's the way we want to look at the face of the corpse," he said.

" Tck-tck-tck ! Such a thing ! And why so should ye want to look at the face of the corpse ? "

The dark man spoke. " We're not sure but that it isn't an old fisherman out of the west we have."

" Aye, or maybe an army pensioner."

" Or maybe a rotten horse-coper."

" Or a dirty tinker-man."

Robby D'Arcy was whimpering. " D'ye know what hour of the night ye have at all ? What would the new dean say if he heard it ? "

" Get the keys of the dead-house," ordered the blind man.

" If 'twas th' ould dean maybe he'd understand ye. D'ye know who ye're dealing with ? This is a man out of a college. I don't understand him myself, I tell ye. I'd advise ye to go home with ye'erselves."

" Get the keys of the deadhouse, I tell you," said the blind man.

" If 'tis a thing he finds out about it he'll rip ye asunder off the altar a' Sunday. Aye an' maybe he'll strip the soutane down off my own back."

The glass cross-door behind Robby D'Arcy opened and his wife appeared. She was a woman as tall as the sky. She had an old overcoat thrown across her night things. Her mother was a Sheehy woman from Friary Lane. The wife must have been listening to the conversation through the door, for she said to her husband :

" Get the keys for the respectable men at once."

Up cocked the blind man's face towards the woman. Tommyo lifted his hat and said, " A bed in Heaven to you, Martha Sheehy." " Amen to that," said the tall woman, answering the prayer for her own mother's soul.

Robby D'Arcy sighed and lighted a lantern. We moved down the alley by the side of the chapel between the grey towering walls. We grew terribly lonely even though there was a crowd of us there together. The moonlight came over our shoulders, pierced the iron gate of the dead-house, and tweaked a reflection out of our grand silvery mountings.

The parish clerk placed the lantern on the little altar and opened its window to let the light splay out. Through the back of the lantern the light came through a round window of red glass and made a circle of red on the white marble altar.

We were a long time unscrewing the coffin-screws. Someone had the wit to bring a timber key, and he made fair progress while the others were fumbling with their fingers. When the lid finally came away we were all at pins and points with one another as each side wanted to give the lid to the other side so as to obtain the first view of the corpse. The dark man's side prevailed on the other side, as his many helpers disdained to take the coffin lid. The parish clerk brought the lantern to the open coffin and then removed the kype from the face of the corpse.

Yes, it was Peadar all right. At first we were doubtful enough about it, but whatever way it was the light shifted it gave him his old face. Not a wisp of doubt about it then; Peadar all right, poor Peadar who now had the terrible astringency of death and the authentic aristocracy of the corpse. The death-rust was on his lips and in his nostrils. The smell of earth came up and filled the dead-house.

The blind man's fingers were on the dead man's face, recognising it. Then the satisfied fingers moved down to the habit and rustled it with increasing disdain. " Habit, how are you ? " scorned Tommyo. " You could shoot straws in and out through it." Now the angry fingers were on the breast. " No holy picture either," he said. " No tassels ! " The light fell on Tommyo's indignant lustreless face. His left hand was on the lining of the coffin. " Ho ! sixpenny cotton and sawdust ! God help the poor, the rich can beg ! " Then with an intensity as the fingers of the right hand probed deeper into the habit, " Nothing next the corpse's skin. God again help the poor ! "

" Tck-tck ! " said the parish clerk. " Can't ye be satisfied now that it's Peadar ? Can't ye put on the lid and go away for ye'erselves ? Ye'll never stop till ye get us all into trouble. If 'twas th' ould dean now . . ."

Old Tommyo groped backwards and seated himself on a long stool running along the wall. The mouth of the lantern followed him, and since his hat was now removed he was like an apostle. He came to a sudden decision, " One of ye will go up to Martin Meehan's and get under-clothes and a decent habit, one with tassels and a picture on the breast. Also a pair of good brown socks. My word is good for more than that."

Robby D'Arcy was on the brink of crying with exasperation. " This is too much of a thing altogether. I let ye in on condition that . . ."

" I'll give out the Rosary while the messenger is gone," said the blind man, groping down on the cold floor and beginning to intone the Creed. One by one the men blundered awkwardly down.

When the messenger came back the men took the corpse out of the coffin and placed it on the stool. Someone brought the lantern closer. One thing we saw and we were glad to see it — the corpse had been washed as clean as a dog's tooth and the scapular was round the shoulder. The men dressed old Peadar in the fine underclothing, and over it they drew the grand habit with the picture and the tassels. They put the good brown socks on his feet, and then at the last, when Peadar had been replaced in his coffin, it was Tommyo who pulled the new rich kype down over the face and knotted the lifeless hands on his own large rosary.

The parish clerk wasn't sorry to see the last of us.

The following day all the people of the Lane mustered to the funeral. One man had left off drawing manure; another had given up grading eggs; another had ceased cutting turf in the bog outside the town; another had stopped plucking chickens in a fowl-yard. Yet another had washed his bloodied hands in a butcher's porcelain trough as soon as he heard the dead-bell banging out from the steeple. The funeral was a good one, even though the clothes of some of the mourners were soiled with dung and feathers and blood. A hundred yards before us walked the priest, his white cypress catching all the light in the dull street. The blind man was directly in front of the coffin. I was in front of him, and again he had his hand on my shoulder. Behind us I could hear the men changing fours frequently and even jostling subduedly for places under the coffin. That, I knew, was the best possible sign of a good funeral. The blind man ignored the halts, with the result that we were soon fifty or sixty yards in the lead walking in mid-road. We found ourselves alone with all the townspeople gawking at us. At first I felt ashamed, then suddenly pride began to choke me when I realised that I was the leader of all those beautiful people.

THE DANCER'S AUNT

THE children who were to dance the minuet in the concert kept wandering out on to the balcony of the Town Hall. Now and again they leaned over the railing to call to friends in the Square below. The boys were dressed in paper doublets and paper ruffs, while the girls resembled ornamental clapper-bells come animate. One little girl leaned dangerously over the railing; a school-teacher ran out from the concert-hall and clutched at her, saying, "Nellie Dennehy, you're the boldest child!"

The concert was at its height. I was against the wall in the middle of the hall — in the one-and-sixpenny seats. Behind me the people spilled up and up towards the ceiling; the throng at the very back recalled a crowd-drawing one had once attempted — blob upon blob upon blob scrawled horizontally, till the wrist ached. These people in the cheaper seats at the back of the hall seemed to like movement for its own sake. They were always in flux. The people in the middle moved naturally, and only when movement was necessary. The people at the front were statuesque.

Three strong men were on the stage. They were very good strong men. Above and below their tights their skins were painted a yellow that was unnecessarily yellow. This was because they were local strong men.

I had a point of vantage against the wall. Thus I could examine front, middle, and back at my very good leisure, without ever seeming over-conspicuous. Waves of heat pulsed through us, and where the smoke was visible against the lighting, it was seen to be carefully eddying.

In the row just behind me, and about four chairs from

me, I saw a tiny woman of indeterminate age. A tall child of twelve or so was crushed beside her on the same chair. The child had her arm around the woman's shoulders, ostensibly for the purpose of balance, but I noted that there was a large element of affection, even of protection, in the gesture. Underneath her tweed coat the child was dressed in Irish costume. The tiny woman kept herself so much forward on the edge of her windsor chair that I knew, without verifying it by staring, that she was a hunchback. Child and woman had identical faces. But while the woman's had gone on from sweetness to harshness, the child's had proceeded from sweetness to sweetness. I recognised the child — she was the daughter of a road-steward who lived a mile or so from the town. I guessed that the woman was the child's aunt.

In her nervousness and uneasiness the woman kept opening and folding and creasing the concert programme. Now and again she'd turn to the child and say eagerly : " Only three more now, Kathleen." Then, " Kathleen, you're second next." Then, " Kathleen, girl, you'd better go up." The girl seemed as wholly composed as the aunt was agitated. At last she rose. The aunt squeezed the child's hand as she passed out to the cluttered passage-way.

Kathleen was announced. The announcer said quickly : " Miss Kathleen Hanrahan. Exhibition of Irish step-dancing. Hornpipe followed by a jig." No more. But instantly I felt a boil of uneasiness ripen at the back of the hall. Turning towards the people there and sensing them keenly yet carefully, I felt a spring-tide of exultation rise in them. All my blobs were swaying and muttering. And when I turned again the girl was at the back of the stage, standing still with her right foot a little forward. She was waiting for the music to come to her.

All of a sudden the people at the back began clapping

and clapping. I was puzzled to find a good measure of vindictiveness in the applause — a sort of to-hell-we-pitch-ye challenge emanating from the sound. Looking at the girl again, I saw that she was completely mistress of herself. And I said to myself: " Somewhere here there is a plot. Here there is something more important than the essentials which please the eye. Here something, a code, a person, a type, a people stands embattled." Then, in a flush of clarity, I saw that the child had been set up to represent things greater than she realised. And I said: " Little woman, there is a formidable array against you."

And all the time the unnecessary clapping was going on. Then instantly I saw the meaning of the clapping, so, quick-as-wink as fierceness surged through and through me, I changed my jacket and mentally screeched for my own. And I said: " I'm for you, little woman, I'm for you!" Then again in silence to myself: " God grant that this little road-steward's daughter shall hold her own."

There was no clapping at the front and only a wan spatter of sound in the middle. The dancer's aunt was clapping as one claps who is unused to clapping, with hand coming fully congruent on hand, and the finger-tips joining prayerfully under the chin. The people beside her were so many stone statues with shame sculped for ever in their faces. Then, out of spite, I did a thing I'm genuinely proud I did. I clapped, and as I clapped I could feel my face lighting up in front of me until at last the fierceness flowed into my fingers. Then I forgot my shame, and my face quenched as abruptly as it had flamed. Kathleen stood there at the back of the stage, accepting the applause easily, without gratitude or ingratitude, taking it as one would an apple from a dear friend.

The stout fiddler began to play. His eyes were aimed down along his strings at the dancer's shoes. The girl flowed into the music. Before long we discovered that she had everything a dancer should have. Allied to precision she had the carriage. She had the three cardinal marks of a great dancer : the time, the rhythm, and the execution. Moving gloriously, she covered all the boards at her disposal. She and the music were one. She was neither inferior nor superior to it. She had taken her mark with her eyes, and had hung her eyes upon it so that the intrinsic splendour of her face should not distract us from the beauty of her flowing feet. We sought for the barely detectable buoyancy high in her chest which was her chiefest weapon against gravity. Anxiously we probed for a flaw. Was the drum of the left heel and toe overstrong — over-compensating for the natural weakness of the left foot ? Again and again we found ourselves impatient as we waited for the lock. And as she stood erect over the oiled hinges of her ankles we scuttled back to our prime enthusiasm. The medals on the black velvet on her breast winked splendour ; the buckles on her shoes winked splendour on splendour.

We looked across the rows at one another and grew warm in the realisation that after all these years a barony of dancers had thrown up a great dancer. We wanted to go out before she stopped dancing, and boast of the wonder to every stranger in our streets: to the couples on tandems, to the commercial travellers, to the land commissioners, to the Civil Servants from Dublin, to the superintendents of the Intermediate Certificate Examinations. We wanted, ever-so-pitifully wanted, to catch them by the elbows and say : " Oh, we have beauty too. I tell you we have beauty. What have you seen of us but old men winnowing the seed-trays of bird-cages with weak breaths ; what have you seen of us but boys nail-breaking the paint-blisters on doors ; what have you seen of us but file upon file of hooped men thinning turnips in the time of the sun's terror ? But behind these and beyond these, oh, we have beauty too."

Then each of us in the hall, within the periphery of his personal quietness, began to hold intimate converse with Time. " Time," we said, " stand still for her. Stand still for this ever-so-precious little woman. For her alone. You cannot break her as you have broken all the others on your five great wheels : on the wheels of poverty, of child-bearing, of loneliness of heart, of tyranny of the fields, of anxiety for tipsy men late at fairs. Time, stand still for her. To us she is everything. So we want to hold her for ever just as she is to-night. Now at last we have beauty. Time, hear us protesting from our shabby valley. To us she is everything. Everything that is delicious to ear and eye. She is our Age of Innocence. She is our Book of Kells, she is our Spring Song, she is our Un Carnet de Bal, she is our Venus of Milo. She is our near approach in sight to what the Litany of the Blessed Virgin is in sound. She is a poem by Campbell, she is a woodcut by Kernoff, she is a window by Harry Clarke. To us she is everything. Time, O Time, stand still for her. God knows and God knows it again, we have precious little beauty to brag about. So having found beauty, do not censure us if you see us exulting. Time, O Time . . ."

In the ease consequent upon the senses' clamour a meaningless appellation ran into my head. It would not go away even though I wanted to put it away. " Chimney of Honey," I said, and kept on saying it in spite of myself, loving the cool flowing of the vowel sounds over the *n*'s much as one loves the flowing of spring water over polished stone. " Chimney of Honey," I said, and in my peevishness I found my right hand physically raised to put away a word-image. So I yielded to the sensuality of the appellation and kept on saying: " Chimney of Honey, Chimney of Honey, Chimney of Honey."

Sensing the end of the dancing I turned my face to the back of the hall. Sweet, wicked, and premature the applause broke upon me, striking me blow upon blow in the face. But gradually, as they listened belligerently through the spaces in their own thunder, the people at the back of the hall found that they had no foes to fight, that capitulation was complete. For by now the people in the middle and at the front were clapping too. That was the wonder — our town together as never before. Together it was a trim unit, trim, say, as a straw-bound bale standing in a corner of a railway station. I promise you from my heart out that it was exhilarating to find us all for once a unit; Bank Terrace and Friary Lane making common cause of laughter; The Height and Old Fair Street embracing incontinently across backways and clothes-lines and condemned houses. That was a well-spring of enthusiasm indeed. For before the dancing had begun the town was in three erect thirds : the supercilious third, the neutral third, the enthusiastic third. But now it was the town as a unit versus everything outside the town — versus the world if needs be. And all the time we were bragging in our hearts and repeating over and over : " We have beauty, too, oh, we have beauty too."

The girl danced again, and at the end of her dancing there was no internecine element in the applause. One could easily find the pulse in the applause, as easily as one could find the beat in soldiers marching. Quickly it came racing past like this : Beat-beat-beat-and-then-hosanna ! Beat-beat-beat-and-then-hosanna !

She came threading down the passage-way with her coat thrown across her shoulders. The people who were standing there crowded upon the girl to place their glad hands upon her. As she came near my row I looked back at the aunt and found the woman's face quivering. Pride had now enfiladed the whole row behind me. Then, as the child passed in, the aunt snatched at her and put her two arms around her. Now they were mouth against cheek, and the similarity of the two faces was heart-breaking. The aunt kept saying: "Oh! Kathleen! Kathleen! Kathleen!"

A piano-accordion player came out on the stage. He was tall and dark and one found it difficult to keep track of his nimble fingers. All the while the plate of mother-of-pearl on his instrument kept levering the light across us in great blades.

THE HOLY KISS

IN certain parts of the country the first kiss of a child on his First Communion morning is considered a great treasure. This kiss is called the Holy Kiss and it is generally reserved for the child's mother. If it so happens that on that morning the mother is confined to bed through childbirth or illness, the aunt, or whoever accompanies the boy or girl to the church, is careful to hoard the kiss on the road home lest indeed its preciousness should be filched by a sentimental neighbour or an inconsequential relative. Arrived home, the guardian of the treasure leads the child to the mother's bedside and says: " Here, Mother, take your Holy Kiss ! "

And how eagerly the kiss is taken ! The bare arms leap out on the child, twine about the child, and the kiss is snatched with a passion far outmatching the marriage kiss which it exceeds by the same measure as the spirit transcends the body. It is as if the mother were to say: " Here, Glory be to God, I have reaped the first of conscious purity. I am greedy to snatch the lips that have held the Lord. Here is the reward of travail."

Little Tommy Donoghue lived with his grandmother, Mary Donoghue, in a cottage outside the town. Just Tommy and his grandmother. Tommy was six and his grandmother seventy-six. Despite the disparity of age the two understood one another perfectly. Mary Donoghue had the great brown eyes of Grandmother Wolf. She had a ditch-apple face ; the knob of a cyst was a landmark on one of her russet temples. The wisps of white hair sticking out from under her black shawl were tufts of bleached hay sticking out of a hayshed. She was lean, hardy, and comparatively agile for her years. Little Tommy was a funny bit of a thing with steel-rimmed spectacles balanced on a comical nose. The child's father, Tom Donoghue, had been killed felling a tree in a neighbouring demesne. Tom had been old Mary's only child, and she had cried bitterly at his death, a good deal more bitterly than Tom's wife, Bridie. Still the old woman had the comfort of little Tommy — after a time Tommy and Tom seemed one and the same person to her. She ceased to mourn the father, for it seemed as if suddenly and surprisingly Tom had somehow shrunken down into Tommy, and the pleasures and apprehensions of his youth were hers to experience anew. Bridie Donoghue, Tom's wife and Tommy's mother, had lived with the old woman for a few years after the accident. Then the young widow had married hurriedly and secretly, without informing her mother-in-law of her intention to do so, and had gone to live with her husband in a cottage about seven miles away. Tongues began to prattle at the sudden wedding, not without justification it must be admitted. Afterwards old Mary could not bear to hear her daughter-in-law's name mentioned, and it became the predominant terror of her life that some day she would return and claim little Tommy. The old woman resorted to unusual subterfuges to ensure that the boy should forget his mother. The news that Bridie had given birth to a child, afterwards to a second child, pleased the old woman greatly — she hoped that those new links would bind Bridie more closely to her new home. But old Mary's sense of security was shaken when the child returned from town one day with a bag of sweets that he said had been given to him by his mother. The old woman put the big bag of sweets on the mantelpiece. She was very silent for the rest of the day.

THE HOLY KISS

When Tommy came of age to make his First Communion the old woman was all ado. She took to standing at the school gate during playtime to pick out Tommy from the hundred other roaring boys. She burrowed deep in the red check bag in the cupboard of her room and took out a small hoard of bank-notes tied with string. She bought black patent-leather shoes for the boy and kept polishing the toe-caps with an assiduous sleeve. She bought white socks and kept smoothing and smoothing them and putting her head sideways to look at them. She bought a grey-green tweed suit (he had only worn jerseys up to this) and a mustard-coloured tie and a white silk shirt. She gave him *My First Prayer Book* which had a long gilt-embossed cross on its snow-white cover. She bought a small white rosary in a little white bag. The old bones took to creaking loudly as she rushed hither and thither. The boy practised his first Confession on her a few times and she heard him out solemnly. He asked her if she knew when midnight was, and his little comical face grew infinitely more comical when she pretended not to know. When the First Communion morning came she polished him up wondrously till he shone. Then she led him to church.

Clouds scudded across the May sky; now and again the morning sun smouldered through the high smoke of heaven. The breeze had the remembrance of winter's sharpness in it. The children with their mothers huddled outside the church gate. The mothers were holding heavier coats for the little ones and they all looked hither and thither as they waited for the teacher to give them the signal to enter the church and take up their allotted places. Now and again the wind lifted the girls' veils and revealed shy downcast faces. At last the teacher came to the church door and signed to the children to enter. They all filed in and took their places — the boys at the Gospel side and the girls at the Epistle side.

The priest read the Mass delicately and clearly, as delicately and clearly as he had read his very first Mass. At times during the Mass the children sang hymns. When the Communion bell rang, the children filed up to the altar, each child walking slowly as if bearing a brimming vessel of liquid. The first file stood against the rails, and as the priest moved from child to child the teacher moved with him behind each Communicant to ensure that the Host was swallowed before the boy or girl left the rails. As the children received, the voices of the choir moved caressingly over them. The priest intoned leisurely, cutting the edges of his words clean. Old Mary Donoghue had been kneeling with the mothers at the rear, her eyes fixed firmly on Tommy as he walked up to the altar. Then to her chagrin she noticed that Tommy was first in the second line of boys and had moved far away to the altar's end out of her sight behind a pillar. If she remained where she was, the old woman realised, she would miss the memorable sight of the Host touching the child's lips for the first time. So, moving urgently, she clambered out of her place, walked up the passage, and with mouth agape peered affectionately to the extremity of the rail where Tommy was standing. When she had seen what she had gone out to see, she turned, widened her hands suddenly in a touching movement of thanksgiving, and thumped back into her seat. Her old mouth twitched as she walked. The mothers were watching her through slitted eyes. But they did not glance at one another amusedly.

Then the sun leaped down from the high windows on its long legs and brought the gilt gate of the sanctuary to finest gold. Through the low stained-glass windows a different, a more sober sun filtered and drew swaths of red and purple and blue among the varnished pews. Here and there amid the mosaics on the sanctuary walls arbitrary squares began winking. Then the wind rose and the church drained of colour.

When the Mass was ended the bright and dark flood of children broke upon mothers whose affections had multiplied. Everyone, young and old, was smiling, and the warmth of comradeship flowed freely among them. Old Mary squeezed Tommy's hand till it must have hurt, but the child did not squeak — he laughed up through his spectacles at his proud grandmother. The old woman braced herself and then suddenly stooped and looked about her. But no mother was kissing her child there in the House of God. Mary tightened her shawl about her with one hand, grasped the boy with the other and began to hurry out of the little church.

Suddenly the old woman's face, that had been set in joy, began to splinter and break. She stopped short and her grasp on the boy's hand tightened. Below at the doorway she saw the child's mother standing beside a pillar, her eager features pivoting this way and that to find her son among the well-dressed children. Old Mary at first grew terrified, then she grew fierce. The intolerable pressure on his hand made the boy turn his face upwards to his grandmother's, and when the old mouth came down exultantly upon him his lips ripened up for the Holy Kiss. But, inexplicably, his grandmother's face stopped short of his, and her mouth began twitching furiously. The child was puzzled at the denial and he put his comical head askew. Then he saw his mother by the pillar, and sunlight streamed into his face. His grandmother began mumbling brokenly: " Hadn't I Tom's, alanna ? Hadn't I Tom's ? An' shouldn't that be enough for me ? " Then she snuffled and wiped her eyes in a corner of her shawl. She thrust the boy forward through the press of people towards his mother. The mother came away from the pillar, spread out her arms to receive her son, then bent fiercely and snatched the Holy Kiss.

Mother and grandmother each took one of the boy's hands. Without speaking they walked out into the windy street. Whenever the sun caught their faces the women's eyes began to glitter like breaking glass.

SING, MILO, SING !

THIS is a simple class of story and the chances are that it isn't worth the telling. It's about a man's wife asking him to sing her a song, and his singing it. Only, as far as it is possible to know, she didn't hear it — for she was dead when he sang it.

The husband's name was Milo Burke and the wife's name was Norrie. Milo was tall, heavy-jowled, bushy-haired and dark-complexioned. He was a noted local singer. He slouched rather than walked. He drank, and his reason for drinking was not readily apparent. He was no good for the world. His age was twenty-nine and his wife's twenty-five. She was small — delicately but strongly made. She was flaxen-haired, and when she smiled she resembled a Norwegian. To see her face when it was smiling was to see it at its best. When she was standing she had a trick of placing one shoe down squarely and raising the other shoe-sole so that only the back of the heel rested on the floor. They had one daughter, Nora, a heavy child of six who resembled her father.

These three people lived in a broken-down public-house at the end of the village of Teerla. The village street was wide, and Burke's house lay at one end of it. The house gave one the impression that it had been built elsewhere on a frame with wheels beneath it and then drawn directly athwart the village street. That is, until one saw where the roadway had escaped to the right just before running right under the building. There was a small grimy shop-window, over which precariously hung a board with the name Burke printed dismally on it. The whole village smelled of decay.

When Nora was six years of age, Norrie Burke gave birth to a second child — a baby girl who survived birth by three days. Then there was the little doll's funeral, the playing at laying out, the tiny candles, the tiny dress, the white doll's coffin with tapes to carry it, and the pathetic grave that a man would dig in ten or twelve minutes. What people attended the funeral attended more from curiosity than from sympathy or respect.

Norrie took the child's death badly. After a few days she found herself caught up in a disease that only women should discuss. She suspected her imminent death in her cold sweating members. Finally she read her death-warrant in the doctor's face. When he had gone she composed herself as best she could, then called " Milo! Milo! "

The heavy boots came up the squeaking stairs. Now more than ever this thundering in the narrow house offended her. The noise made her wince. Hard on her husband's heels came a neighbouring woman who was in and out tending the sick woman.

" 'Tis all right, Mary," she said to the woman. " I want to talk to Milo."

Mary punched the pillows and arranged them behind her. " Don't wear yourself out, leanav," she said.

" Shut the door behind you, Mary, and don't let little Nora come up."

When they were alone the sick woman turned to her husband who was standing awkwardly at the bedside.

" Sit down, Milo; I want to talk to you."

He sat gingerly on a finely made chair.

" Move closer, Milo." He did so.

After a pause, " I'm going my road, Milo. You know that. The doctor told you."

Milo examined his large stupid hands. His face was indicative of little emotion. After an effort he began in a colourless voice, " I wasn't such a good husband, Norrie."

The sick head coquetted wanly : " Who said you weren't, Milo ? Did I say it ? Answer me, Milo ? "

Again in a voice that was incapable of lustre : " I didn't bring you luck, Norrie. What with the drink and everything. What did I bring you but misfortune ? "

" You brought me your singing."

The man was silent and kept examining his hands as if they were novel to him.

" Milo ? "

" Well, Norrie ? "

" Do you remember the day I met you first ? It was on the pier of Inver. Seven years ago last 26th of July at a quarter-past four in the evening. Do you remember, Milo ? Myself and Kitty Dawson were sitting on the pier wall, and the quiet waves were slapping the cement behind us. A canoe was going out to the islands. In the front of it was a big bundle of hay. The mountains far away stood up out of the heat-mist. You came down the pier with all the other girls and fellows. One of them had a concertina. I took particular note of you — you were trailing behind like a sheep. Your big mohall of hair, your blundering boots, your heavy lugs and your stone-dead eyes. Do you remember, Milo ? "

The man tired of looking at his palms. He turned over his hands and began examining the large hairs on the backs of them.

" Kitty Dawson nudged me and you passin'. I skitted right into your face. Even then your eyes didn't come alive. You passed us out and trailed after the others as they went to the end of the pier. You looked more awkward from the back than you did from the front. And then I lost interest in you until all the fellows and girls gathered in a ring around you. I heard them saying, ' Sing, Milo, sing ! '

" And then, Holy God, you sang. Out into the sea.
Do you remember, Milo ? "

The man kept turning his hands to see all sides of them.
He said nothing.   His face was utterly composed.

" I followed you then, Milo, until I got you.   And
through drink and misfortune and trouble I had no pay-
ment but your singing.   I was well paid, Milo."

The man said stolidly, " I wasn't a good husband,
Norrie. . . ."

" No, no, Milo. How many times did we talk all night
long until the green morning walked in the windows.
And now and again, if I asked you, you sang with your
head under the bedclothes so as not to wake the child.

" And how many times did I walk home from the
concerts with you after you had sung.   And all the women
were jealous of me and I having hold of you by the sleeve.

" And how many times did we go into the woods
together and walk by the path under the hazels until we
came out on a lump of white gravel over the river.   And
then you sang against the snarling water.

" Milo ! "

" Well, Norrie ? "

" I want you to promise me something."

The man did not answer.

" It isn't the drink — it isn't fair to cage a man in that
sort of a promise.   Nor 'tisn't about getting married again,
because that's not fair but as little.   Nor it isn't about the
child, because I know that whatever happens it's your
nature to be good to her.   It's a different thing entirely."
The woman checked her swallowing and said : " The
night I'm being waked, Milo . . ." She stopped.

Milo looked at her bovinely as if her terrible emotions
had not the power to hinder or hurt him.   Steadied by
his non-display of grief she began again in a steadier
voice :

" The night I'm waking. . . . You'll sing for me. Won't you, Milo ? "

" I will, Norrie."

" You promise, Milo ? "

" I promise, Norrie."

" As sure as God is your judge ? "

" As sure as God is my judge ! "

In Teerla, gentle and simple can tell you how Milo Burke kept his word to his wife. The night of the wake was still and windless — such a night for singing had never been before. She was laid out in her blue Child o' Mary cloak and white veil. She looked contented. Small wonder that, since the stones of the road know that a woman dying out of childbirth is certain sure of Glory. By some means or another it had become public property that Milo was going to sing. No one begrudged him doing so, no more than they begrudged the cat her mew or the sheep her bleat. The wake-house was thronged. The very last of the drink of the shop was going — Milo himself drank but he didn't get drunk. Out in the village the people who had remained at home to mind the houses kept coming to the doors to watch Burke's casement windows. The windows were open, and the watchers could see the mourners passing and re-passing in the lighted wake-room.

About half-past ten Milo came into the wake-room and, standing with his awkward hands more or less by his side, began to sing :

> " I'll take you home again, Kathleen,
>   Across the ocean, wild and wide,
>   To where your heart has ever been,
>   Since first you were my bonnie bride."

The first note he uttered sliced to silence the speaking house. In the back bedroom his child leaped straight from sleep to wakefulness, and beating down those who had come in to pin her, said, " Hush ! I want to hear my Da singing."

So divorced from his song was the singer that his voice took on a body of its own. The people listening in the village included an old man standing before a pergola and a girl and her lover who stood beneath some pollarded poplars.

The song called the dead woman jewel, darling, treasure, calf, secret, share and bright white love.

It told the people how to be beautiful though ugly, how to be rich though poor, how to be happy though sad, how to be young though old.

When the song was finished, Milo retreated into a corner of the room and remained there for the rest of the night, quite silent.

THE WALLFLOWER WOMAN

SHE was as dumpy as a marquee. Scarcely anyone remembered seeing her raising her eyes from the ground. Her clothes were so shapeless that they could have been made of grey canvas. She was middle-aged, but her nondescript apparel and her senile gait made her appear older than she really was. In her hand she invariably carried a reticule so stuffed with articles that it appeared to parallel her own shapelessness. A black straw hat was plugged haphazardly down over her forehead. Once an old friend of her father's had stopped her in the street and said: " Excuse me, but you're wearing two hats." The dumpy woman seemed genuinely grateful to her informant and had shown no signs of embarrassment.

One day she was standing on the Convent Cliff. Here it was that her resolution had come upon her. She was looking down at the dull backs of the houses and at the great grey stores. She noted well the colourless walls, the eaten and faded brickwork, the fatigued buttresses and the ruptured gables. Suddenly she said: " Look, I will tie a bright scarf to the throat of this sober town."

Richie Hogan often earned the price of a pint for participating in the miracle. Whenever the wall was too high she got Richie to hold the ladder for her. I remember one day in particular when Richie was holding the ladder for her. It was down on the slobland near the Castle wall on the riverside. A team of us boys stood on the metal footbridge. Slight as the bars were, they disguised us by breaking the contours of our faces. We watched dumpiness struggle up the ladder. She was sowing the wallflower seeds in the crevices of the ancient wall. We watched ever so carefully. We saw Richie Hogan quaking from his poll to the soles of his drunken boots. When precariousness was at its peak we began to hoot and jeer. We sang out: " Humpty Dumpty sat on a wall; Humpty Dumpty got a great fall." Richie Hogan leaned his drunken strength against the bottom of the ladder and corkscrewed his neck as he tried to sight us. His empurpled face and primrose eyes did their best to intimidate us. He looked at a great stone in the muck and again his eyes measured us. We continued to jeer. Then we aimed our jeerings at Richie himself. " Richie Hogan the Bogan the High-Cock Stogan," we screamed. That cock didn't fight either. Richie Hogan's company had him gagged. As a last resort we trumpeted through our hands : " Wallflowers, wallflowers, growing up so high . . . especially Richie Hogan. . . ." But the dumpy woman ignored our taunts and continued to plug pellets of clay into crevices, cracks, crannies, chinks and fissures. Tiring of the unproductive baiting, we danced across the bridge to the Fair Field where we played Ball i' the Cap, Hullahoo and Queenio.

Each succeeding April found us more thoughtful. Standing on the footbridge we could see the long walls of the town curling with the flames of the wallflowers. Tawny and yellow and crimson and orange. In and out through the greyness of the limestone the colours raced. Then we thought : " Why, she has tied a bright scarf to the throat of the sober town."

Nevertheless it took us a long time to christen our bewilderment contrition and longer still for us to call our contrition pride.

Strangers asked us questions about the wallflowers — a Monsignor from Milwaukee, a horse-coper from the West of Ireland, a painter of statues in the Convent. And then, learning our lesson from the weather-vane of common gossip, we found leisure to brag of our wallflower woman.

" Sssh ! " we said to one another, " it isn't right to speak that way about the Wallflower Woman. Look at the long walls of the town curling with the flames of the wall-flowers."

Her death made little impression on us. She was a Protestant ; we were Catholics. She wasn't prayed for at Mass at all. If she had been prayed for at Mass we'd have found out her name. They took her to her church at a queer time of day ; they buried her at a queerer time of day. We were at school on both occasions, and there was the grand gawk gone waste ! Important-looking people came by train in the morning ; they went away by train in the evening. At luncheon-time we saw a man wearing a silk hat. He was standing outside the hotel. That was all we saw of the funeral.

Rory Sullivan mitched from school that day. Rory Sullivan's stories weren't worth a hatful of crabs. He said he was at the Wallflower Woman's funeral. He said that the Rector turned his eyes to the sky and said : " I hear a voice from Heaven." But Rory Sullivan was a flaming liar and we were sure he was making game of us. 'Twas a heartscald that it wasn't Jackie Roche that had mitched — he'd have brought back a story with a fair colour to its skin. We had cold comfort in what Rory told us.

In April the townspeople came out on the grass of the Convent Cliff. They said, " Will you look at the wall-flowers ! " " If you were lowest in your heart wouldn't they raise you up." " Well, well, wasn't she a great-hearted poor creature." " Look, even away up beyond the market I can see them blazing — at the back of the wheat store, on the railway wall, on Jack-Jer's gable-end, and on Heenihan's old mansion." " Well, wasn't she great entirely ! " " I'd say ' Lo'th have mercy on her ' if I thought 'twould be the least good to her." " And the way we used to laugh at her." " But sure if that drunken wretch Richie Hogan saw you layin' a finger on one of those wallflowers, wouldn't he open you with an axe!" "Ha! ha! Richie inherited the wallflowers." "They'll be there for ever; they'll never die out. Like eternity. For ever and ever."

Peter Breen was ten years of age. He seemed perpetually hungry, delicate, and cold. Smiling old men sitting on stools in the Lane would chin the shined curves of their sticks and say: "Faith, Timothy Breen's son isn't long for this side — he's a Knockawn Rider." They said this of anyone who was delicate, inferring that he rode bareback with the fairies around the fort in the Knockawn.

Peter Breen had three bastions to protect the clue to his soul that lurked in a pinpoint in the pupils of his eyes. First bastion was the cheap-rimmed pair of Board of Health spectacles that were always askew on his nose. Second bastion the eyelids — matter-matted and carmine. Sadists were always intrigued and consequently trapped at this second bastion. Third bastion the pale, pale pupils in the jaundiced irises. Then the vital point behind the three bastions. Peter Breen — ten, hungry, delicate, and cold.

Listen to me: I vividly remember this incident happening. We youngsters were collecting for a football. From early morning until evening we had trailed around from door to door, an impertinent gaggle of ragamuffins, pack-treacherous as greyhounds, shouldering one another into shops, shushing one another from irresponsible laughter, and rapping over-loudly at knockers. Through it all ran our all-in-one-breath cry: "Gis-somethin'-for-a-football-please-sir (or ma'am)." If there were customers in the shop the shopkeeper would whinny funnily to us, gauge us narrowly as he tried to find our fathers in our faces, knife us on the small block of a smaller joke, and finally give us a penny. I remember one old lady bending down over her derelict counter, thrusting her saffron face horribly close to mine, and saying : " Wisha, a weenach, I'm as poor as a church mouse." We found her curious refusal intrinsically interesting, so we congealed in a cluster around the counter and said : " But how is a church mouse poor, ma'am ? " And the old woman said : " O leanav bawn, what has he to ate but stumps o' pinny candles ? " After hearing this I had to struggle against a temptation to take a fistful of breadcrumbs to the chapel on Sunday.

By dinner-time we had four and fourpence. The ball was eleven shillings. We decided to start collecting again after dinner and arranged to meet at Hannon's Bakery. When I came back I found the other lads there before me. They were arguing loudly among themselves. Peter Breen stood a few paces apart from them. His head was down and he was shamedly kicking a hollow spot in the concrete near the base of the bakery gable. The first thing I re- marked was the glug-glug his boot was making. The rest of them turned their faces full on me to see what side I'd take in the dispute. One of them ran towards me with the glee of cruelty on his face, gave a fiery hop-step-and- a-jump, executed a mock-adoration act with tautened neck, pointed at Peter Breen and chanted : " Wallflowers, wallflowers, growing up so high." Peter put his head down lower and continued tipping the hollow spot on the wall. Then they all spoke together. I said nothing. I walked over to Peter Breen and, as he lifted his eyes, for the first and last time in my life, I penetrated his poor ramparts. What I saw within made me side viciously for him. And then the water poured down over his white face and licked into his mouth. " He's crying with temper, lads," I said, defending him.

Now I shall set down here the names of us fourteen

boys. Because of what we did afterwards I am vehement to the point of fierceness in wishing that our names be recorded. Besides Peter Breen and myself there were the two Brownes — Tom Joe and Michael, Archie Sheehy, Jack Delaney, the two Callaghans — Denis and Fran, Pa Gallagher the policeman's son, Nick McGrath, Ulick Connor, Dick McKenna, Jackie Roche and Paud Stack. There they are, the living lumped together with the dead.

Peter Breen had his way. The whole fourteen of us spent the balance of the day scrabbling at the grave. Archie Sheehy's father was working for the Council so we stole the town picks, the town shovels and the town spades. Our fine four and fourpence went into wallflower seeds. We never cried halt till the soil of the grave was as fine as meal. Peter Breen was scurrying here and there among us, making friends with his little enemies and saying that those who had jeered loudest at him had done their digging the best. We let Peter sprinkle the seeds in broad strips, first the red, then the yellow, then the tawny and last the orange. We stuck the empty packets on sticks on the grave. We threw light bushes across it and tied rags to rods to keep the birds away. Down the town that night there was talk of the Well-Laners tearing them up again — just to spite us. But it all came to nothing. The thunder of the Penny Catechism and the terror of consecrated ground were more than a match for the Well-Laners.

Again and again the Aprils came. The caretaker of the graveyard had sheared and trimmed the plants until there was a solid slab of wallflowers over the grave. We took pride out of going to funerals for the sole purpose of hearing the people remarking it. After all these years I can still recall the clinkers of the graveyard path crunching under my boots, can come around the corner of a tomb as large as a labourer's cottage, can suddenly chance upon that block of coloured grandeur, can place myself in silly ambuscade, can hear with pleasure the oh-oh-oh-oh of wonder run along the mourning people. I'm glad now we didn't buy that football. I'm gladder still that the sonorous Catechism and the wonder of holy ground bludgeoned the Well-Laners. I'm glad I saw Peter Breen's soul embattled behind his pitiful ramparts.

That's all ancient history. This dull evening, having nothing better to do, I took my stick, whistled to my terrier and went for a stroll around the town. Once again I found myself mentally collecting for that football. Hard on my heels trooped the quick and the dead. Once again I put my face against the face of the old woman who was as poor as a church mouse, once again I saw the shopkeepers search for our fathers in our faces. As I daydreamed thus my feet instinctively led me to the long bakery wall: after a good deal of tapping, the ferrule of my stick found the place where the bakery fire had sucked in the bricks and thus made a little kettledrum of the plaster. Placing my shoulder against the wall, I played Peter Breen's part in our boyhood play. I filched his proposal from him and found unspeakable joy in the theft. Glug-glug went the wall against my boot just as it had done forty years ago.

When at length I raised my conscious eyes I saw Garrett Cregan the smith eyeing me quizzically from the door of his forge. His look embarrassed me, since I wouldn't for the world have it noised around the town that I was already in my dotage. I walked away with a counterfeit briskness. After a time I came out on the Convent Cliff and oh, man dear, how my heart lifted when I saw that everywhere the wallflowers were lighting their Chinese lanterns in the grey evening.

THE GLITTERIN' MAN

MICKY DOYLE the half-poet was telling a story at the wake. It was a labouring man's wake. Old Maurice Heaphy it was who was dead. Maurice had been living with his unmarried daughter Mary in a labourer's cottage on a by-road.

A few shawled women were murmuring in the wake-room ; there was a sprawl of men out in the white naked kitchen where only one thing had the fabric of richness to it, and that was the fire. It was a good turf fire. Badly needed it was too, although August itself was there.

There were eleven men in the kitchen : ten labouring men (Micky Doyle the poet is counted as a labourer) and one farmer. The farmer's name was Edmond Heffernan. He was there only because the man who was waking that night had worked for him for a number of years. Nine of the men were ranged on long stools along the walls, while the farmer, looking as though he begrudged every second that he was present, sat independently at one side of the fire. Directly opposite him sat Micky Doyle.

While he was telling the story, Micky's face was directed primarily at the farmer and secondarily at the men at the wall behind the farmer. Micky was faring badly with his story-telling. The men at the wall had heard the tale repeatedly, and their faces lacked the hue of interest, yet they considered themselves bound to offer some pretence of attention and appreciation. Not so with the farmer, who listened with a type of tolerant hostility. The labourers, indeed, would also have shown this type of hostility if they had had the courage to do so. True, they were bound to the poet by uncertain bonds of loyalty, but more than that they feared the man's tongue. He was capable of pillorying a person, a family, a tribe or a townland. Once, indeed, a woman leaning over a half-door in the village of Cloonafoor had laughed at the weary poet. Micky had straightaway pinned poor Cloonafoor to the wall much as a collector would pin a butterfly. At fair or at races or at pattern, mischief-makers kept chanting over porter at the people of Cloonafoor :

> Cloonafoor, both mean and poor,
> A church without a steeple,
> Where ignorant boors look over half-dures
> To jeer at dacent people.

The poet had a small face made wholly, it seemed, of wind-stirred sand. The red sand, say, of Fanore in Clare. And his two eyes were two living things that one chances upon suddenly in sand. That he was sensitive to the inattention of his audience goes without saying. The tepid boredom of the labourers he chose to construe as a type of wry homage. He could stomach that. But his tiny bitter eyes kept narrowing fiercely at the pattern of opposition that Edmond Heffernan was cutting. The prospect of this hostility spreading to the men at the wall was insupportable to the poet. Reciting slowly, he reached that portion of the story where Patsy Moore the Gambler met the dark stranger late one night. The stranger had dared Patsy to gamble with him. " A tall glitterin' man the stranger was, and when they reached Patsy's little cottage, Patsy lighted the oil-lamp. And then they sat down to the table to gamble, Patsy Moore and the Glitterin' Man. . . ."

(By right, the poet thought, at this stage in his story his listeners should have plucked up their ears, leaned forward, exclaimed, spat or shuffled as appreciable evidences of quickening interest. But what little movement there was, was wholly unrelated to the story. As for the farmer, he was obviously sneering through the money-box slit on both sides of his pipe.)

Micky Doyle paused, ostensibly to redden his clay pipe with a coal of fire pincered in the tongs, but in reality to arrange the details of his plan. Over the whitening coal his eyes concentrated to two points of menace. He lidded his pupils lest they should betray him. When he began again his tone of voice had subtly altered. Vestiges of intrigue crinkled on his temples.

" Little or no talk between them! Only the quiet deadly playin'. Once when it came to Patcheen's turn to deal the cards, didn't he turn up the Ace of Hearts to himself! And the Glitterin' Man said nothin'. This put Pat's dander up. ' Blast you for an ignoramus,' says he, ' wouldn't you have the common manners to say " A ring of gold on you " to a man that's after facin' the Ace o' Hearts ! ' Even at that the Glitterin' Man said nothin'. An' then, whatever the hell fiddlin' Patsy had and he robbin', the Ace o' Hearts fell out of his fingers to the floor. . . ."

By sneering audibly Edmond Heffernan had filled this important hiatus. The men at the wall looked shrewdly from the poet to the farmer. Now, they seemed on the point of allying themselves with the farmer. Micky Doyle was alive to the danger of his position, and although it was patent that his climax was failing him, it was still more obvious that he had resources of intrigue. This sense of confidence alone held back his timorous allies by the wall.

". . . fell out of his fingers to the floor. An' he groping on the floor for his card, didn't Patcheen spy the two legs of the Glitterin' Man ! An' God between us an' all terror an' affliction ! but weren't they cut an' cloven like the two huffs of a cow ! "

There was no echoing ring of amazement to the poet's ring of triumph.

THE GLITTERIN' MAN

To encompass his design it now suited Micky Doyle to pretend that he considered his listeners dull. With grand deliberation he chose to halt and seemed to grope mentally in an effort to illustrate this incident in his story. He leaned across towards the farmer and gestured stagily with his hands. " Now, Mr. Heffernan," says he, " we'll pretend that I'm Patsy Moore and that you're the Glitterin' Man." With that he stooped slightly and glanced at the farmer's boots. Instantly the men at the wall tautened. Then, as if they were possessed of a common volition, they brought their backs out from the whitewashed wall.

The farmer tried to draw his boots in under him. But the chair he was sitting on was a labouring-man's chair and the cross-rung denied the farmer's boots asylum.

All the men in the kitchen were now on the alert. Alert and vibrant. Here, Glory to the Man Above, was a grapple ! The men's faces became so many glass jugs of chuckling ale. Edmond Heffernan's eyes were two red coals in a raked fire. His mouth grew astringent. It pursed obscenely. His lips writhed around the pipe-lip. Every puff of his came out as a living threat.

Softly, eggingly, out from the wall in trumpery wonder, a man queried, " Like the two huffs of a cow ? "

" Like the two huffs of a cow ! " repeated Micky Doyle. His eyes were still holding the farmer's face. And then, as if he lacked the power of controlling them, the eyes slid down slowly to the farmer's boots. Quickly the poet stuck his clay pipe into his brown mouth and drew the knife-blade of the index-finger of his right hand across his left palm. This to illustrate the act of cleaving. Again the eyes began sliding — only this time they were piping twenty eyes downwards with them. But the poet, dearly loving the glory of the indirect, peremptorily recalled his errant eyes when they had reached the farmer's fob. The labourers' eyes blundered away down : discovering the trap over-late they stampeded like startled cattle.

The slit of the farmer's mouth widened and he blurted :
" Isn't the kitchen wide for you, Mister Doyle ? " The
tone he used was such as few had heard him use before.

The poet was now in counterfeit abjectness. First he
ventured a disconsolate yet tentative glance at the reactions
of his allies at the wall. Then the " Tck ! Tck ! " of his
penny contrition. " As if . . . as if I'd offend a child
. . . a child . . . sure, what was I doin' only . . . only
lettin' on that you were the Glitterin' Man an' that I was
Patsy Moore the Gambler ? "

" An' isn't the kitchen wide for your Glitterin' Man ? "

The poet pouted down at the fire. " I can't say now
that I like this class of talk. Sure what harm was it itself
if . . ." The poet broke off and gave the men at the wall
a further sharp glance before he continued in emboldened
tones. Now he directly addressed the men on the stools
and ignored the farmer. " Mind ye, my friend here might
be by way of being a strong farmer itself. An' he might
even have the grass of twenty-five or thirty cows. But
to-night I'd have him understand that he's talkin' to a
poet. In the mornin' I'll be by way of bein' a labourin'
man again, please God, an' this man here'll be by way of
bein' master of his grand red cattle. But to-night . . .
to-night . . ."

No one spoke. They were all watching the poet's
hands. The right hand seemed to be caressing the farmer,
deprecating idle funny words, but the left hand, the
murderous left hand, was doing nothing if it wasn't
nudging the men along the wall.

Micky went on, a shade more of vindictiveness in his
voice. " To a poet ! This class of talk to a poet ! In the
ould days things were different. Oho, but there was a
change in Parliament then, I warrant you. In the ould
times maybe a poet'd take it into his skull to quarter

himself on a farmer . . . on a strong farmer with fine red cattle. Quarter himself for maybe a month or six weeks, and the strong farmer daren't put in or out on him either — with the dread. Hiyeh! An' then maybe at three o'clock in the mornin' the poet'd take a mad fit of screechin' for the most outlandish things in the world. Cat's eggs, maybe, or hen's paps. . . ."

Out from the men ran a brown brook of laughter. Suddenly the brook began brawling, broke its banks, and licked and bubbled as a great wave in the white kitchen.

The farmer had his back to the wave of huh-huh-huhs. The noise hissed softly down to silence. It was as if the thinning, hurrying flood had run on and on and finally lost itself in speaking sand.

The pipe-pulls were audible for a span. A man prompted softly. . . . " About the Glitterin' Man? "

Micky drew himself back physically as if to parallel a mental reversion. " Aye! about the Glitterin' Man." Followed the relishing smack of narration and the lifting of the voice to a suitable level. " Well, when Patsy seen the two huffs on the other fellow his colour went from him. When he was up again he reached back in his chair till his breath would come up in him. But Patsy Moran the Gambler was no sop in the road! No, indeed, he was nothin' else but an iron able lad. And as soon as ever he had gathered himself, he says to himself: ' Now I know who's sittin' down card-playin' at the one table with me. An' Mr. Glitterin' Man, if your two legs are cut like the two huffs of a cow itself . . .' " Again the eyes idling downwards: again the right hand soothing and the left hand inciting. " Cut like the two huffs of a cow itself! " he repeated, succumbing to the pretence that everyone had suddenly grown hard of hearing.

The farmer took his pipe out of his mouth and extinguished it with the fearless spatula of his thumb. He slammed the dottle home into his palm. Those were actions readily construed as threats. He pocketed his pipe. His method of doing so constituted a further threat. He shifted his chair harshly. This was perhaps the finest threat of all. There followed an eager lull — the lull of hounds before slipping.

One of the men at the wall had the singular valour of faking obtuseness. Out past the vertices of the farmer's ears the words burned, " Is it the way, Micky, his two legs were cut like a cow's huffs ? " Micky wisely ignored this query.

" The Gambler was talkin' under his breath an' sizin' up his man. ' Cut like the two huffs of a cow itself,' he says, ' I'll play you an' I'll play you, Mr. Glitterin' Man, whether or not the first crack of the mornin' finds me rottin' an' rollin' an' roarin' inside in the red belly of hell ! ' So away with Pat the Gambler as cool as you please, dealin' an' forkin' an' jinkin' an' shufflin' an' crownin' an' cuttin' an' leadin' an' robbin'. An' smart an' all as the Glitterin' Man was, he wasn't able to get the upper hand of Patcheen Moore."

Three men at the wall spoke.

The first man said : " Good man ! Good man, faith ! "

The second said : " Good man, Patcheen Moore ! "

The third said : " Wisha, glory on you, gamblin' man ! "

The poet continued : " An' just as 'twas brightenin' for day they heard a cock crowin' two solid miles of ground away. Then what did Patcheen do but slap the cards down fair and square on the deal board. An' then he said in a roarin' voice, ' See here now, Mr. Glitterin' Man ! ' "

At this the poet pointed his right index-finger full into the farmer's face. Then the billows of laughter again went seething about the kitchen. Edmond Heffernan got up, his chair-movements detonating like cannon-fire. Incoherencies jerked out of his magenta face. "Ah! to hell and to hell I pitch the lot of ye! To hell and to hell . . ."

For a time the kitchen was all futta-fatta and hubbub. Then softly the splendour of the men at the wall ebbed and they were left drained and abject. They hung their heads under them. Women's voices began bubbling up in the wake-room. Mary Heaphy, the dead man's daughter, came to the room door and began concertina-ing with her long anaemic fingers. "Vo! vo! vo! vo!" she went sorrowing. At length the joining of her hands in supplication under her chin set a period to her lamenting. She sent the soft sickle of her voice swishing over the heads of the labourers. Then to the farmer: "Oh! the respect, Mr. Heffernan . . . the respect. . . . For a thousand crowns of gold . . . oh, Mr. Heffernan, as sure as your poor mother is in her grave . . . oh, the respect . . . gold . . . into my warm hand. . . ."

Edmond Heffernan exonerated the woman with copious gestures. He looked turbulently on the meek bowed heads. Then he clumped out into the night. He ill-secured the door behind him, and one of the younger men crossed speedily and latched it. One by one the faces came up. They focused on the foxy face of the poet. Micky Doyle caught the tongs and lifted a small lively coal to his pipe. When the coal's glow had reached his face he looked archly at Mary Heaphy. All the faces then turned to the woman. For a moment she hesitated — then the white mouse that was her smile emerged, and the gentle fans of her fingers moved softly before her face. What she was implying was: "We, we, we. Yes, ye, me and the poet are one. We, we, aye, and my poor father that's waking. We, we, we." The men were gratified and offered the poet their communal glance of pride. Then, inexplicably, they abandoned him.

They commenced to speak among themselves without tonal let.

One said: "That little fawn-and-white greyhound bitch I seen you havin'. What way, now, would she be bred?"

The other answered: "Well, then, if it's a thing that breedin' is any standard she should have . . . She's by Cotton Frock outa Lanny. You might remember that the dam of Lanny. . . ."

The poet was in no way aggrieved at being thus abandoned. After a shrewd glance around the kitchen he curled downwards into his súgán chair and fell asleep. He twitched in his sleep like a hunting terrier. Seeing him twitch thus the men ceased from conversation and exchanged proud affectionate looks.

Morning was on the world when the poet awoke. Though the fire was blazing up into his face he found his back anaesthetised by the cold. On Mary Heaphy's invitation he sat at the head of the table, wolfed a few pointers of griddle bread and drank three mugs of scalding tea. Then he lumbered to the wake-room door, where he thundered to the board floor and prayed gracelessly. Mary Heaphy was leaning against the bin drinking a cup of tea. Micky Doyle shook hands with her and left. He got his hay-fork in the outhouse, slung it on his shoulder and walked out into the renovated world.

The sun was already promising a fervent day. In field on field upwards on the rising ground to his right the ripe wheat was speaking, gardens of it here and there already in stooks. In one field of perhaps ten acres men were fiddling with a reaper, waiting for the dew to dry out of the standing corn.

When the poet reached the dark running ribbon of the

main road he started to whistle. Then he turned north and walked briskly for perhaps a mile. He saw Edmond Heffernan's place above him in a grove. Micky Doyle smiled as he turned in the boreen that led to the house.

Edmond Heffernan was out in his great wheat garden. All around the wheat a path had already been cleared for the reaper-and-binder, and the sheaves from this opening hurtled into the brambles. The reaper-and-binder owner had disappointed him, so Edmond's son Tim had attached the reaping-attachment to the mowing-machine, affixed the platform and the goad and inserted the second and lower seat for the sheaver. He had then yoked the horses and removed the súgán rope from the knife-blades, and inserted the serrated knife in the slot. Tim now sat on the lower seat with a short askew rake in his hands. His right shoe was on the reaping bar. The father sat on the higher guiding seat. With a prodigious crackling the machine spurted forward and attacked the standing wheat. The son dipped and re-dipped in the act of sheaving. Immediately the machine began crackling, three men detached themselves from the hedges and fell to binding in its wake.

The poet came down the long upper field, crouched under the paling and, with an innocent and independent movement, drove the fork deep into the grass of the headland of the wheat garden. Slowly he removed his jacket and hung it on the fork. He let the roaring machine pass him, then moved in and began to bind in its track. Passing the waiting poet, Edmond Heffernan had shouted unnecessarily at the horses. The labourers automatically spaced one another to yield Micky Doyle working span. While they worked they glanced at one another expectantly. Micky worked competently and speedily, though his was a thistly patch of corn. The ground was again clear when the machine crashed around once more. The labourers bowed their heads and moved out obsequiously from the approaching horses.

Suddenly the clamour ceased. There, perched on the high seat, was the farmer. He was glaring at the waiting poet. One man at the end of the swath had not quite finished his quota of sheaves; now he grew statuesque with his knee on the unbound sheaf. The farmer's son looked up curiously at his father.

" Get off my bloody ground, Micky Doyle ! " Edmond Heffernan trumpeted.

Micky grinned unctuously. The palms of his hands pleaded innocence. He shifted feet and looked amusedly at the labourers. He read denial in their faces.

" I won't tell you again to get off my ground ! "

The poet gave way slightly, eyed the son and the labouring men, then pushed his hat high on his forehead and looked up fully at the sky. " Sure, isn't the sun shinin' now, man ! " he laughed. All the men looked up as if the sight of the sun was a novel experience.

The farmer threw the reins to his son, leaped off the machine and stalked towards the poet. The working-men were watching keenly — the end man still frozen on his sheaf of wheat. At the last moment the brown poet turned unhurriedly and walked to the headland. The farmer stopped and watched him go. At the headland Micky slowly put on his jacket and tugged up his reluctant fork. Then he crouched under the wire and walked up the pasture. Every now and again he threw a dog's eye backwards. No one in the wheat garden moved. Micky reached the five-barred gate, mounted it and straddled it. He stayed sitting on the top bar for a tantalising minute. Suddenly he pointed up at the sun in the sky and commenced to laugh richly. The farmer made as if to move upwards towards the gate, but something his son said checked him.

THE GLITTERIN' MAN

Micky leaped from the gate, put the fork on his shoulder and clattered down the boreen. When he reached the dark main road he swung southwards into the sun. After a time he came to an arcade of demesne beeches. Looking up at the wonderful translucency he fell to considering how many years the beeches had given to the fashioning of that lime-green place of remembrance. Then with tilted olive face he began to whistle thoughtfully. He ceased abruptly when he grew conscious of the fact that over him and around him and about him was beating the immoderate enthusiasm of the birds.

THE BREADMAKER

NOREEN spilled the flour from the saucer to the losset, then slowly sieved it through her fingers. She clapped her hands dustily and walked to the yawning bin, with its hoard of golden meal and silvery flour. She extracted a pinch of soda from a drab paper bag, then locked the pinch in the palm of her left hand. Back at the table again, she crunched the soda over the flour. Now for the salt. Soda, salt, butter! All in ? Then she walked to the dresser, took up a jug of sour milk and sniffed it. Her left hand was groping abstractedly for an empty jug while her eyes were examining the milk. She hummed as she sent the sour milk careering in a viscid bubbling waterfall from full jug to empty jug and back again. The ingredients of her cake had spoken in different voices : the flour had uttered the faintest flicker of a whisper, the soda had rustled as a nun's dress, the dampish salt had evoked water from the bases of her teeth, and now the thick milk gurgled with a lewd drunken joy. " Glug-glug-glug," it said, as the swallowing of a fat old toper. Laying down the jugs, Noreen gathered the feet of her irregular hillock of flour and made a rough crater at the top. Then she poured the milk into the mouth of the little volcano. Bubbles winked and broke, winked and broke, winked and broke. Short lives they had ; one solitary violet-indigo-blue-green-yellow-orange-and-red wink and life was over. Birth, prime, old age. Pouff — so !

The old man and the old woman were seated by the fire under the dark chimney in the farm-house kitchen. The old man was opposite the girl who was making the cake, arrogantly watching her movements out of his red, wicked eyes. He noted every feature of the pretty face that was framed in errant ringlets, and noting, he scowled. Scowled again as he looked at the interloper. Turning his face to the fire he railed inwardly at the thought of his big idiot of a son. What right had Johnsey to go against his parents ? What call had he to break the law that was there since time-out-of-mind that decreed that parents should match younglings in pub snugs ? What title had he to burst out laughing when a person mentioned the sanctity of a solicitor's settlement ? A settlement was a grand thing entirely at the end of old folks' days. Sure it read as finely as a prayer and it gave spent people a last grandeur and importance : " Reserving unto the said John Joseph O'Sullivan, Senior, and to his wife Anne O'Sullivan during their lives the east room in said dwelling-house with full right of ingress and egress through the kitchen of said dwelling-house. . . ."

Oho ! the old man mused, but this purty-faced lassie had spoiled all that ; a clever little scheming slut if ever there was one ; a regular doxy who had cajoled their fine broad Johnsey to the altar ; a cute little cabaire with her white apron-strings making the Cross of Calvary on her back. A white apron might be all right in the doctor's house in town where she was in service, but here in a farmhouse . . . ! A bould little madam, faith, she was, and the divil a stim of shame on her to walk into a snug warm place without a copper to cross herself with. An' what harm but the money badly wantin' to fortune off Nellie in Dublin ! Ah, but the good God was in His high sky and she'd be tamed for it. Cut the ear down off him if she wasn't tamed for it before Christmas night was in the door. . . .

His wife, who was rocking herself forwards and backwards on the súgán chair opposite him, looked apprehensively at her man. Seeing the bitterness in his face, her head revolved on unmoving shoulders, the better to view the breadmaker. Then with a trembling hand she groped among the voluminous folds of her skirts. A slash of red flannelette showed momentarily, and then the old hand emerged grasping a shiny penny mustard-box. With nose twitching peevishly in anticipation, the old wife extracted a pinch of snuff.

" Go ndéanfaidh Dia trócaire ar h-anaman na marbh," she intoned, as if it were a curse instead of a prayer.

" Amen ! " said the breadmaker lightly, if not provocatively. The old woman resented the " amen ". More so the old man, since it was his prerogative to answer her. A collie was lying with his nose in the cold ashes. It had one eye blue and the other brown. The old man struck it full across the forehead with his stick. " G'our that ! " he said savagely. The dog fled howling, shaking his head humanly and sniffling strongly through its nostrils.

Open-mouthed the old woman swayed on her chair· Sneezed.

" Dia linn," she wheezed instinctively.

" Dia linn is Muire," chirped the breadmaker, even before the web of spittle from the crone's chin to her chest had broken.

Recovering from her sneeze the old woman scowled. The old man scowled in sympathy with her. The dog whimpered from the doorway.

" Poor Chep," Noreen said, " poor oul' Chep."

For all the gay mask on her face the newly married girl was deeply troubled. She knew well how completely the old pair were allied against her. Worse still, she fearfully recalled the flaming lie she had told Johnsey, her own big soft Johnsey. That night under the ivy of the parsonage wall, when, with her moonlit face upturned to his, he had entreated her not to laugh at his question. For himself he didn't care a ramblin' damn, but she knew that the ould wan'd keep pickin' at him till he'd get an answer. Could she bake a cake of bread ? And Noreen recalled in horror how glibly the lie had come to her lips and how easily she had added to the lie. Who else baked all the bread in Dr. Mangan's ? Was it for her good looks Dr. Mangan kept her ? Would he like to ask Mrs. Mangan if he didn't believe her ? And then, before her false dignity could run away with her, Johnsey's lips were sealed on hers and the incident was forgotten.

Retribution had now come upon her with a vengeance. Noreen became her own accuser. She who had never whitened her hands with flour in her life, who had done little else at the doctor's except to bob and bow to the red-faced and white-faced patients. To tell the truth of it, what was she but a la-di-da who had nothing to do but say " yes'm " and " no'm " and " ma'am, if you please ", with an occasional mincing variation of " Who shall I say called ? " And to make matters a hundred times worse, 'twas the first decade in that bogawn Johnsey's bead to boast of her breadmaking prowess to his mother. And, of course, the headstrong Johnsey refused the account of a match from the Fitzgerald girl of the New Glebe, who was a sow of a woman for all her father's long-tailed purse. Noreen faltered. Here she was, the liar, making a liar of Johnsey before his mother, who was the best breadmaker in the seven parishes. For men are born with " green hands " and they are gardeners ; and people come into the world with rhythm at the tip of tongue and finger and they are musicians ; and now and again, once in a generation perhaps, God vouchsafes to grant a woman power over fire and flour, and she is a breadmaker — The Breadmaker. Such a one was the old crone on the hearthstone — Johnsey's mother. Sure there· wasn't a housewife in the barony but begrudged her her gift. Going by the road with their men, in the orange-red market-rails, the jealous women would open the wings of their shawls to blind their men to red-white discs of bread on O'Sullivan's sill. All kinds of bread came lickalike to old Annie Jack — " stampy ", griddle bread, potato cake, whole-meal bread, currant bread, caraway-seed bread, soda bread, or the golden, crumbly, meal bread called " paca ", after the good ship *Alpaca*, which was the first ship to bring maize to Ireland in famine days. Aye, all breads came second nature to Annie Jack Sullivan — The Breadmaker.

As if divining the girl's thoughts, the old woman glanced again over her shoulder at the face of the bread-maker, then at the ungainly lump of dough on the losset. She turned again to the blaze and, leaning forward, she emitted the full of a tablespoon of spittle. It flattened to a starry design on the broad flag of the hearth. Venom-ously she drew her boot across it as if to show the contempt a true breadmaker had for the white poison of the shops. And already her mind was framing bitter equivocal phrases with which to wound the new breadmaker. Long-loved jibes rolled in her mouth and jostled one another to secure first place in the queue of maledictions on her tongue's tip.

The oven was squatting on the embers. Into it Noreen threw the ungainly mass of dough, made the sign of the Cross on it with a knife in the name of the Father, Son and Holy Ghost, stabbed once in each of its four quadrants. Then she lifted the lid with the tongs and put the cover on the pot-oven. Next she squashed red coals on the lid. With heat-reddened face she straightened herself. 'Twas done ! Flesh and blood could do no more. Now her cause was beyond human strivings. Her fate was in the lap of God : her firstling was leaping in the womb of fire.

Now to wait. The old breadmaker, the young bread-maker, the old breadmaker's bitter man.

Now to wait.

THE BREADMAKER

Hens' meat to be got. Noreen got it. Bonavs and sucky-calves clamouring for their food. Noreen fed them. The black braddy cow to be milked before the red, udder-troubled herd lumbered down from the bawn field. Noreen milked her. Then she went into the kitchen to raise the cover of the oven to see how her cake was doing.

The old woman leaned forward farther and farther as Noreen took the tongs in her hand. The old man's jaws fell apart and a thin quick dribble ran down on his greasy lapels. Noreen muttered to herself as if she had forgotten something, smiled impishly and laid aside the tongs. Then she almost ran out to the piggery, to vent her pent-up laughter. The old woman clucked angrily in her disappointment. The old man grasped his stick firmly, and the watchful dog, who had resumed his place in the ashes, fled yelping before the blow could fall.

Again the fireside pair settled themselves to wait. Their eyes were glued on the oven. After a space Noreen came in again and busied herself mightily with the stitched delf on the dresser. Laying aside a large ancient dish, she took up an alarm-clock which would go only when lying on its face, studied it minutely, then raised her gaze to the black roof-joists as if she were solving an abstruse problem. The old woman looked at her with a false smile that did its best to be triumphant. The old man was torpidly scraping dirt from between two floor-flags with the ferruled end of his hazel staff. Noreen smiled benignly at the poll of the old man and rather archly at the face of the old bean-a'-tighe, though within her tremulous breast she could hear a voice piping shrilly through the halls of Heaven for the succour of a saint who knew something of the craft of breadmaking.

At long last she tightened the soldier-sashes of her apron, which were so becoming in the house in town, but

which seemed so completely out of place in the rude farm
kitchen. She sighed at the change in her way of living,
but smiled as she thought of her fine man above in the
ploughland, with the animate draught-board of gulls and
crows about his shoulders, and the red loam falling freely
like meal from his silver coulter. She grew warm and
moist at the feeling of security, the feeling of strength, the
feeling of safety the touch of his body ensured. But for
him she could scarcely have the valour to wage this smiling
silent battle against the peevish pair by the fire. Not a
battle, she hastily amended, but a long weary war, with
no ally by her, to be ended only when the old couple were
side by side in their coffins in the Kill of the Bees.

Ceasing some wholly petty business about the kitchen,
Noreen pursed her lips and emitted a faint sound of
annoyance. " Tck-tck ! " she went, as if upbraiding herself for her forgetfulness. The old man's patience seemed
to have become frayed in the passage of arms. Noreen
was now between the old couple, with the tongs in her
hand. For a moment she toyed with the notion of laying
it down again, but seeing that the collie was now hemmed
in on the hearth — it seemed instinctively to accept her
propinquity as proof of sanctuary — she routed the idea
from her mind. With great deliberation she inserted the
tip of the tongs in the loop of the lid and lifted it. The
two were craned forwards in their súgán chairs, the old
man tapping eagerly on the hearthstone with his stick, the
old woman swilling saliva through her toothless gums.
Up, up, came the cover, slowly, with the greyed coals
quivering on its top. Up ! Then the old crone gasped,
venomously released her spit and sank back. The old
man threw himself back heavily. It was then Noreen lit
with laughter. The cake, God bless it, was so big, so
lovely, so golden-brown. Oooh ! A cloth. Tilt. Tilt
carefully. She knuckled it on its back and laughed at the

little resonance. Tested it with a knife-blade and almost crowed when the blade came clean.

The Virgin never swathed Jesukin as carefully as Noreen swathed her cake. First, with pride and reverence she lifted it high above her head, as one would a child, the better to gloat on its beauty and fine limbs. Then, when it was well wrapped in a cloth, she placed the cake standing on edge on top of the bin.

In an access of impishness she broke out into a song the townies sang. She had only half of it, but the words " blue ukulele " were recurrent in the refrain. Well she knew that the words sounded abominably in her country mouth, but nevertheless she sang it as a crude, hateful paean of victory over the old pair.

After Noreen had gone out into the farmyard the old man leered across at the deposed breadmaker. Old Annie Jack masked up her face in a narrow vindictiveness and sniffled like a wet hound. She pulled a crude kype up over her hair in token of defeat, then fumbled in her skirt. The corners of her nose went crinkling again. Suddenly the old man's leering expression changed to one of peculiar loyalty. He looked back at the shrouded bread behind him. Then he looked craftily at his wife, who seemed sunken in the deepest senile despondency. He tapped on the flagstone to draw her attention; then, with his brightened eyes on the doorway, he leaned back and with a sudden push of his stick sent the cake skittling to the floor. It fell helplessly on its side : its swaddling clothes parted to show a broken cake spilling its steam on the air. The old woman cackled dryly and searched feverishly in her clothes for her snuff-box.

But the old man had not reached the end of his bravery. He raised his cracked voice.

" Hey, girlie ! " he called.

The dog left the ashes and with a sudden snap took a

hunk of the hot bread. Carried it under the table. Laid it on the floor. Licked it gingerly. Looked around with greedy canine sagacity. Growled.

" Well, sir ? " The breadmaker was framed in the doorway.

Solemnly the old woman lifted a pinch of snuff to her nostrils. " Go ndéanfaidh . . ." she began. Then the laughter broke on her.

THE CORN WAS SPRINGING

THE boy heard the young footsteps behind and beneath him. Then he heard the tittering like tearing paper. When the footsteps stopped he dared not turn round though he was aware that the eyes behind and beneath him were gimleting holes in his shoulder-blades. As he turned, a fistful of spalls was thrown in his face : a sharp stone caught him on the cheek bone. He blinked his eyes protectively. When he opened them again he had a memory of two dresses whisking beneath his little scaffold and vanishing through the chapel door. He heard the inner glass door swish open. Within the chapel the first footsteps of his attackers were excited and irreverent. The door was a long while closing, as it was controlled by an apparatus designed to prevent it slamming. Then he heard the footsteps within grow reverent and meek and innocent. The boy put the back of his hand to his cheek where the spall had nicked him ; when he withdrew it there was a small sign of blood on the point of the knuckle. He resumed his carving on the hood moulding around the doorway. As he worked he hummed menacingly through his teeth :

I'm sitting on the stile, Mary, where we sat, side by side,
On a bright May morning long ago when first you were
    my bride.
The corn was springing fresh and green . . .

Through the song and the noise of the mallet his ears were most alert.

The convent, with the chapel to the right of it and the schools to the left, was wonderfully clear in the pure air of the May morning. The three buildings formed a quadrangle with an open side or mouth. This mouth was turned to the south : thus the sunlight of the young summer was trapped in the garden beds before the convent door. In the middle of the beds was a statue of Our Lady. Around the base of the statue was a bed of tulips, already alight with vivid blooms which leaped up from a carpet of forget-me-nots. The façade of the convent proper was scrawled over by the angry cords of Virginia creeper which in autumn whooshed the sober building into a red-gold blaze. The high convent peeped over the ivied wall into the village, the single street of which fell downhill to peter out in a mutter of thatched cottages at the base of the hill.

The planks on which the boy was seated were supported by two six-foot trestles. The youngster appeared to be about seventeen years of age. He was wearing a soiled white coat. A pair of goggles was pushed high up on his forehead. He had an open, even a merry face. Soon his anger ebbed in him and he began to forget that he was waiting for his assailants to emerge. He focused his attention on the mallet and chisel. This was the first time the foreman had entrusted him with important work of this nature and it behoved him to be careful. He continued to sing softly, but the malice had now vanished from his song : "The lark's loud song is in my ear and the corn is green again." The mallet wasn't a whit too heavy for his hand : it was accurate, obedient, and kind, going where he asked it to go. Funny to listen to the old stone-cutters talking of mallets. Holly was good, American hickory better, but neither the one nor the other could hold candle-light to the wood of the female crab-tree. The old fellows on the job were a study. Matthews was so accurate that the others said jokingly that he could carve faces on the shoulders of a lemonade bottle ; Flanagan was peerless at lettering a tombstone. But they had their faults :

THE CORN WAS SPRINGING

Matthews was deplorable at foliage and Flanagan was hopeless at the angle-cut to get shadows. The foreman, Finucane, was the best all-round man in the province but he was unpredictable in mood, and if he were ill-tempered he couldn't carve soap. They were all superstitious to an extraordinary degree, and if a mallet fell from a scaffold every man on the job watched to see if its handle pointed to the gateway, for if it did there was trouble ahead. Their conversation was invariably trade-proud and esoteric ; to a man they were contemptuous of tailors.

The boy again heard the footsteps behind him. Crunching on the limestone spalls. He knew immediately it was the foreman. The man stayed watching him for a moment before he spoke gruffly. His cap hid his eyes.

" Well, how're you doing ? " The foreman was as lean as a mustang. He had a small brown moustache.

" Fine, sir."

" That's it ! Go on, go on ! What are you afraid of ? You're working on the freeway." Finucane put his hand in behind one of the trestles and with his fingers caressed the foliage carved on one of the terminal bosses. This was his own work. On the boss were the letters I. H. S. on a bed of leaves. The caressing appeared to afford him keen satisfaction. Coming out in front of the doorway again he kicked the spalls away. " Keep the path clean underneath you and don't let people be dragging that stuff up the middle of the chapel," he said. Then he gave a grunt indicative of a grudged satisfaction of the boy's work.

As the foreman turned to go away he spoke with a half-smile. " Mother Xavier is in the garden — she's gathering more leaves." He turned down the short cement pathway that led to the road. As he walked away he kicked more of the spalls aside.

Finucane must have heard the nun coming, for scarcely

had he gone than Mother Xavier came round the corner of the chapel with a great ado of hissing and trundling. She was a gigantic woman with an enormous, bespectacled face. It was almost impossible to determine her expression, as she had a trick of sealing up her eyes by reflecting the sunlight on the lenses of her spectacles. Her face was pale and the mouth indeterminate. The tremendous girth of her body made playthings of her rosary and girdle. Through the creakings of her approach the boy made a last effort to sift the noises that he fancied were coming from within the chapel. His effort was unavailing, for no sound could be heard above the clacking of the nun's rosary and the great rustle of her moving garments. The boy looked down into the twin circles of reflected sunlight that hid her eyes. Then he saw that the old nun was carrying a handful of leaves.

" Aha, young man ! " Mother Xavier wheezed. The boy stopped working, and as a mark of respect dipped his goggled forehead towards his mallet-head.

" Well, did you find out what kind of leaves they were ? "

" I did, ma'am — I think they're hop leaves."

" Hop leaves ? " she complained. Grumbling, she moved to one side and peered through the stilts of the trestles at the foliage carved on the terminal boss. Then, " They don't look like hop leaves to me. I don't know much about hop leaves. Why didn't he put vine leaves or some other kind of leaves on them ? "

" I couldn't exactly say, ma'am."

" Tck-tck ! Well, maybe he knows his own business. And maybe he doesn't ! Now isn't that a nice leaf ? " She was handing him up a sycamore leaf that was splendid in its young green leaf and red stem. The boy took it gravely and, catching it by the stem, revolved it appraisingly between his thumb and forefinger.

" That's a lovely leaf, ma'am."

" And that ? " She handed up another leaf.

" That's a grand leaf, too, ma'am."

" And that ? — and that ? — and that ? "

The boy said they were all beautiful leaves.

" And will you tell me why he didn't put those leaves on the boss instead of his old hop leaves ? "

The young stone-cutter said he couldn't exactly say.

Suddenly the great nun became conscious of the boy as a boy. Her face grew a shade softer.

" What's your name, sonny ? " she asked.

" Jamesy Dunphy, ma'am."

" And where are you from ? "

He told her that. Also his age. That his father and mother were alive. That he was the eldest of six. That his mother had had an operation for gall-stones. That the baby was as good as gold, except the time that he had the whooping-cough, when he got up any amount of phlegm. That he had an aunt a radiologist in an hospital in Lancaster. That his father had bound him to a stonemason. That he pulled the goggles down on his eyes when he was working on a certain class of stone.

This information received, the old nun delivered judgment. " God bless you, Jamesy, but you're a great boy altogether. Your father and mother should be proud of you ! "

The boy had no reply to this, except to attempt a faint smile. This smile was killed decisively as he heard a low squeak from the chapel door. His sudden tautness communicated itself to the old nun, who immediately moved herself to a position where she could peer in the doorway. She continued to look in suspiciously. Just as she was about to investigate the squeak further two other nuns came walking out of the pathway that wandered through the flower-beds. One was a tall, graceful nun of thirty-five or so, who had the accurate features of statuary allied to the capital complexion of rude health. Her companion was a tiny old nun with a bright scarlet face so pointed that it instantly reminded one of a small song-bird. On catching sight of Mother Xavier this small old nun sprang to the attack. She turned her face to the tall nun beside her.

" There she is now, Reverend Mother, pestering the poor little boy," said tiny Mother Catherine.

Mother Xavier gathered herself for attack. Herself and Mother Catherine were old friends who played at being old foes. For many years they had taken every second term at being Reverend Mother. At last they had been successful in their pleadings for a younger nun in command. They were now testing the new Reverend Mother, playing at being enemies in her presence, simulating contrariness and even dotage; not infrequently taking refuge behind barriers of obtuseness in order to witness her reactions of perplexity. It was all a game, and the new Reverend Mother thoroughly understood the rules. She knew that the two old nuns were probing her for that kernel of royalty that must of necessity be present in every woman who seeks to rule a community of women.

So Mother Xavier, playing according to the rules of the game, bridled in the midst of her fat. She employed her old subterfuge of taking refuge behind the light-laden lenses of her spectacles. She tucked her leaves up her capacious sleeves, and mock-fumed at the venom of the little woman's onslaught.

" The Lord give me patience ! " she breathed.

The young Reverend Mother extended her arms in a wholly delightful gesture. " Hush, mothers, hush ! " she chided. The boy was tapping softly, one eye on the newcomers so as to be ready with his salute if they addressed him.

Then two traitorous leaves began to sneak down out of Mother Xavier's sleeves. They were buoyant and took a long time to fall to the ground. Mother Xavier saw their treachery reflected faithfully on Mother Catherine's face. Mother Catherine opened her mouth and made the preparatory noises of a song-bird who hears singing afar. Her opponent pursed her mouth as a prelude to retaliation. The young Reverend Mother took them by the arms and drew them softly away. " Something I wish to ask you both . . ." she said. She guided them as a dancer moves a partner. They seemed unwilling to part company with their anger. As the three nuns moved among the flower-beds the boy watched them curiously. In his own mind he compared them to a hillock of black serge on the move. He heard the two old voices clash on one another ; then the oil of the young nun's speech was poured between.

When they had gone, the girls came out of the chapel. One, a black-haired girl of fifteen or so, scurried skittishly out from beneath the scaffold and rushed to the doorway that led to the road. The other, a tall girl of about seventeen, with ripe-corn hair bushing on her shoulder blades, walked out slowly. She was obviously a disdainful but graceful minx. Despite the apparent valour of her carriage, the indefinable impression of unsureness in calves and ankles was unmistakable.

Jamesy Dunphy lowered his hammer and eyed her fully and severely. Watching her move away from him he said nothing, for he was shrewd enough to know that if he stayed motionless the girl would turn round. She did so, a good deal sooner than he had expected. Finding herself fully apprehended, she faced him as bold as brass. The boy ran his hand down the moulding in the direction of the terminal boss, thereby subtly implying that the carving of the foliage was his unaided work. The tall girl was still staring. Their glances were locked for a little while.

" D'you see me ? " asked Jamesy. The words of themselves seemed harsh, but the intonation was soft.

" I do."

" You'll know me again when you see me."

More than a hint of her tongue appeared. " A cat can look at a queen," she said.

" Can a cat fire stones at a queen ? "

She looked around at the light spalls. " Stones ! " she said contemptuously.

A pause. The boy over-earnestly returned to his work. Again the sound of young footsteps behind him, picking their way among the spalls.

" What are you doing ? " she asked.

" Can't you see what I'm doing ? "

She was about four yards from him now. She was peering at the boss on the left-hand side of the doorway. " Did you do that ? "

" Huh-huh ! "

" You did in your eye ! "

The boy said evenly, " And who do you think did it so ? "

" You didn't do it — that's one sure thing ! "

A pause. Then the boy spoke out of the corner of his mouth. " Run away, little girl, and do your lessons ! "

" Lessons ? I'm in Intermediate ! "

The boy's face creased in its film of powder. He said a curious thing. " Trace the character of Banquo."

Her eyebrows lifted in genuine amazement. " Did you do Inter. ? "

" Uh-huh ! "

" An' what are you doing picking old stones if you did Intermediate ? "

The boy gave her a look of concentrated scorn.

" Here, buzz off ! " he said.

" I'll buzz off if I like."

There was a sudden agitated whisper from the doorway at the roadway. " Kitty! Kitty Kavanagh! Reverend Mother is over in the playground. She's watching you ! "

A momentary wiggle of fear came into Kitty's eyes. She looked across the flower-beds and saw Reverend Mother walking up and down on the nearer edge of the school playground. She stepped backwards and placed the head of a bush in the line of vision between herself and the nun. " Ah, she can't see me at all." She threw the defiant words across her shoulder.

" She's after looking over at you, Kitty," wailed the dark girl. Then in terror and uprighteousness, " I'm going away."

" Who's stopping you, cowardy-cat ? "

But the young Reverend Mother had seen the girl. The speed of her gait increased as she debated within herself whether or not she should reprove Kitty Kavanagh for her forwardness. She found it difficult to reach a decision, for her own memory was harrying her without respite. Then, as now, it was a bright May morning. The slow, soft effervescence of the apple-blossom was foaming in the vat of the orchard ; Bernard had come striding through the trees, his head every now and again was bending engagingly. She was picking rust off the garden seat with her finger-nail. Bernard came nearer and nearer, bringing with him the treasures of his carriage and eyes and hair. Again and again the vision sprang out from the ambush of the years. The young Reverend Mother groped for her beads and ran them through her fingers as she walked.

The Great Parlour was on the second story of the convent. The lower half of the windows had been raised to their full extent so as to let in the May air. Within,

the two old nuns were seated behind the table watching
the young Reverend Mother and Kitty Kavanagh.
Mechanical impulses of their lips compelled them to call
the girl " Baggage ! Minx ! Madcap ! Hussy ! " but their
imprecations had no validity. They continued to watch,
with such immobility that they might have been sleepers.
They were independent of eagerness and anger and sur-
prise. Their souls were beyond invasion. Long ago they
had made a truce with life, and life had respected the terms
of the bargain. Now they were two old gentlewomen of
God who were superior to the memories of tulle and music
and huzzas. From their holy stupor they continued to
watch as they had watched the village below them for
more than fifty years. They knew themselves for what
they were — two old leaks by which the tremendous confidences of tormented wives had been vented. They continued to watch, with such an extraordinary concentration
as almost passed muster for obtuseness. But they were not
obtuse. They had seen too many novices with smiling
distances in their eyes, and finger-tips for ever seeking their
ear-lobes. They had seen too many ringleted cherubs
grow up and meet seduction, too many angular imps
enlarge and become country empresses. They had strong
precedents to guide them : they themselves had distilled
lamplight on far hills and the litmus bloom of rhododen-
drons to inadequate drops in the eye-corners. They had
recognised themselves in everyone with whom they came
in contact, until personal pain was lessened by division and
subdivision. A shot in the boundary elms would have
startled them ; a rat gnawing in the partition would have
terrified them. But the remoter phenomena of people's
emotions they perfectly understood.

Mother Xavier had now no sunlight to gild her glasses,
and there behind the lenses was discovered the reason why
she herself had been selected Reverend Mother. Now

more than ever was Mother Catherine a bird of God. But what kind of bird was she ? She was neither His falcon nor His magpie nor even His beloved black hen. Age had granted her the boon of interpreting aright the authenticity of curious hallelujahs. A slow, sad smile slitted her beak. She continued to regard Kitty Kavanagh, and, as she watched, she saw the girl's dead mother and dead grandmother stand behind, directly behind, the flirting child. Just so they had coquetted and pirouetted and flirted. And had they been the worse for it all? No, a thousand times no. (The soft silver gongs of first love were ringing through the sunny convent and were strangely welcome.)

The two old nuns continued to watch in stubby pattern ; their etiolated faces framed in the black passe-partout of their veils and their facial bones thrown into relief by the light reflected from the inverted fans of their gamps. Their amazing power of self-identification was now being exerted to the full.

Just then the foreman stole past the dark-haired sentry at the gateway and took in the situation at a glance. He saw the boy and girl, the nuns behind the open window and the striding Reverend Mother. His decision was swift. " Hey, come off it ! " he roared at the boy.

The girl stood, a cool spectator, enjoying the youngster's shame. The foreman did not intimidate her. Her sense of amusement heightened as the boy went round the corner of the chapel, to work on large rough stones lying beside the gooseberry bushes. As he went he had the wit to hum to himself, " And I'll not forget you, darling, in the land I'm going to. . . ."

A breeze came up out of the good green fields. It prinked and pranced like a flighty filly. Suddenly it stood stock-still, and instantly the bright May morning was motionless. The young Reverend Mother moved up through the tulip beds on her way to the main door. Her face had the lustre of prayer-book gilt. The old nuns remained regardant until such time as the approaching nun was out of sight beneath them. Then each awoke to find that her mind had been a box within a box within a box.

THE RING

I SHOULD like you to have known my grandmother. She was my mother's mother, and as I remember her she was a widow with a warm farm in the Kickham country in Tipperary. Her land was on the southern slope of a hill, and there it drank in the sun which, to me, seemed always to be balanced on the teeth of the Galtees. Each year I spent the greater part of my summer holidays at my grandmother's place. It was a great change for me to leave our home in a bitter sea-coast village in Kerry and visit my grandmother's. Why, man, the grass gone to waste on a hundred yards of the roadside in Tipperary was as much as you'd find in a dozen of our sea-poisoned fields. I always thought it a pity to see all that fine grass go to waste by the verge of the road. I think so still.

Although my Uncle Con was married, my grandmother held the whip hand in the farm. At the particular time I am trying to recall, the first child was in the cradle. (Ah, how time has galloped away! That child is now a nun in a Convent on the Seychelles Islands.) My Uncle Con's wife, my Aunt Annie, was a gentle, delicate girl who was only charmed in herself to have somebody to assume the responsibility of the place. Which was just as well indeed, considering the nature of woman my grandmother was. Since that time when her husband's horse had walked into the farmyard unguided, with my grandfather, Martin Dermody, dead in the body of the car, her heart had turned to stone in her breast. Small wonder to that turning, since she was left with six young children — five girls and one boy, my Uncle Con. But she faced the world bravely and did well by them all. Ah! but she was hard, main hard.

THE RING

Once at a race-meeting I picked up a jockey's crop. When I balanced it on my palm it reminded me of my grandmother. Once I had a twenty-two pound salmon laced to sixteen feet of Castleconnell greenheart; the rod reminded me of my grandmother. True, like crop and rod, she had an element of flexibility, but like them there was no trace of fragility. Now after all these years I cannot recall her person clearly; to me she is but something tall and dark and austere. But lately I see her character with a greater clarity. Now I understand things that puzzled me when I was a boy. Towards me she displayed a certain black affection. Oh, but I made her laugh warmly once. That was when I told her of the man who had stopped me on the road beyond the limekiln and asked me if I were a grandson of Martin Dermody. Inflating with a shy pride, I had told him that I was. He then gave me a shilling and said: " Maybe you're called Martin after your grandfather ? " " No," I said, " I'm called Con after my Uncle Con." It was then my grandmother had laughed a little warmly. But my Uncle Con caught me under the armpits, tousled my hair and said I was a clever Kerry rascal.

The solitary occasion on which I remember her to have shown emotion was remarkable. Maybe remarkable isn't the proper word; obscene would be closer to the mark. Obscene I would have thought of it then, had I known the meaning of the word. To-day I think it merely pathetic.

How was it that it all started ? Yes, there was I with my bare legs trailing from the heel of a loaded hay-float. I was watching the broad silver parallels we were leaving in the clean after-grass. My Uncle Con was standing in the front of the float guiding the mare. Drawing in the hay to the hayshed we were. Already we had a pillar and a half of the hayshed filled. My grandmother was up on the hay, forking the lighter trusses. The servant-boy was handling the heavier forkfuls. A neighbour was throwing it up to them.

When the float stopped at the hayshed I noticed that something was amiss. For one thing the man on the hay was idle, as indeed was the man on the ground. My grandmother was on the ground, looking at the hay with cold calculating eyes. She turned to my Uncle Con.

" Draw in no more hay, Con," she said. " I've lost my wedding ring."

" Where ? In the hay ? " he queried.

" Yes, in the hay."

" But I thought you had a keeper ? "

" I've lost the keeper, too. My hands are getting thin."

" The story could be worse," he commented.

My grandmother did not reply for a little while. She was eyeing the stack with enmity.

" 'Tis in that half-pillar," she said at last. " I must look for it."

" You've a job before you, mother," said Uncle Con.

She spoke to the servant-boy and the neighbour. " Go down and shake out those couple of pikes at the end of the Bog Meadow," she ordered. " They're heating in the centre."

" Can't we be drawing in to the idle pillar, mother ? " my Uncle Con asked gently.

" No, Con," she answered. " I'll be putting the hay from the middle pillar there."

The drawing-in was over for the day. That was about four o'clock in the afternoon. Before she tackled the half-pillar my grandmother went down on her hands and knees and started to search the loose hay in the idle pillar. She searched wisp by wisp, even sop by sop. My Uncle Con beckoned to me to come away. Anyway, we knew she'd stop at six o'clock. " Six to six " was her motto for working hours. She never broke that rule.

That was a Monday evening. On Tuesday we offered to help — my Uncle Con and I. She was down on her knees when we asked her. " No, no," she said abruptly. Then, by way of explanation, when she saw that we were crestfallen : "You see, if we didn't find it I'd be worried that ye didn't search as carefully as ye should, and I'd have no peace of mind until I had searched it all over again." So she worked hard all day, breaking off only for her meals and stopping sharp at six o'clock.

By Wednesday evening she had made a fair gap in the hay but had found no ring. Now and again during the day we used to go down to see if she had had any success. She was very wan in the face when she stopped in the evening.

On Thursday morning her face was still more strained and drawn. She seemed reluctant to leave the rick even to take her meals. What little she ate seemed like so much dust in her mouth. We took down tea to her several times during the day.

By Friday the house was on edge. My Uncle Con spoke guardedly to her at dinner-time. " This will set us back a graydle, mother," he said. " I know, son ; I know, son ; I know," was all she said in reply.

Saturday came and the strain was unendurable. About three o'clock in the afternoon she found the keeper. We had been watching her in turns from the kitchen window. I remember my uncle's face lighting up and his saying, " Glory, she's found it ! " But he drew a long breath when she again started burrowing feverishly at the hay. Then we knew it was only the keeper. We didn't run out at all. We waited till she came in at six o'clock. There were times between three and six when our three heads were together at the small window watching her. I was thinking she was like a mouse nibbling at a giant's loaf.

At six she came in and said, " I found the keeper." After her tea she couldn't stay still. She fidgeted around the kitchen for an hour or so. Then, " Laws were made to be broken," said my grandmother with a brittle bravery, and she stalked out to the hayshed. Again we watched her.

Coming on for dusk she returned and lighted a stable lantern and went back to resume her search. Nobody crossed her. We didn't say yes, aye or no to her. After a time my Uncle Con took her heavy coat off the rack and went down and threw it across her shoulders. I was with him. " There's a touch of frost there to-night, mother," said my Uncle Con.

We loitered for a while in the darkness outside the ring of her lantern's light. But she resented our pitying eyes, so we went in. We sat around the big fire waiting — Uncle Con, Aunt Annie and I. That was the lonely waiting — without speaking — just as if we were waiting for an old person to die or for a child to come into the world. Near twelve we heard her step on the cobbles. 'Twas typical of my grandmother that she placed the lantern on the ledge of the dresser and quenched the candle in it before she spoke to us.

" I found it," she said. The words dropped out of her drawn face.

" Get hot milk for my mother, Annie," said Uncle Con briskly.

My grandmother sat by the fire, a little to one side. Her face was as cold as death. I kept watching her like a hawk but her eyes didn't even flicker. The wedding ring was inside its keeper, and my grandmother kept twirling it round and round with the fingers of her right hand.

THE RING

Suddenly, as if ashamed of her fingers' betrayal, she hid her hands under her check apron. Then, unpredictably, the fists under the apron came up to meet her face, and her face bent down to meet the fists in the apron. " Oh, Martin, Martin," she sobbed, and then she cried like the rain.

THE END